The War in the Nueces Strip

The War in the Nueces Strip

DON WORCESTER

A DOUBLE D WESTERN

Doubleday

NEW YORK   LONDON   TORONTO   SYDNEY   AUCKLAND

A Double D Western
Published by Doubleday, a division of
Bantam Doubleday Dell Publishing Group, Inc.
666 Fifth Avenue, New York, New York 10103

Double D Western, Doubleday,
and the portrayal of the letters DD
are trademarks of Doubleday, a division of
Bantam Doubleday Dell Publishing Group, Inc.

Library of Congress Cataloging-in-Publication Data

Worcester, Donald, 1915–
The war in the Nueces Strip/Don Worcester.—1st ed.
p.   cm.
1. McNelly, Leander H., 1843 or 4-1877—Fiction. 2. Texas
Rangers—History—Fiction. 3. Nueces River Valley (Tex.)—History—
Fiction. 4. Texas—History—1846–1950—Fiction. I. Title.
PS3573.0688W37   1989

813'.54—dc19   88-32211
                                                                              CIP

ISBN 0-385-23854-1
Copyright © 1989 by Don Worcester
All Rights Reserved
Printed in the United States of America
June 1989
First Edition
OG

I am willing to take a good many chances, but I certainly would not live on a stock ranch west of the Nueces River, at any point from the mouth of Devil's River to the mouth of the Rio Grande. I think the risk is too great—so great that scarcely any compensation would pay for it. My position in command of a company of troops I do not consider half so hazardous as that of those living on ranches.

Captain LEANDER H. McNELLY, 1875

The War in the Nueces Strip

I

It was late April 1875 when I first saw Captain Lee McNelly, and at first glance he wasn't impressive, not at all like I'd expected. He stood only about five-and-a-half feet tall and didn't weigh over 135 pounds. His long brown hair and beard contrasted strangely with the paleness of his face. Could this little preacherish-looking man be the famous guerrilla leader who'd given the Yankees fits in Louisiana? It didn't seem possible. I almost had second thoughts about joining his Ranger company.

A tall man with a blond beard was seated at a table in front of a tent, looking over some papers. The Captain stood near him, hands in his jacket pockets, chewing on an unlit black cigar. He wore a good beaver hat and calfskin chaps, and his pistol belt was hand-tooled.

"Looking for me, son?" he asked, taking the soggy cigar from his mouth.

"Yes, sir, if you're Captain McNelly, sir."

"I am. Want to enlist?"

"Yes, sir." He looked me up and down, and right then I noticed something about his eyes. They seemed to read you, to take your measure, to see everything about you. I felt like a naked kid who'd climbed out of a swimming hole and found strangers looking him over. Whatever there was to see they saw, and so did Captain.

"Yours?" He nodded at the Colt .45 on my hip.

"Yes, sir."

"Can you use it on a man?"

"I've never had to before, but lately we've lost so many cattle to rustlers I'm ready to use it. My pa is Aubrey Carter."

The Captain turned to the big man at the table. Before he could put the question, the man spoke. "I know of Aubrey Carter, sir. If this lad is cut from the same cloth as his pa, he'll do to take along." He rose and held out a huge hand. "I'm John Armstrong, First Sergeant. You must be Concho."

I nodded and shook his hand.

"Sign him up," the Captain said. To me he added, "Pay is thirty-three dollars a month in state scrip. You furnish horse and gear and gun.

The state'll supply grub and bullets. You'll need plenty of 'em where we're going."

Sergeant Armstrong wrote my name on the roster. The Captain bent over the papers on the table, his thoughts already on other things. Accepting my dismissal, I looked over the camp. There were about fifteen men present, sitting or standing alone or in groups of two or three. I didn't recognize anyone, and none of them paid any attention to me.

A tall, powerfully built young fellow came up the road from Burton. His horse looked glad it wasn't still pulling a wagon or a plow. The saddle was sorrier-looking than the horse, and the rider wore old square-toed boots, patched pants he'd outgrown, a shirt that had served beyond its time, and a floppy-brimmed hat. He had Farm Boy written all over him, but he had a pistol stuck in his belt and he looked you straight in the eye. He dismounted and ambled up to the Captain and Sergeant Armstrong.

"Captain McNelly?" He seemed to be asking both of them, uncertain which was the Captain.

"Yes. What can I do for you?"

"I'm George Burnham, but they call me Josh. Pappy served with you in Louisiana. I come all the way from Georgia to see you, and now I hear you're hirin' men."

"Burnham. I remember him. Good man. Want to enlist?"

"Yes, sir, I do, sir."

The Captain looked up and down that big frame, then turned to Sergeant Armstrong. "What do you think?"

"I'd take a chance on him, sir." The Captain nodded, and Josh's name went on the roster below mine.

When Josh left the table I walked toward him. A short, stocky man with a black beard was eyeing me, and he spat in front of me as I walked past him. "Ain't no call for lettin' greasers in the Rangers," he said to a man squatting on his heels beside him. "I ain't never seen one of 'em worth a damn." I acted like I didn't hear him or see him. It wasn't the first time I'd been taken for a Mexican, but it was the ugliest. I was so mad my ears were ringing when I got to where Josh was standing, still grinning broadly. When he saw me he stopped smiling. "Are you a scout for the Rangers?" he asked. "I mean . . ."

"You mean you take me for a Mexican and that's not good enough to be a real Ranger along with you cotton choppers." He tried to say something but I wasn't listening, and before I knew it we were swinging at each other. I was really fighting with the black-bearded man. Josh was about six feet two, four inches taller than me, and he packed a lot

more muscle. Luckily for me, Sergeant Armstrong stepped between us before I got my head knocked off. I escaped with only a bruised cheek.

"If you're goin' to be Rangers you'll save your fightin' for the enemy," he told us. "What are you fighting about?"

"It's my fault," I admitted, gingerly touching my cheek. "Someone called me a greaser. Then he," I nodded toward Josh, "asked me if I was a scout, like I'm not good enough to be a regular Ranger. That's when I blew up. It really wasn't at him."

"No, it's my fault, I guess," Josh said. "Pap was in Captain's company in Louisiana, and they had a *Tejano* or Mexican scout who could follow tracks where no one else could see 'em and he used a lassoo like he could make it talk. I was goin' to ask him to teach me those things."

We both laughed and shook hands. Sergeant Armstrong looked around, I guess trying to spot the one who'd called me a greaser. "I'm not goin' to ask you who it was," he said. "That's something you'll have to handle on your own." He left us.

"You said your father served with Captain during the war?" I asked Josh.

"Sure thing. The Captain's a bigger hero around our place than General Lee. I didn't know anything about the Rangers till this mornin'— just rode all the way from Georgia to see him and maybe shake his hand. Feller at the post office said he was out here hirin' men. He took me on! Biggest day of my life!" He grinned again. "Are you a real Texan?"

"Yes. My grandfather came here from Kentucky about 1830 and married my grandmother. Her folks were Spanish and had a big land grant; she inherited part of it. My father came from Tennessee about '46, right after Texas became a state, and a few years later married my mother. So I'm about half Tennessee, a quarter Kentucky, and the rest Spanish. I speak the lingo well enough to pass for a Tejano, and I guess to some people I look like one."

"How come you to join up?" he asked me.

"Lately we've been losin' a lot of cattle and horses to the Cortina bandits from across the Rio Grande. The other ranchers told Pa to see Governor Coke and ask him to do something before we lose everything. I went with Pa, and the governor said, 'Son, the legislature has authorized the Special Force for the Suppression of Crime and Lawlessness for that very purpose. There's only one man in Texas who can deal with those raiders, and that's Captain Lee McNelly. He's allowed up to fifty men and he knows how to pick 'em. I'm givin' him a free hand and those river bandits are in for a surprise. He's settin' up camp outside

Burton, so if you really want to do something about rustlers, head on over there and sign up with Captain McNelly.' So here I am."

"What kind of horse you got?"

"Luckily I rode my best cowpony to Austin, a little coyote-dun mustang that can run the legs off any critter around, at least after a mile or two, and he can do it day after day. Toughest pony I ever rode."

"Look at mine." Josh nodded toward his old wagon horse and his poor excuse for a saddle.

"Maybe some farmer will swap you a saddle horse for him."

"I hope so. At least Captain let me sign on, and right now that's all that matters. Wish Pap could've knowed about it, but Sherman's men killed him and cleaned us out of everythin' we owned. A bunch of our neighbors gave up and headed for Texas. I helped Ma with the farm for a while, but when I turned nineteen I followed 'em. Figured I'd see Captain, then catch me some cattle and start a ranch. It's plain luck I got here just when he was lookin' for hands."

Josh and I sauntered among the others, but they hardly looked at us and went on with whatever they were doing. They weren't much for talking to strangers. As they sat around in twos and threes, and a few by themselves, several were oiling their guns. We were the youngest of the bunch, for I was just a year older than Josh, and I guess they figured we weren't dry behind the ears. Josh was bustin' to talk with someone and find out what we were going to do. He walked up to a man with graying hair who was hunkered down sharpening both edges of a mean-looking knife that had a foot-long blade and a copper handle. Josh watched him awhile, and he seemed friendly.

"My name's Josh Burnham."

"Sho' nuff." The man rose to his feet and walked away.

We learned later that he was Jim Boyd, one of the best knife fighters in the West.

Josh didn't give up easy. He was feeling good, like all of a sudden he wasn't a fuzzy-faced kid any more and would have to shave or grow a beard. He walked over to another man who had his gear spread out on a piece of canvas along with a boxlike thing that looked like a camera. I hung back a little.

"Wonder where we're headin'," Josh said to strike up a conversation.

The man rose, looked at Josh with a smile, and said, "Ain't you heard?"

"Nope."

"It's sort of secret, but we're going wherever Captain says. That's where, and nowhere else."

"I asked you a question. I can't make you answer, but I can damn sure stop your smart-aleck talk." Josh took a step toward him.

The man laughed and slapped his thigh. "You'll do, son," he said. "You'll do for sure. You'll either get the job done or go down trying."

Then he turned serious. "None of us know, but if I were bettin' I'd say we'll go to Corpus Christi first. They've had a heap of trouble there lately from them raiders. They crossed the river like an army, burned three or four settlements 'round Corpus, killed some folks, and generally raised hell. I was there last week and the citizens were forted up like they expected more of the same. I bet Captain tries us out on that bunch." He spat in the dust. "Name's Parrott. Reckon we'll be seein' plenty of each other."

"Do you know that man with the black beard?" I asked him.

"That's Blackie Smith, or at least that's what he calls himself. I could swear I saw him in Corpus and figured he'd just come up from the lower country, right where we're headin.' Why?"

"He figures I'm a Mexican and he's not very high on them."

Parrott looked thoughtful. "Better keep an eye on him, son. If he came up from the lower country and Captain knew it he wouldn't have signed him on. But I heard him say he was from over Nacogdoches way. I wouldn't turn my back on him if I was you. We'll find out soon enough if he's up to something." We shook hands with him, and then he turned his attention to his gear.

Word had spread that Captain was looking for men, and they rode in from every direction as if drawn by some mysterious power. Captain and Sergeant Armstrong looked them over closely but asked few questions. They didn't accept everyone. In fact they turned down many more than they took in.

A couple of youths rode noisily into camp, dismounted, and swaggered up to the table. Each wore two guns, and they were obviously trying to look tough. "We come to join up with the Rangers," one said. "Where do we sign?" Captain and Sergeant Armstrong exchanged glances.

"Sorry," Captain said. "We can't use you." Looking like they'd been insulted, the two boys wheeled and stalked off, spurs jingling noisily. They mounted, pulled their hats down, and spurred their horses. As the animals broke into a run, their hind hoofs sprayed us with gravel.

Those who signed up were quiet men of all shapes and sizes, men who wore their guns as if they'd been born with them on, like they were part of their clothes. Most wore good hats and boots, but their clothes weren't new by a lot. They were bearded or stubble-faced, a hard-looking bunch. Some were ex-soldiers who had been with Captain before, and most were in their twenties or early thirties. They sized up one another silently, like male dogs. Their glances weren't hostile, but they weren't exactly friendly. I figured that they recognized something in each other's eyes and were satisfied. They damn sure didn't look like men you'd try to push around. Josh and I could tell that Captain knew how to pick fighting men, and we were proud as hell he'd taken us. We aimed to make damn sure we didn't disappoint him.

While we waited around camp with nothing to do, Corporal W. L. Rudd came and hunkered down by us. He was a little redheaded Englishman who'd been a private during the war. The others called him "Colorado Chico," or Little Red. He was from London, and I sure liked to hear him talk. And he was mighty proud to be a corporal. "You chaps know anything about Captain McNelly?" he asked. I'd heard a little about his war record, and Josh told him what he'd already told me.

"He was born in Virginia and studied to be a preacher," Rudd told us, "but he developed consumption and his folks sent him to Texas to rest up and get well. About that time the war began and he's never had much chance to rest. After the war he married Carrie and raised cotton on a veteran's headright—a land grant—here in Washington County. He was in the State Police for a time, but left 'em. But I've run on too long. Just remember he's a stickler about upholding the law and he doesn't accept excuses for failure, and you'll get along fine."

Only one other man in camp was real friendly to us, and he was also young, about twenty like me. His name was Sonny Smith, but it could have been Sunny, for he was always in a good mood. "I figure to learn all I can about bein' a lawman from the best," he explained. "Then I'll go back to Lee County, run for sheriff, and get married. My girl says she'll wait for me, but she's a worrier, afraid I'll get killed. I don't aim to."

About sundown Dad Smith, the wagon master, hollered something and the Sergeant ordered us to fall in. That was army talk, and right then it was easy to tell who'd soldiered before—they lined up elbow to elbow. Josh and Sonny and I watched and did what they did, not wanting to let on how green we were. The Sergeant counted us. "I make twenty-two, Captain," he said.

"Does that tally?"

"Yes, sir."

"Count off by eights," Captain ordered in his weak voice. "Number eights, forward two paces. You men will be acting corporals until further orders. You're responsible for the men in your dab. Post a guard of four men in three-hour shifts, beginning at the head of the line. Bed down at the ready, at ten-pace intervals behind your horses."

Ex-soldiers understood these orders. Josh, Sonny, and I watched them and figured out what to do without asking. The corporal of our dab, which meant our squad, was Polly Williams, or at least that's what he was called. His brown hair was beginning to turn gray, and he'd obviously served in the Army at some time. He knew a lot about Captain, and I thought maybe he'd served with him, but he never said. Our dab ate together.

When Williams woke me for my turn at guard duty, he said, "Standing guard in this outfit means just that. Stand. Don't even hunker down. We ain't in enemy country yet as far as we know, but we're under war orders. If you're caught nappin' on guard, Captain can't order you shot but he'll boot you out with a black mark that'll follow you the rest of your life. Captain doesn't sleep much, by the way."

Breakfast was cornmeal mush, a slice of side meat, and coffee, and that was all for the day. Josh wasn't used to drinking coffee—said it'd been pretty scarce in Georgia since the war.

About suppertime we were ordered to line up again. More men had come and signed up, and there were now forty-one. Captain called for John Robinson and L. B. Wright to step forward. "These are your first and second lieutenants," he said. Robinson was a slender, dignified-looking Virginian who seemed to know what he was doing. Wright appeared real young to be a lieutenant. He had a funny way of making a straight line with his eyebrows and wrinkling his forehead.

Captain called next for R. P. Orrill and Linton Wright to step forward. "These men are sergeants. You've already met John Armstrong, First Sergeant," he said, nodding toward the man who'd sat beside him at the table. Armstrong had quite a bit of schooling and was plenty smart. A powerful, handsome Kentuckian, he looked to be about six feet one. Like Captain he sported a mustache and goatee, but Captain's were dark and Armstrong's were blond. All in all he looked like a real Texas Ranger ought to look. The men called him "McNelly's bulldog," and that was high praise. Except for the difference in size, we soon learned that Captain and Sarge were pretty much alike, especially when it came to fighting. Of all the little McNellys, Sarge was my favorite—when he led us into a scrap it was just like Captain was by his side.

"Old Orrill," as he was called, was a lanky Mississippian with a long neck and scraggly blond beard. When he talked it looked like his Adam's apple was walking up and down his long neck. Although he drawled and seemed to move slowly, he was always where he needed to be. He and Josh got to be great friends. Sergeant Wright was a short man, real businesslike, but he never talked much.

"Be ready to move in fifteen minutes," Captain ordered. I had my gear rolled up in a blanket, and it took only a minute to tie it behind my saddle. Josh was already waiting, for he had nothing to pack but an old army blanket. Sergeant Orrill picked two men and the three of them rode ahead on the road to Corpus Christi, fanning out to scout the way. We followed. No one mentioned that we hadn't eaten since morning. Those who knew Captain had learned long ago that when he was on the move, eating could wait.

We must have been quite a sight when we set out in a column of twos just before sunset. The scouts were out ahead of us on either side of the road. Captain, the lieutenants, and the sergeants rode at the head of the column, and after them came the rest of us following our corporals. We were forty-three in all, counting Captain. Hats were of every kind from Captain's good beaver to Mexican straw sombreros to Josh's floppy-brimmed hand-me-down. Mounts ranged from so-so saddle horses and mustangs to Josh's old farm horse. I couldn't see how we'd ever catch up with well-mounted bandidos. We were sure one ragtag, bobtailed outfit, and if looks meant anything we weren't much of a fighting force. As we rode along I wondered what I was doing there.

On the way to the coast we stopped and set up camp outside Cuero. "Why're we stoppin' here?" I asked Corporal Rudd. By then we knew he was one we could talk to, and one who'd level with us.

"The Taylor-Sutton feud's about to break out again, after being quiet for nearly a year. Both sides are gathering forces and they seem jolly well ready to shoot it out. We've got other things that need our attention right now, but Captain figures we'd better cool them off first."

It was early afternoon when Sarge Armstrong ordered us to line up. Captain stepped in front of us. "The Taylor and Sutton men are gettin' ready for war," he said in his soft voice. "None of 'em are worth keepin' alive, but we're goin' to send them home for the sake of decent folks."

He took half the company and headed north, and I was glad to see that Blackie was with him. I sure didn't want him behind me if there was any shooting. Lieutenant Robinson and Sarge Armstrong and the rest of us headed south. After a couple of miles we saw a big bunch of men sitting on their horses under some oaks. There were about twenty of us and maybe fifty of them. They watched us approach, rifles across their saddles. Only three of the Rangers had rifles.

I figured Lieutenant Robinson and Sarge would stop us out of rifle range and then have a parley with the leaders, but we rode up to within pistol shot. Three men came out to meet us. We all had our hands resting on our guns, for it looked like Lieutenant Robinson was fixin' to get us killed.

"We're Texas Rangers," he told them. "Captain McNelly orders you to return to your homes. He's disbanding the Sutton men right now."

"And if we don't?" one of the leaders asked.

I looked over that bunch, wondering just what we would do if they decided to fight. There were at least fifty rifles pointed our way. Most of the men were young, and all were trying to look mean. From what Rudd had told us we knew they didn't care much about lawmen.

"Captain McNelly and his men will come shortly to see if you've obeyed his order, but we don't aim to wait for him. Our orders are to treat all armed bands as outlaws, and we'll do just that. Suit yourselves," Lieutenant Robinson replied.

I hardly breathed while they drew back and palavered. They outnumbered us and they had rifles, so it wouldn't be an even fight. We'd get some of them, but most of us would be killed for sure. I didn't like the looks of it one bit. They argued and jabbered and waved their arms like they were working themselves up for a scrap. I glanced at Lieutenant Robinson and Sarge. They just sat there cool as you please like they weren't a bit worried. I figured they must have lost their minds.

Finally a bunch of the Taylor men turned their horses and loped away, then more followed. The leaders cursed and then rode after them. I took off my hat and wiped the sweat off my face as we headed for camp.

"Wonder what we got ourselves into," Josh said quietly as we rode side by side. "They could have killed all of us if they'd decided to fight. Nothing we could have done about it."

"If this is the way it's goin' to be we damn sure don't belong in the Rangers," I said.

We didn't have much time to think about it, for it was getting dark and we headed on for the coast. But we sure had doubts that Captain and Lieutenant Robinson knew what they were doing.

II

Riding only at night, we reached the coast before daybreak one morning, then followed along the upper end of the bay to Corpus. It was a fair-sized town with a couple of big general stores and a lot of little shops. The place seemed mighty quiet that morning, like it was Sunday and everyone was in church. We saw few men and no women or children. "Looky there," Sonny Smith said, pointing to a man dangling at the end of a rope tied to a tree limb. The rope was tight around his neck and his head sagged to one side. I felt sick at the sight of him.

A rancher named Pat Whelan and a posse of eight men had had a scrap with bandits on the Little Oso, Sheriff John McClure told us. They'd killed three of the bandits and captured one, but lost two of their posse. They'd brought the captive to Corpus, where the crowd grabbed him and strung him up to that pecan tree in the plaza. "I wasn't here or I'da stopped it," the sheriff told Captain. Now everyone was worried, for the country was swarming with bandits, some parties as large as a hundred men. The people of Corpus were forted up for an attack, like we used to be during the Comanche Moon in the old days.

Sheriff McClure told Captain that in March several hundred bandits had crossed into Texas at Eagle Pass, then split up into bands of from fifteen to a hundred. It looked like they were trying to drive all Americans out of the Strip. One band had swept through Duval County toward Beeville, and others had headed toward Goliad and Refugio. One bunch ran off seventeen of Cornelius Stillman's best saddle horses, but when a posse captured two of the bandits and turned them over to Stillman, he let them go. He was a justice of the peace, but he knew the bandits would come back and kill him if he didn't turn the two men loose. That's how bad it was.

A big band of raiders had approached Corpus, capturing and robbing everyone they saw, the sheriff continued. One was Mrs. Sidbury, who was on the way to town with her hired man Santos driving her carriage. The bandits saw a small trunk and ordered Santos to hold up everything in it, one thing at a time, while they crowded around and watched. It was sure embarrassing for her to hear them snickering about those lacy things women wear out of sight. But Santos was game and loyal. There was a little box of valuable jewelry in the trunk, but he pawed around like he couldn't find anything else and they didn't look for themselves. Lucky for him they didn't, for they'd have shot him dead.

One big party had captured ranchers Mike Dunn and Jim Lane and held them for a week. Dunn was there and told us his story. Those bandits had robbed and burned ranches all the way to Nuecestown, he said. When they entered town they made the two ranchers ride in front to stop any bullets fired their way.

At Fred Franks' store an old Mexican who worked for Franks had been standing in the doorway. The bandit leader, an Anglo outlaw, ordered him to join them. When he refused they dragged him out and hanged him. After looting Franks' place, Dunn said, they headed for Tom Noakes' store. Noakes and his children escaped through a secret tunnel. The bandits helped themselves for a while, then set fire to the store. Martha Noakes had been hiding, but she ran to their living quarters in the back of the store to save her featherbed. The bandit *jefe* grabbed her and ordered her to show him where their money box was hidden. She refused. He quirted her hard across the back, but she just hung onto her featherbed and said nothing. She was one game woman, Dunn added. We'd already figured that.

Captain chewed his black cigar, and I knew he was mighty upset over the whipping of Martha Noakes. "What'd he look like? Describe him so we'll know him on sight."

"That won't be hard, Captain. He's some taller than most, with hair about the color of old saddle leather. In some knife scrape he got slashed across the face, and it left a deep scar from hairline to chin on the right side. Dresses like a regular dude. You won't mistake him."

"I aim to find him," Captain said, "and send him where woman-beaters belong. Anything else you can tell us?"

"They took eighteen Dick Heye saddles, all of them decorated with silver conchos," Dunn answered. Heye was a San Antonio saddlemaker who liked to stud his saddles and bridles with lots of silver. I'd seen a few of them and knew you could recognize one about as far as you could see it.

"Describe them," Captain ordered, "so all of us will know one when we see it." Dunn did as requested. Sol Lichtenstein, who owned the biggest store in Corpus, told Captain he had some of the saddles on order. Captain thought a minute, then said, "When those saddles come, Sol, don't sell any until I tell you differently. It ain't going to be healthy to be found ridin' one."

Captain turned to Sarge Armstrong. "Be sure everyone will know those saddles when they see them. Then order 'em to empty those saddles on sight," he said. "No palaverin' with the riders. No askin' where they got 'em. Empty 'em. Leave the men where they land and bring the saddles to camp." His voice was weak and soft as usual, but his words were chilling. That order caused Captain some trouble later. We emptied a lot of those saddles, and in every case it was an outlaw who'd been sitting in it, someone whose name was on the list of wanted men. The trouble was that some of them had influential friends. Bad hombres usually do.

Captain chewed his unlit cigar a bit, then turned to Sol again. "The state didn't give me any money, Sol, but I've got to have rifles and ammunition, and some grub."

Sol pointed to his store. "There's the best stock you'll find between Santone and Brownsville. Pick out what you need. Anything you want."

"You may never get paid for it," Captain said. "The carpetbaggers left more debts than money in Austin, and the legislature might call it a war in the Nueces Strip, but they ain't willing to spend much to stop it."

"Let me worry about that. I'd rather give it to you than have them bandits steal it. Take all you need and sign a receipt. Tom Noakes would do the same if he had anything left."

Old Sol grinned and continued. "You're in luck about rifles. Last ship brought us a big batch from the East—all the newest repeaters—Henrys, Spencers, Winchesters."

"How about Sharps?"

"Sharps? We used to keep a few on hand for buffalo hunters, and we took some in trade for Henrys. We're probably stuck with at least thirty. Ain't much call for them these days, now that the buffalo's gone."

"I want 'em."

"I thought you were hunting bandits, not buffalo. Sharps are heavy to carry and they're only single shot. They'll bring down a buffalo, but if you miss a buffalo, he'll give you time to reload. If you miss a man you're in trouble."

"I don't need men who miss."

The store had thirty-six Sharps and Captain took them all. Sol was sure glad to see them go. I'd never handled one before. That .50-caliber rifle barrel looked big enough for squirrels to store acorns in; the bullets were as big as my thumb. When that gun roared, something was bound to drop; if you missed a man the wind from the flat-nosed bullet would probably blow him over. But if you missed, he wouldn't give you time to reload for a second shot.

That, we found, was Captain's way of fighting. He got you there and gave you a big chance, but then it was up to you. We soon learned never to pull the trigger unless the target was square in our sights.

We loaded the wagon with plenty of boxes of pistol and rifle bullets and sacks of frijoles, cornmeal, and coffee. The grub wouldn't be fancy, but at least we'd eat every now and then. Sheriff McClure came back while we were loading the wagon, and stopped to talk to Captain.

"I forgot to ask if Adjutant Steele mentioned my wire," he said. "I told him that five ranches had been burned in a week, and asked him when you were comin'."

"I didn't see your wire, but he sent word to head here as soon as possible. Were the ranches Anglo or Mexican?"

"Mexican, every last one of 'em. I don't know if they were burned by raiders or posses. Whelan's posse bragged that they'd killed eleven men last time they was out. It's gotten out of hand. That's why I sent for you. If these posses keep on killing Mexicans we'll have a civil war, and can't say I'd blame 'em."

"I knew a lot of Mexican ranchers when I was here in '72," Captain said. "They're Texas citizens, and almost to a man they're as much against the raidin' as Americans." The sheriff agreed.

Pat Whelan was talking to Sol Lichtenstein. Captain walked over to them. "Disband your posse at once," Captain ordered Whelan. "All others are to be disbanded, too, unless Sheriff McClure deputizes them."

"I'll try," Whelan answered.

"I didn't say try. I said disband them." Captain's tone made a shiver run up the back of my neck.

"They may not want to disband."

"That's right, they may not." Captain chewed his cigar. "They may have a little private killin' to do and want a posse for a shield. You notify every one of 'em that as of this minute any armed bands we run across will be treated as outlaws."

"We'd be glad to help you, Captain."

"When I want your help I'll sign you up. Huntin' outlaws is full-time work, and we've been hired to do it. Get that word to the posses. We mean business."

Later I saw Captain's report to Adjutant General Steele: "The acts committed by Americans are horrible to relate; many ranches have been plundered and burned, and the people murdered or driven away; one of these groups was described to me in Corpus Christi as having killed eleven men on their last raid. I immediately issued an order disbanding the minute companies and all armed bands acting without authority of the state. Had I not disbanded these companies it is possible and very probable that civil war would have ensued as the Mexicans are very much exasperated. I think you will hear from us soon."

It was late afternoon when we headed out of Corpus, and we rode all night, most of the time in a heavy rain. Water several inches deep covered the ground in every direction; it didn't seem to have any place to run off. The going was hard for the horses and even worse for the wagon mules. They sank in the mud at every step, and that black gumbo had to be scraped off the wagon wheels every quarter of a mile. There was no place we could stop, so we just kept slopping along in the water and mud, moving but not getting anywhere. We made only about twelve miles that whole night.

After the sun came up we saw a little rise on the plains that was out of the water and we headed for it, but when we got near we saw it was crowded with cattle, deer, jackrabbits, alligators, and rattlesnakes. It looked like they must have had a truce for bad weather; as far as we could see they seemed to be getting along together. We were looking for high ground, too, but Captain decided not to join them.

Scouts Horace Maben and Parrott signalled Captain to come forward. When we rode up to them we saw two Mexicans hanging by their necks from a wooden bridge across the Little Oso. Captain turned red. "Outlaws didn't do that. Some possemen paid off an old grudge," he said.

I found out later that the two men were the Vásquez brothers, owners of some of the best grazing land around. For years Anglos had tried to buy their land or to drive them off it. Plucky and determined, the two Mexicans had fought for what was theirs. I made a mental note to come back someday and see who had grabbed their land and cattle.

After we crossed the bridge the ground was dry and solid. Captain dismounted, loosened his cinch, hooked his pistol belt over his saddle horn, and walked on, leading his weary horse. He gave no order, but we all did the same, tired and hungry though we were. After the rain the air was moist, and mosquitoes that seemed as big as bees attacked the men and horses in swarms. "We'll rest up at Ban Katy," Captain said.

We got to what was left of Banquete by mid-afternoon, and while we hobbled our horses and turned them out to graze, Dad Smith started a fire. Soon we had hot coffee, and biscuits that must have been around a long time though not quite long enough to be petrified. We soaked them in the coffee and wolfed them down while he cooked some meat.

Before Anglos had come to the area, Banquete was a Mexican center, with fiestas and Saturday night fandangos. During the Civil War it had been a Confederate supply center. Now it was a ghost town, with everything in ruins but a little adobe chapel. It was the jumping-off place for men on the run heading for the lower country, and it was where sheriffs pulled up and turned back. The sheriff's deadline, they called it. Any man who made it to Banquete knew he could get to the border without running into lawmen. There wasn't a fence anywhere, and ranches were far apart. The stage between San Antonio and Brownsville had made it a stop for changing teams, but the horses kept disappearing. Now the stage stopped only to leave mail for ranchers in the area.

Banquete was deserted except for an old codger called W6 Wright. W6 was a grizzled old rascal who looked like a buffalo hunter. He'd showed up one day and claimed some land—said his Winchester gave him title to it, and nobody argued. Then he began branding mavericks W6. When any mail was left there, old W6 looked after it. When he saw our camp he paid us a call. "Howdy, Cap," he said. "What brings you to Ban Katy? Headin' for the lower country?"

"Mebbe."

"How many men you got?"

"Forty-two."

"Betcha a hundred you don't take forty-two in with you all the way."

"I don't bet."

"Betcha a hundred you don't bring twenty out."

"I don't bet." Captain turned to leave.

"Wait a minute, Cap. The stage driver left you a box of books from the governor." He led the way to the old chapel while I wondered how he knew what was in the box. We found the lid had already been pried off. "I thought they was mail order catalogs," W6 explained, "but they ain't. They're descriptions of some of our citizens, a whole passel of 'em, who seem to have gotten into a little trouble with the law somewheres."

Captain began thumbing through one of the books. "I ain't in there, if that's what you're looking for," W6 said. "I already looked. If I'd seen my name I'd be across the Rio Grande and dried off by now."

We all crowded around, real curious. "Is that there book full of names?" Josh asked. The look Captain gave him cooled down his curiosity and put a bridle on his tongue. Corporal Rudd nudged him in the back, but that wasn't necessary; he'd already been squelched good. Captain gave copies to Lieutenants Robinson and Wright and the three sergeants. He took one for himself and then had us put the box in the wagon.

Some of the Rangers who'd been with Captain earlier figured the books described men wanted by the law before or after coming to Texas. Captain had drawn up such a list when he was with the State Police under Governor Davis. He had resigned when he saw how the carpetbaggers intended to use the police. Now that they were out of office, Governor Coke had added a bunch of new names and had the list printed.

We rested and our horses ate their fill. Next morning Captain and old W6 talked some more before we set out. The bandits who'd raided the area around Goliad had taken their loot and headed for the river crossing at Las Cuevas, but W6 said that a big party had passed by Banquete on its way down the coast. This was the bunch who'd plundered and burned Noakes' store and had taken the Dick Heye saddles. They were probably heading for Brownsville and Matamoros.

We rode toward Brownsville on the old Taylor trail made by General Zachary Taylor just before the war with Mexico. Even though the country was open, with few places where an ambush was likely, Captain had scouts out ahead and on both sides. Each of us had his cartridge belt full of pistol bullets, and his pockets bulging with Sharps cartridges. The farther we went the more nervous I got, but I didn't aim to show it. I looked at Josh, and I could tell he too was wondering what we were in for.

After two days' travel we stopped at Santa Gertrudis, a settlement of a hundred or more people on Captain Richard King's huge ranch. The main ranch house had a high tower where a pair of men kept watch at all times. The lookouts spotted us a long way off and sent out scouts to see if we were bandits. They led us to the edge of the ranch buildings, where Captain King rode out to welcome us. From a distance he looked like Captain McNelly's twin.

Captain King had come to Texas during the war with Mexico, and had run a steamer up the Rio Grande. He and Mifflin Kenedy, a fellow ship captain from the East, had started raising cattle in the 1850s and were partners for a time. They had had plenty of trouble with the river bandits, and the ranch house was like a fort. In one room there were stacks of cartridge boxes and eighty Henry repeating rifles, well oiled and ready for use.

We unsaddled and turned our mounts into a corral, where vaqueros fed them. Captain King looked the horses over. "How in the world did you get this far on those nags?" he asked. "You must have had to walk and lead them."

"Yes, but they're all we have," Captain replied, "so we got this far on them."

"You'll never catch those Cortina men on them. Too many of 'em are riding my horses," I heard Captain King say as the two men walked toward the ranch house. They put us up in a bunkhouse that night but first filled us up with good beef stew and coffee. Mrs. King and her niece Caroline Chamberlain refilled our cups whenever they were empty. She was a right pretty little gal and I thought Josh would drown in coffee just for the pleasure of having her refill his tin cup. "Ain't he something," Sonny Smith said. "I do believe he's been bit by the love bug."

That night, after we'd bedded down, Josh seemed kind of quiet, not joking a lot like usual. "What's on your mind, amigo?" I asked him. "You wantin' another cup of coffee?"

He grinned sheepishly. "I been thinkin' of askin' Captain King for a job," he admitted.

"You mean quittin' the Rangers and stayin' here?" I couldn't believe it.

"It's just a crazy thought that snuck up and hit me when I wasn't lookin'. If I was to quit Captain they'd set the hounds on me. Captain King would never hire anyone who walked out on Captain. Probably wouldn't even let him spend the night here."

I agreed with that, and closed my eyes. Josh was so full of coffee he wasn't a bit sleepy. Anyway, his mind was on other things.

"Wonder how long it would take me to learn cowboyin' and work up to foreman," he said. He was still talking when I fell asleep.

When I looked out in the morning there was a corral full of King Ranch cowponies, and the Rangers were roping them and leading them out. I caught my own coyote dun, for I knew he was all the mount I'd ever need. Captain King looked at him and asked, "Sure you don't want to swap ponies?" I shook my head. He smiled. "Looks like a good one," he said.

Josh, who had a lariat but couldn't rope a fence post with it, was standing by the corral, staring at the excellent horses, which were all part thoroughbred. Captain King spoke to one of his vaqueros, who flipped a loop over the head of a rangy sorrel gelding and led it out to where Captain King and Josh stood.

"Where're you from, son?" Captain King asked Josh.

"Georgia, sir."

"How come you happened to hire on with Captain McNelly?" Josh told him as King looked over his worn-out old farm saddle. King spoke to the vaquero, who left and returned with a stock saddle and a rifle scabbard. While the vaquero saddled the sorrel gelding, Josh gazed at it in admiration.

"Like him?"

Josh nodded. "How much is a horse like that worth, sir?" Captain

King smiled. "Don't worry about that, son. Wherever Captain McNelly takes you that horse will get you there. He's a good, sound animal with plenty of staying power and enough speed." Josh was the happiest lad I ever saw as he swung into that saddle.

The Rangers had saddled their new mounts, but Captain was still looking at the horses in the corral; he was watching a big bay gelding that was obviously mostly thoroughbred.

"That's Segal," Captain King told him. "You want him?"

Captain slowly shook his head. "He's worth at least five hundred dollars. What a horse! But I couldn't ask you for him. The state would never pay you what he's worth."

"I'd rather give him to you than have those bandits get him. Most of those devils are already riding my horses and I want to do at least as well by you, Captain."

When we rode out of Santa Gertrudis we didn't look at all like the motley crew that Captain had rounded up in Burton. It does something to men to be straddling good horseflesh, and all of us were now well mounted. I glanced at Josh and Sonny; both looked ready for anything. Although we wore the same clothes as before, we sure looked like a different outfit. Leading the way was Captain on Segal, one of the best horses I'd ever seen.

It was amazing the way Captain had taken charge of the bunch of us, mostly strangers to him, and in a couple of weeks had us ready to follow him into a fight even though we'd be outnumbered. Some of them had served in his scout company in Louisiana, so they knew what he could do. Most of us had heard stories about how he had outfoxed and out-fought the Yankees, and that helped. But even if we hadn't known anything about him, after a couple of weeks in his Ranger company we'd have followed him anywhere. Josh and I figured now that he'd known all along that none of the Taylor or Sutton crowd would fight.

Captain never wasted a word or made an unnecessary move; it was like he always knew exactly what to do. I can't explain why, for I don't have an answer. I guess we could see that he was a natural leader with plenty of experience, but it was partly a feeling we got just by being around him. He could tell you what he wanted and you'd do it without wondering if it would work.

I heard later that some of the men were on the dodge and the names they used weren't the ones they were born with. One was supposed to be Frank James, but if so I never knew which. Captain signed them on because he figured they'd take orders and wouldn't run from a fight. Mostly he was right.

By now I'd figured that Captain had a mind of steel and had ice water in his veins instead of blood; that he was a man who didn't recognize pain and who either had no feelings or hid them well. I tried to imagine what it would be like to follow him into battle.

III

Mounted on Segal, Captain led the column while we loped along in single file, with scouts ahead and on our flanks. About mid-morning I smelled smoke, and it didn't smell like a campfire. We soon came to the smoldering ruins of Rancho La Parra, set afire by bandits or a posse the day before.

While we sat looking at the burned-out buildings, a party of men rode up behind us and stopped just out of pistol range to size us up. They had rifles across their saddles, ready for use. Sarge rode toward them. "We're Texas Rangers," he called. "Come forward."

When they heard we were Rangers they trotted right up, and we saw they were a mixed bunch, Anglo and Mexican ranchers with their cowboys and vaqueros. A big man rode up to Captain.

"I'm McFaddin from Cameron County," he said. "You be Captain McNelly. I met you when you was here in '72." Captain nodded and shook his hand. "A vaquero from La Parra rode in last night and told us a bunch of Americans had attacked the ranch," McFaddin continued. "Those posses are every bit as bad as Cortina's raiders from Mexico. We raised what men we could and come to protect the folks here. I see we're too late. Damn! We don't hold with the murderin' and cheatin' goin' on 'round here. I suppose they hit other ranches too."

Captain nodded. "I've ordered the posses to disband," he said. "We'll kill any armed bands we run into, Americans or Mexicans. You folks can go on back and leave it to us. I'll send for you if I need help. I know you're one man I can trust."

"That's good enough for me," McFaddin replied, and they rode back the way they'd come. Almost by accident I'd noticed that when McFaddin was talking to Captain, Blackie had pulled his hat down over his eyes and turned his back.

We moved on, and a couple of hours later Sarge Armstrong galloped into the open. He circled his arm twice and pointed south. We guessed he'd spotted riders coming our way.

Captain gave some cavalry signal, and the three corporals ahead of us moved their men to the left, while Corporal Rudd and the other two turned to the right. We hadn't practiced that maneuver, but the excavalrymen knew what to do and the rest of us copied them. We formed a crescent, with about five paces between riders. Captain twirled the chamber of his pistol and tested the trigger action, so we all did the same.

Up ahead, Sarge and Jim Wofford sat their horses on opposite sides of the trail. When a bunch of men rode toward us, Sarge held up his hand. They stopped, and then he and Wofford escorted the leaders to Captain. They were local ranchers Hines Clark and Martin Culver with a big posse they'd raised.

Culver rode up to Captain, all smiles and friendly. "Captain," he said, "we got about a hundred men, all white. Nary a Yankee, nigger, or Meskin among them. Real God-fearin' white men."

"Did you overtake any raiders?"

"No, they got plumb away, back across the river."

"Who burned La Parra?" Culver shrugged but didn't answer.

Captain was silent for a minute or two, then pulled a cigar from his pocket and stuck it in his mouth.

"We want to throw in with you, Captain," Culver said.

"I don't want your help. I'm going to disarm these men and send them home." Clark and Culver looked at each other; then Culver said, "They won't do that."

"Then I order you to. Disarm and disband them."

"They won't do it for me."

"They will for me," Captain said, chewing on his cigar. We'd already learned that meant he was getting warmed up, maybe hot.

"We'll have to vote on it."

"You have ten minutes. If you don't decide to lay down your arms and surrender to the regular law of Texas, my Rangers will lay them down for you."

"Meanin' we're the same as outlaws?"

"I can't prove you're outlaws right now, 'cause I don't know all you've done. But in ten minutes you will be for sure. You'll be reckoned as armed outlaws, and we've been ordered to kill any we find. Tell your men we'll do just that."

Clark and Culver rode back to their posse while Captain pulled a watch from his vest pocket and glanced at it. I sneaked a look at the posse and could see there was a lot of jawing going on. One of them was counting us. Captain didn't even look at them. I was wondering what he'd do if they refused—they outnumbered us at least two to one, maybe more. If I'd known him better I wouldn't have had any question about what he'd do. He'd do what he said he would.

That was the longest ten minutes I ever sat through, holding my breath most of the time. I glanced at Josh; he looked like he was also doing some heavy thinking, and he was a bit pale. Sergeant Armstrong appeared perfectly relaxed, like he wasn't a bit worried, and that made me feel some better.

Captain put his watch back in his pocket and threw away his soggy cigar. In almost the same motion, he pulled his pistol from the holster. All the rest of us little McNellys drew our guns, but I've got to admit I wasn't eager to use mine right then.

At that moment I learned one of the many things Captain taught us just by what he did. If a peace officer deserves to be respected, men will respect him. I doubt that there was another lawman in Texas who could have done what he did. Those men knew they could kill all of us, but they also knew that there wouldn't be many of them left to brag about it.

One of the possemen rode up alone and handed Captain his pistol, butt forward. Captain holstered his gun and told the man to keep his, but to use it only to defend his home. I quietly breathed one big sigh— things had been pretty touchy. The other posse members filed by one at a time, each one stopping until Captain signalled for him to move on. When that posse surrendered it meant that Texas law had finally come to the lower Nueces country, and that it would be obeyed and respected. Clark and Culver sullenly rode up last. Captain said nothing but waved them on. Word got around fast, and I heard later that some people swore that Captain was only bluffing. Those were people who didn't know him. No one there, Ranger or posseman, believed that. Captain didn't give an order unless he intended to enforce it. If Clark and Culver had thought he was bluffing they'd probably have tested him. But they saw the look in his eye and knew damn well he meant what he said.

When the posse had moved on we spread out in a line and continued our march. There wasn't much brush at first, just occasional islands of it and mottes of oak trees, but we were approaching brush country that was a bushwhacker's delight. There, it would be foolhardy to ride out in the open without knowing whether men were hiding among the oaks or in the brush and looking at you down their rifle barrels. That's why Captain had scouts ahead of us.

That night we camped in the Mota Tablón, a big oak grove. We had no campfire, no coffee, no food. If you were a McNelly you ate only when Captain ate. We took our turns at guard and slept when we could. In the morning Dad Smith fried some salt pork in cornmeal and made coffee, and we ate all we could hold, not knowing when the next meal would be.

"Captain mentioned being here in '72 and McFaddin said he met him then. What was that all about?" I asked Corporal Rudd.

"Congress sent a committee here to investigate the cattle war, and the committee hired Captain to bring in witnesses to testify. Some of the ones who did were killed later by bandits. The committee decided that Cortina was responsible for all of the raiding, but I'm not sure. They listened to his enemies, who may have laid it on a bit heavy."

After breakfast we fell in and Captain walked back and forth along the line. "We're in outlaw country, and you'll be sent out on scouting patrols," he said. "As far as we're concerned there are only two kinds of people here, outlaws and law-abiding citizens. Treat all law-abiding folks with respect, regardless of color, shape, or size. Don't enter a house unless the owner invites you in. Don't take a melon or an ear of corn unless he offers it. If his dog barks at you, don't shoot it—get away from it. Let 'em know we're friends and here to help 'em.

"As for the other kind, arrest 'em and bring 'em to camp. Horseback or afoot, alone or in groups, arrest 'em and bring 'em in. Until further orders, apply the old Spanish *ley de fuga* or law of flight to all prisoners. That means if one tries to escape or his friends try to rescue him, shoot him on the spot.

"Any questions? Anyone got anything to say?"

A man in Polly Williams' squad stepped forward, eyes on the ground. "Captain," he stammered, "this plans to be longer than I figured. I got some stock I better look after—"

"You want a discharge?"

"I reckon I do."

Captain seemed to have expected this. He pulled a paper from his jacket pocket, wrote on it, and handed it to Lieutenant Robinson. "Scratch him off," he said.

Four more stepped up and asked to be discharged.

"Turn in your rifles and any other state property you have," Captain ordered. "I can't force you to, but I'm askin' that you go back to the Santa Gertrudis and swap these horses for your own nags."

After they left Captain gave each of us a copy of the books he had gotten in Banquete. "If you have any trouble bringin' in a man and have to leave him on the ground, try to identify him in this book and then scratch his name," he told us. The book was crammed with names and descriptions of criminals from all over. The ones in big black type, we were told, were the "swapouts," those who swore they wouldn't be taken alive.

"These outlaws," Captain said, "have been plunderin' and murderin' decent folks. They don't acknowledge any law, either that of the United

States or of Texas. We're here to set them right, and they won't be easy
to convince. But I'll never send you into a fight. I'll lead you in. Any
questions? Anyone got anything to say?"

No one else wanted a discharge, so Captain nodded to Lieutenant
Robinson to get us on our way. We headed west from the Mota Tablón,
with four scouts out ahead and others on our flanks. We'd left the
Taylor trail a mile or two behind when Deaf Rector signalled that men
were coming from the south. We stopped where we were.

Rector and Adams escorted a column of men toward us; they were
Captain Neal Coldwell and his Ranger company, part of the Frontier
Battalion.

Captain rode up to Coldwell and shook his hand, though Coldwell
didn't seem pleased to see him and his men didn't speak to us. "I got a
message from headquarters by army telegraph," Coldwell said, "ordering us to report back. Maybe they figure you can do better there than
we did. Good luck. We arrested the raiders with stolen cattle and turned
'em over to the sheriff. Fat lot of good that did. They posted bond and
were back in business by the time we got to camp. Not one of 'em was
ever tried or convicted. I've got my doubts about that sheriff."

"Our comin' here doesn't mean anything like you're thinking," Captain told him. "The legislature created this Special Force to come down
here so all of the Frontier Battalion companies can fight Comanches
and Lipans. They know at headquarters that you and your men have
done everything you could possibly do."

That thawed the ice a bit, so we all dismounted and squatted in the
shade to talk awhile. "The troops also caught a bunch of them from
time to time, but none of us could get them to talk," Coldwell continued. "Those bandits are smart and well organized, and they've got spies
everywhere. They know when you move and what you're goin' to do as
soon as you do. They're bigger than the law and they know it." Captain
chewed on his cigar.

"Is Cortina behind it all like everyone says?" Captain asked.

"No way of tellin' for sure. I guess he's still a local hero to the
Mexicans for tryin' to protect 'em before the army and Rip Ford's
rangers ran him across the river. And since he whipped the Brownsville
boys twice they still hate him and blame him for everything that happens. All I know for sure is that he has a contract supplyin' beef to the
Spanish army in Cuba, and that he buys stolen cattle. Whether or not
he has a hand in stealin' 'em I can't rightly say." He shook hands with
Captain again and mounted. "I hope you have better luck than we did,"
he said. "I really mean it. This country needs to be cleaned up." They
headed off along the trail we'd followed.

The governor had sent Captain with a commission and the authority to enlist a company, but without money for supplies or anything else. And Captain was expected to do what neither the U.S. Army nor Coldwell's company had been able to do—end the killing and plundering in the Nueces Strip. Coldwell and the Army had followed the rules laid down in Washington and Austin, which was why they hadn't gotten anywhere. But the Strip had to be pacified if it was ever going to be safe for law-abiding folks, Mexicans or Anglos.

Captain had an advantage over the others—the governor trusted him and had told him to do whatever had to be done. If he was on the trail of raiders and they crossed into Mexico he could follow them. None of the others had that kind of authority. The outlaws made their own rules, and they didn't take prisoners unless they had some temporary use for them. "What's good enough for them is good enough for us," Captain had said when he ordered us to shoot any prisoners who were trying to escape or whose friends were trying to rescue them. A few Rangers felt that was going too far, but they kept quiet about it and intended to obey orders. They wouldn't have been little McNellys long if they hadn't.

After Coldwell left, Captain changed his plans. He was sure Cortina's spies knew that Coldwell's company had been pulled out, but he figured they might not know about us yet. He pulled us back and hid us in some oaks a few miles north of the Rancho los Indios headquarters. He kept the patrols out, but they stayed under cover and out of sight.

I had just gotten to sleep that night when Corporal Rudd touched each of us on the shoulder and whispered, "Get ready to move." Five minutes later the entire command set out in a column of twos behind Lieutenant Wright on his little black stallion. We rode all night, and at daybreak we hid in an oak motte near a spring called El Sauz, the Willow. We stayed there all day, while scouts rode out to see what they could find. Someone brought in a stranger to us, old J. S. Rock, a Brownsville scout who'd worked with Captain in '72. He signed on with us.

Next day some of us were sent out as lookouts, to hide on the highest ground and watch for anyone. Sergeant Orrill took Josh and me to our spot. We hid our mounts in the brush and picked out the tallest mesquites to climb.

"What if we see someone?" Josh asked, a quaver in his voice.

Sarge Orrill smiled. "Orders are to bring 'em to camp, son."

"What if there're several?" I asked.

"Makes no difference. Orders are still orders. Bring 'em to camp."

"And if they won't come?"

"You've got guns. You know what they're for, don't you?" We didn't answer that one, and I guess we both hoped no one would show up, but an hour or two later we saw a rider coming along on a mule.

"I'll get him," Josh said, scrambling down. "You stay here and keep watch." I could tell he was as nervous as I was, but he was determined to show he could carry out orders. He was so edgy that his horse sensed it and jumped around while he was trying to mount. Nervous men make nervous horses.

I kept my Sharps trained on the man, but my finger was sweaty. Josh overtook him, and they seemed to be having some kind of a palaver. I was too far away to hear them, but I gathered that the man was speaking in Spanish, and that neither of them understood a word the other said. Finally Josh aimed his pistol at the man and pointed toward camp.

That night I talked to him and learned that he was a young Mexican on his way to get married in the chapel at Rancho los Indios. His girl and the padre had been waiting there. We kept him in camp helping Dad Smith until we were ready to move, and then let him go. He didn't wear a gun, but he might have spread word about us, and Captain didn't take any chances—you can't tell a spy by his looks. "I sure feel sorry for him, and even more for his gal," Sonny Smith said. "She probably thinks he's run out on her or been killed."

Matt Fleming, another of our lookouts, rode in that evening with a strange-looking man who still wore his gun and wasn't under arrest. He'd spotted Fleming and asked to be taken to Captain. He was old Jesús Sandoval, and he knew Captain and Rock. Captain signed him on immediately, and we got word he would take charge of all prisoners. I figured he must be our jailer or something like that.

Old Jesús was a sight. His skin was parched like old leather and his light blue eyes seemed to throw off sparks. His hair and beard were red and scraggly, the beard flecked with white, the hair reaching his thin shoulders. He looked like a crazy man, and I guess in a way he was. He'd testified before the congressional committee, Rudd told us, and for that bandits had carried off his wife and daughter. Now he lived only to avenge them by killing raiders—for him it was a holy war, and he didn't care if they were Mexicans or Anglos. He and Old Rock knew that country, knew every trail, spring, and river crossing. Captain and Rock spent most of the day covering the country round about, and that evening, when all the scouts were in, Sarge Armstrong lined us up.

"Two good men have joined us," Captain said, "Old Rock here and Haysoose. They know the trails and they'll take us where the shootin's good. If two or more of you flush out some bandits, whether they're runnin' or holed up, put yourselves at five-pace intervals and shoot only at the target in front of you. Don't shoot to the left or right but straight ahead. And don't shoot at all until you've got your target good in your sights so you can't miss.

"Never walk up on a wounded man. Pay no attention to a white flag. That's a trick bandits use on green hands. Don't touch a dead man except to identify him. And treat all law-abiding folks with respect." Captain's voice was so weak we could barely hear him at either end of the line. He didn't look or sound like a fighting man, but when he spoke we held our breath and our horses seemed to quit switching their tails and stomping, like they were also listening. Captain was that kind of man.

At dark we moved out, following Old Rock and a few scouts. The moon was at first quarter, and for a while gave us a little light. We rode slowly and finally stopped at the deserted Rancho las Rucias, about ten miles from the Rio Grande. The ranch had been one of the big Spanish land grants, but border troubles had forced the owner and his family to leave. Everything was in ruins, even the corrals.

It was now mid-May and the Rio Grande was low and easy to cross in many places. The rustlers were busily taking advantage of this opportunity. We learned through a friend of Rock's who worked at Cortina's headquarters at Matamoros that they were shipping five thousand head every month, and that Cortina was paying from two to ten dollars a head for stolen steers. I didn't know it at the time, but the man working for Cortina was a Ranger sergeant who'd gone to Matamoros like an American renegade. There were a lot of them with Cortina.

We sent out patrols from Las Rucias for several days, but none cut the trail of stolen stock. Josh and I accompanied Corporal Rudd on a scout about twenty miles upriver, while others went downstream and toward Los Indios. No one had anything to report.

One day, while we were in camp waiting for action to start, Lieutenant Robinson suggested we have some target practice. Most of us picked a tree that couldn't fight back, fired a shot from about fifteen feet away, then gradually backed up to about fifty feet.

Josh got carried away, like he'd heard about some gunman who could shoot accurately from a running horse. When he galloped toward a tree and blazed away at it, all of us—even Captain—stopped to watch. That made Josh plenty nervous, but he came on the run again, boring holes in the atmosphere. If he hit a tree it was an innocent victim, not his target. When he went to the supply wagon and asked Dad Smith for more shells, Captain followed him.

"Sell him some," he said. "Two bits a round."

"Is his credit good?" Dad Smith asked.

"No. Cash."

Josh holstered his pistol and looked at his shabby boots. Captain spoke again. "George," he said in a fatherly tone, "the state will buy you all the shells you need, but don't waste 'em. Practice, for you sure need it. Just don't put on a show."

After that, Josh practiced like the rest of us did and hit his target as often as any. Captain watched him for a few minutes, and I saw him smile as he walked away, like he knew there was a real man in that big kid.

We sat around camp the rest of the day doing nothing. The older men seemed to sense that we'd see action soon, and they did little talking and no joking. Rock and Captain were often together, but not even the lieutenants knew what they talked about. Later Robinson admitted that if they knew three minutes in advance what Captain was going to do they felt lucky. I guess he didn't want anyone stewing about what was coming. Men who get all worked up over something aren't the best of shots, and if they worry long enough they might even talk themselves out of fighting at all. Captain knew what he was doing when he did our worrying for us.

Dad Smith served us only hardtack and coffee for supper, and by then we knew Captain well enough to realize something was brewing. Captain was convinced that men fought better and longer on empty stomachs. If both men and horses couldn't keep going for thirty-six hours without eating, they didn't belong in his outfit—they weren't fit to be called McNellys. We weren't convinced that a meal now and then would prevent us from fighting, but we did what Captain did.

We'd just bedded down on the ground when we heard a rider coming. A guard took him straight to Captain and Rock, so I figured the rider was probably Jesús or another scout. Then the guard came back down the line and told fifteen of us to saddle up. Old Rock led off to the north and we followed, with Lieutenant Robinson in command.

Old Rock was no easy man to follow for he led the way at a lope, splashing through lagunas and climbing up slopes, occasionally heading straight through thorny brush that almost clawed some Rangers out of their saddles. Old Rock was ducking and clinging to the side of his horse now and then like a brush-popper after mossyhorn steers. I'd chased cattle in the brush before, so I just gave my mustang his head and crouched low, ducking under limbs and shielding my face as best I could. The men on big horses really got scratched up. I was sure glad I hadn't swapped my mustang for a big horse at the Santa Gertrudis.

After a couple of hours Old Rock pulled up on high ground and stopped to let the horses blow while we tightened our cinches. Corporal

Rudd, who rode the biggest horse in the outfit, looked like he had been dragged through catclaws. Although he'd never been heard to complain, he did mutter, "That man Rock acts plumb loco." We agreed but Rock went on, following the Rio Grande until daybreak, when we saw that the river was covered with fog so thick we couldn't see the other bank.

Rock looked around to get his bearings and then spoke to Lieutenant Robinson, who sent Sarge to spread us out in a skirmish line. "If shooting starts," Sarge told us, "stop in your tracks and wait for orders. Don't shoot till I tell you to."

We moved on, and in about an hour we came to a fresh cattle trail. Rock stopped and looked at the tracks, cursing softly. As the fog lifted we could see a dozen men driving the last of the stolen cattle up the Mexican side of La Bolsa crossing. The river there was wide and shallow enough for cattle to wade across. "They got away with about three hundred head, damn them," Rock said. "They have at least fifty men, maybe more."

As we rode into sight one of the bandits took off his hat, half bowed in our direction, and blew us a kiss. An Anglo rustler thumbed his nose and fired his pistol at us. I wondered why we didn't cut loose on them with our Sharps. We might have emptied a few saddles, though I guess Mexico would have considered it an act of war. But it was sure tempting.

Our horses were worn down, so we unsaddled and let them roll and graze for a couple of hours. No one was in a hurry to get back to Las Rucias and tell Captain we got there too late. Lieutenant Robinson was silent and gloomy, and when we went back he rode by himself most of the way. I was wondering what kind of shape we'd have been in if the fifteen of us had taken on those fifty well-armed bandits. But the point was that we'd failed, and Captain didn't accept failure. We might have been in less trouble fighting the fifty bandits.

We straggled into camp just after dark, and Lieutenant Robinson went straight to Captain, who was talking to Jesús and one or two others. I got near enough to hear what was said.

"We missed 'em. They were already across when the sun rose," Robinson told him.

"That's fine," Captain said, "just fine. We're doing almost as well as Coldwell and the Army." He chewed his cigar savagely, and I was glad I wasn't in Lieutenant Robinson's boots. We'd ridden as hard as we could, but they'd run the legs off those cattle, moving them at least fifteen miles between sundown and sunup. Other patrols had scouted downriver almost to Brownsville, but they also came up empty-handed. Cortina's spies had sure known where we were all the time.

IV

All of us got to wondering how Cortina's spies could know we'd arrived and what we were doing. There weren't any high places where they could hide and watch us with binoculars from a distance. That meant there might be some of them hiding close to our camp.

I watched for a chance to talk to Corporal Rudd alone. "How do you reckon Cortina's men always know what we're goin' to do?" I asked him.

"I can't explain it; they probably have men concealed in the brush observing us. Or maybe one of our men is in their employ. I wish we knew."

"I'm pretty good at hidin' out," I told him. "Learned it from an old Indian who used to work for us. How about sendin' me off somewhere, like to Santa Gertrudis or Banquete, and then I can hide out in the brush for a few days and maybe see what goes on."

"Good idea. Let me talk to Sarge."

The next morning while we ate biscuits and sidemeat, Sarge handed me a piece of folded paper. "Captain wants this delivered to Captain King," he said. "Wait for a reply." He winked when he spoke but didn't smile.

I packed some biscuits and bacon in my saddlebag and lit out like I was heading for the Taylor trail. There was a spring with willows around it and a few cottonwoods about a mile from camp, and I circled back to it. I unsaddled my pony and hobbled him. I was sure there wasn't anyone hiding along the way who might have seen me, for my mustang's ears didn't go up like they always did when he smelled a strange man or horse, and I trusted him to warn me.

None of the trees was very tall, but I didn't want to get up where someone might spot me, just high enough to see if anyone was coming. I stayed in one of those trees all day but saw no one. The grass was good around the spring, so my pony stayed close by, and the willows shielded him from the sight of anyone who might ride past. I ate a little and then lay down on my saddle blanket, with mosquitoes buzzing around me and coyotes yipping not far away.

I was up before daybreak and ate a biscuit and cold bacon, wishing for a tin cup of hot coffee. I checked to see that my pony hadn't wandered, and to give him a biscuit and scratch his ears. Then I climbed the tree and watched. The hours dragged by. I climbed down a couple of times to drink in the spring, wondering if I was just wasting my time.

By mid-afternoon I was close to falling asleep when I happened to look at my pony. His head was raised and his ears were up—someone or something was coming. I watched in the direction he was facing, and saw a man cautiously riding around the oaks and brush, obviously keeping out of sight as much as possible.

I slid down, unhobbled my mustang and saddled him, then climbed the tree again in time to see the rider enter a motte of oaks about half a mile away. I figured he must be waiting for someone, so I kept on watching. Half an hour later another rider came from the direction of our camp and entered the oaks. He was too far away for me to recognize either him or his horse.

The first rider probably would head back the way he came, I figured, so I climbed down and rode to the far side of some brush he'd passed earlier. After about fifteen minutes I heard him loping along. When he was about to go past me I rode out, covered him with my pistol, and ordered him to stop. He did.

He was a mean-looking cuss, and for a moment it looked like he'd grab for his gun. I didn't want that, for we needed him alive. "Raise your hands and be quick about it," I told him in Spanish. He raised them slowly, glowering at me like he'd kill me in a flash if he got the chance. I quickly grabbed his pistol and stuck it in my belt, then tossed my rawhide lariat over his head and pulled it tight in case he had any foolish ideas about making a run for it. "Now ride that way," I told him, pointing toward the camp.

There were only a few Rangers in camp as we approached—Sarge, Maben, Rector, and a few others, lying in the shade near the wagon. As the prisoner and I rode up I saw Blackie quietly approaching the camp from the opposite side. He was about to dismount when he saw us. He gave me a look of hatred. "God damn you, Carter," he said. "I'll kill you for this." He turned his horse, dug in his spurs, and was quickly out of sight. The Rangers all scrambled to their feet.

"What's goin' on?" Maben said. "Who was that that took off in such a hurry?"

"Blackie. I saw him and this man havin' a little talk, so I brought this feller to camp." Sarge Armstrong took charge of the prisoner.

"Ask him who he was talkin' to," Sarge told me.

I asked him in Spanish, but all he said was *"¿Quien sabe?"* Who knows?

"When Haysoose gets back he'll sing us a song," Sarge said. "It may not be pretty, but he'll be glad to tell us all he knows before Haysoose gets through with him."

I went to the wagon for a little grub and a cup of coffee, then lay in the shade and fell asleep. It was nearly dark when I awoke. I looked for the prisoner but didn't see him.

"Did he have anything to tell us?" I asked Sarge.

"Sure did. He's a spy for a big raider band that has an Anglo *jefe*. Someone in Brownsville tipped them off that Captain was raising a company to come here, so they sent Blackie to join it. He had us fooled. He's in the book, a thief and a killer, but most of his crimes were in Missouri. They figured that Texas lawmen didn't know much about him and he could get away with spyin' for 'em. Did for a while, and still would if you hadn't caught his partner."

"Where's the prisoner?"

"Haysoose took him."

I remembered that Jesús was to take charge of prisoners, but I didn't know if he turned them over to a sheriff or if he had a prison somewhere.

We loafed around camp the next few days, waiting for orders. Boyd was kneeling on a blanket, shuffling a deck of cards. I could tell by the way he handled those cards that he'd done more than his share of gambling.

"How about a little game to kill time, boys? Name your choice. It's all the same to me." Josh admitted he'd played stud poker a couple of times. I told Boyd it was against my religion. The look he gave me made it clear that he'd try to convert me one day.

Boyd threw his money on the blanket. Josh searched his pockets and came up with two dollars' worth of coins, which he gently placed on the blanket. They didn't kill much time, for in about as long as it takes to saddle a pony, the two dollars were in Boyd's pile.

"Ain't you got any more?" With a sickly smile, Josh said that was all he had in the world. Boyd tossed the coins back to him. "Ain't either of us goin' to spend any money for a while," he said. "You growin' boys need somethin' to jingle in your pockets. When we get somewhere we can spend it I'll win it back for keeps."

For the next day or two Jesús and Old Rock were out. On the third day Jesús rode in at noon on a sweaty horse and reported to Captain. We saddled our mounts while Jesús got a fresh one from the remuda. "Tighten your cinches now," Corporal Rudd told us. "There won't be any rest stops." Jesús and Rock led the way, with Captain and fourteen of us in single file behind them, heading for Los Indios.

We traveled at a fast lope for a couple of hours, then stopped while Rock and Jesús talked with Captain. Then Maben and Rector were sent ahead on the left and Jesús and Parrott on the right. About sundown Maben and Rector brought in a captive who was sitting in one of the Dick Heye saddles. "We thought he might want to tell us something," Maben explained, "so we brought him along with the saddle." They remembered Captain's orders to empty those saddles on sight.

The rider was an American who said he'd won the saddle in a poker game at Neale's ranch. He didn't know anything about cattle or cattle thieves, he said. He was a gambler.

"Maybe he talk to me," Jesús said, his light blue eyes flashing. Captain nodded, then went into his tent. Jesús slapped the man on the side of the head with his pistol, flattening him. He tied the man's hands behind his back, slipped a noose around his neck, and dragged him to a cottonwood. He tossed the rope over a limb and hauled the hombre to his feet, fighting for air. The man drew his chin in tight and was barely able to keep on breathing.

"Let me show you a little trick I learned in California," Spencer Adams said. "We found it unlimbered their tongues pretty fast." He pulled on the rope, raising the man a foot or two in the air, and then let him drop. After about the fourth time the man signalled that he was ready to talk. He said he was scouting for a party that had raided almost to La Parra.

"How many men?" Lieutenant Robinson asked.

"About fifty."

"How many beeves?"

"Around three hundred."

The raiders were coming back between the Taylor trail and the Laguna Madre, closer to the coast than they'd ever gone before. That meant they should cross the Arroyo Colorado in the afternoon or early evening. They'd follow along the edge of Palo Alto prairie and reach the crossing at about sunrise. At least that's what Captain, Rock, and Jesús figured, providing the captive was telling the truth. He was badly shaken and pretty pale, so there was no reason to suspect he was lying.

Jesús took charge of the captive, whose hands were still tied behind his back. He put the man on his horse and mounted his own. Still holding the rope around the man's neck, Jesús led him out of sight. "I wonder where his prisoner camp is," Josh said. It couldn't have been far, for he was back in about half an hour with both horses and no prisoner.

We knew what was coming next, and we were all saddled and ready to ride. But Captain kept us in camp for the night. We never knew what he had in mind, but we didn't ask. I must admit that I didn't fall asleep right away that night. I tossed a bit, wondering how the fifteen of us could take on two or three times our number of well-armed bandits, and how I would do in my first gunfight. I hoped my nerve didn't fail, but I wasn't at all sure.

When Captain had his plans set and was satisfied they'd work, he relaxed and seemed almost like an ordinary human. He knew the raiders were at least twenty-five miles from the Rio Grande, so there should be plenty of time. All we had to do was wait until daylight and then intercept them.

We were in the saddle well before dawn, heading east toward Laguna, spread out in a skirmish line with Rock and other scouts ahead. We all had fifty rounds of Sharps shells in our saddlebags and as many pistol bullets as our cartridge belts and pockets would hold.

The country we rode through was mainly hardpan, with occasional salt marshes and clumps of cedars or scrub oaks. About the time the sun burned off the ground fog, Rock came to the trail of the stolen steers. It was a few hours old; the raiders were driving the cattle hard. We were near the upper edge of Neale's old Rincón pasture when we saw Rock raise up in his stirrups, circle his hand, and point south toward the river. Josh and I looked at each other. I'm sure I was as pale as he was, for we were both plenty anxious. But Sonny Smith appeared as unruffled as ever. If he was worried he didn't let it show.

Rock headed down the trail at a fast lope. With Captain at our head, we followed in a double column about half a mile behind Rock. After a couple of miles Rock rode onto a bit of high ground, circled his hand and lowered it twice—he'd seen the herd. It was about seven o'clock. Right then I wished I had a canteen—my mouth felt like it was full of cotton.

The cattle were still about eight miles away and the raiders were pushing them fast toward Palo Alto prairie. They spotted us and drove those long-legged steers even faster. After about three or four miles they saw we were closing in and drove the cattle onto high ground on the far side of a *resaca*, a shallow basin with a foot or two of water in it. They had maybe half an hour to get ready before we could reach the edge of the water.

Captain galloped up to Rock, then stopped and scouted the raiders with his binoculars. He put the glasses back in his saddlebag and drew his pistol, spun the cylinder, tested the trigger, then reholstered it. Glancing to see that we were in position behind him, he dug his spurs into Segal. That big bay must have cleared twenty feet the first jump, and his hoofs showered us with hardpan cakes. Captain should have remembered he was riding a blooded animal, for horseman though he was he nearly lost his seat. Segal left us so far behind we lost sight of him now and then, though we were all riding hard. When he finally slowed up he was still heading for the bandits. We caught up with him at the edge of the *resaca*, about half a mile from where the bandits were forted up in the brush. There was nothing between them and us but that stretch of shallow water.

We bunched around Captain. "Boys," he said, "over there are some outlaws who think they're bigger than the law. In a few minutes we're going to set them right. This won't be a standoff or a dogfall. We'll win completely or lose the same way. Those outlaws have plundered, raided, and murdered. They've even carried off some of our women as slaves. Not one of them deserves to live another day.

"Follow me in a skirmish line at five-pace intervals. Don't get ahead of the others and get mixed up with the bandits or you're liable to get shot by mistake. Don't worry about the cattle—they won't go far.

"Those are some of Cortina's top men over there, and he says they can whip the Rangers any day. We'll give 'em a chance to see how Rangers fight. Don't shoot until I do and don't shoot to your right or left. Shoot only at the target directly in front of you, but don't shoot at all until you have a man in your sights and can't miss.

"If they stampede, pick out the nearest one and keep him in front of you and take after him. Get as close as you can before you shoot. It doesn't matter which way he goes—stay on his tail till you get him."

While we were bunched around Captain the *bandidos* fired a few shots to scare us off, I guess, but they fell short and hit the water. They were a good-sized crowd, forty or fifty men, and there were only fifteen of us besides Captain and Old Rock. When they shot at us, Captain said, "Seems they're getting nervous. The longer we hold our fire the more jumpy they'll get, and nervous men aren't good shots." I figured they couldn't be any more nervous than I was.

Some of the bandits were still mounted and holding the cattle off to the left, and a few others seemed to be drifting around aimlessly, probably trying to remember something they should be tending to across the Rio Grande. I felt the same way, wondering if maybe my pa needed another hand back at the ranch. Most of the raiders had dismounted and hidden in the brush along the water's edge, facing us. When I looked across that half-mile of shallow water at the line of brush where men were aiming rifles at us, my hands got all sweaty.

Captain still didn't hurry, for he must have figured the waiting was harder on them than on us, though I wasn't at all sure about that. When he was ready, he nodded and we spread out in a long skirmish line behind him. He pointed Segal in their direction and splashed into the *resaca*. We followed. Ahead of us was that long stretch of water, with a line of brush where it ended. Here and there in the brush I saw the sun reflected off rifle barrels, and we were heading straight toward them. Only we didn't have anything to hide behind.

I don't know what the bandits had expected us to do, but when we started toward them it certainly took them by surprise. I saw one man slip out of the brush and run for his horse and I sure envied him. It must have shaken them to see us calmly riding toward them, for at first they stopped firing, like they couldn't believe we were coming straight at them. I say calmly, because that's how we must have looked; at least Captain looked calm. Actually I was scared witless, and all sorts of crazy ideas raced through my mind, like turning back and heading for home. I glanced sideways at Josh. He looked pale. If he'd showed signs of turning back I'd probably have joined him for sure. That's how scared I was. Maybe we were too young to fight.

When we were halfway across they suddenly cut loose at us, everyone firing wildly as if they'd just realized we hadn't turned back but were coming straight at them. Captain held his pistol ready but didn't use it, like he wouldn't let on he knew they were shooting at us. By the time we were within pistol range they were firing more wildly than ever. If Captain had let us start shooting, I'd have been low on ammunition by now, but he still held his fire. That seemed to unnerve them as much as it did me. I couldn't understand why Captain let them do all the shooting. We had plenty of bullets, but there wouldn't be any of us left to use them by the time we reached the brush with so many of them peppering away at us.

Captain nudged Segal into splashing along a bit faster, getting closer and closer. If that didn't panic them I'd be surprised—it scared the hell out of me. Without being urged, my mustang picked up his pace. I fought off the temptation to slow him down.

Several of our horses took hits, and some were jumping around. Corporal Rudd's mount went down, but he pulled his Sharps out of the scabbard and slogged along on foot, with no sign of fear in his face. Our line was less than a hundred yards from them now, and some of them jumped on their horses and sold out; but those hiding in the brush still outnumbered us, at least judging from the number of shots.

Josh's horse went down, but he got his rifle. He seemed to hesitate, like his legs weren't working right, and I was afraid he'd been hurt when his horse fell or maybe he got hit in the leg. I was ready to pull up and help him, but he went on, keeping his place in the line. His horse got up and followed, dragging the reins in the water.

I was holding my breath, wishing Captain would open fire so I could start shooting even if I didn't have a target. Having to hold my fire was agonizing. When we were only thirty yards from them he spotted a target and fired a shot. I saw a man in the brush ahead of me, and cut loose at him. He jumped up but I shot again, and he didn't make it to his horse. I exhaled mightily and kept going. I was trembling all over but I knew now that the battle would go our way.

A man rose to his knees in front of Josh and raised his rifle. He had a scar from hairline to chin, and I knew he was the American hombre who had quirted Mrs. Noakes. Josh levelled his Sharps and just about blew the bandit's ugly head off.

All of us still on horses dismounted at the edge of the brush, crouched low, and kept going on foot. Everyone was firing any time he had a target. The line of brush was about sixty feet thick, from the water to the prairie above. Some of the bandits started for their horses, but most of them didn't make it. We cut them down.

Two of them jumped on one horse and were racing away when Lieutenant Wright shot them with his Sharps. One rolled off one side of the horse, and the other fell off the opposite side. "Dadblame if I didn't get dubs," Lieutenant Wright said, grinning like a boy winning at marbles. "Captain said just to get one with each shot. Reckon he'll charge me extra?" That little joke relaxed us some, though the fighting wasn't over. Josh and I had both made our shots count, and I felt good about that.

There was one outlaw left in the brush in Captain's area. He'd quit shooting, but Captain knew he was still in there, playing possum. Captain hollered to anyone who was listening, "My pistol's empty. Someone bring me some shells!"

The hidden outlaw leaped out, grinning broadly, with a machete in his hand. He didn't grin long, for Captain drilled him plumb center. There were no more men left in the brush now, at least not live ones.

Captain mounted and rode into the open. Lieutenant Wright was near one of the two he'd knocked off with one shot. "He's asking for a chaplain," Wright told Captain. "Must be a war veteran. He wants a preacher by him when his lights go out."

The man had caught the big Sharps bullet in his midriff and was fading fast. Captain quickly dismounted and took a Bible from his jacket pocket. The shooting was still going on around him as he leaned over the man, reading the Bible to him as he breathed his last. That's the kind of man Captain was, part warrior, part preacher.

Over on one side Spencer Adams and Sonny Smith were stalking around looking for hidden outlaws. One jumped up from the grass and ran for his horse. He was trying to mount when Sonny shot him. He fell back and lay like he was dead. Sonny walked toward him, forgetting Captain's warning never to approach a wounded man. The outlaw raised his pistol and shot Sonny. Adams emptied his gun into the man, but it was too late.

Some of the Rangers had followed the fleeing bandits for five or six miles across the prairie, so there were dead outlaws scattered all over when the fighting ended. Josh had grabbed an outlaw's horse branded with the King Ranch's Running W on its left hip, and joined the chase. I went with Boyd and Maben looking for any men still in hiding. We flushed a few out of the grass and dropped them.

Josh told me later that he got off only one shot during the chase and missed, but Corporal Rudd and others had better luck. When there was no one left to shoot Rudd waved our men in and called off the chase. By now it was nearly noon. A lot had happened in the four or five hours since we had first spotted the rustlers.

After Josh and the others came back we doctored his horse as best we could, but we didn't have much in the way of medicine. We pried a bullet out of a Sharps cartridge and poured gunpowder in the wound. If we could keep the screwworms out of the cut the horse would recover. Adams' horse Sorrel Top had caught a bullet in the neck and Adams had taken off his shirt and tied it around the horse's neck, covering the wound. He thought a lot of Sorrel Top.

"Did any of our people get hurt bad?" Josh asked.

"They killed Sonny Smith, and a bunch of the men got hit, none of them bad."

"Killed Sonny?" The shocked expression on Josh's face brought home to me something I hadn't really accepted until that moment—the fact that Sonny was really gone.

"Were you as scared as I was when we were crossing the *resaca?*" I asked Josh. "I'd have used any excuse to turn back. I figured we'd all be killed before Captain ever fired a shot. I really had to fight with myself to keep from turning tail."

"That makes two of us. I was thinkin' about gettin' out of there right up to when my horse was hit. That made me mad. I still wasn't sure I could shoot a man, even an outlaw. But when I saw that skunk with the scar on his face and knew he was the one who whipped Mrs. Noakes, I knew I had to drop him. When I pulled the trigger on this ole buffalo gun I quit bein' a scared country boy. I was a Ranger, a little McNelly."

V

Captain ordered all hands to go into camp outside Brownsville, then headed there himself to report the battle. We tied Sonny Smith's body onto his horse and headed for town, while Lieutenant Wright and Sergeants Armstrong and Orrill went with Captain. Orrill told us later what had happened. They went to the Miller Hotel, and Captain went in to see Miller.

"My name's McNelly," he said. "Lee McNelly. I want two big rooms downstairs for a headquarters."

"What sort of headquarters?"

"Ranger headquarters. We're Texas Rangers."

"Shore 'nuf? We heard some Rangers was havin' a fight out at Palo Alto this mornin'. Was that you?"

"That was us."

"Anybody hurt?"

"Yes. I want two rooms. The state will pay you."

"You say your name's McNelly? Would that be Captain McNelly?"

"That's right."

"Well, why'n hell didn't you say so?" Then Miller paused a bit. "You ain't on the dodge, are you? I don't want my place shot up if anyone comes after you, understand?"

By this time Captain was chewing his cigar. I guess he was tired of all the palaver. "You've got rooms to rent. I've rented these two front ones. We're moving in." Miller didn't ask any more questions.

Whenever the Rangers went to any county on state business they were supposed to report to the county sheriff, even though no local official had any authority over Rangers. The day before our fight at Palo Alto, the two Rangers had brought in a man named Luis Saldaña. We still had orders to bring in anyone we saw, whether or not he was armed. Captain had been away at the time, but had finally come in and looked over Saldaña's papers, saw that he was a deputy sheriff, and let him go.

"Sheriff Green ain't goin' to like this, you holdin' one of his men prisoner," Saldaña had said.

"If he was doin' his job we wouldn't be here," Captain had replied. "We aim to take the fun out of stealin' cattle."

"I understand, but it ain't likely the sheriff will."

After Saldaña had left, Orrill told us he'd learned that the sheriff had raised a posse and that they were riding out in the direction of where we were camped. If they were after Captain they were lucky they hadn't found him. While they were looking for us we'd been having our scrap over at Palo Alto. Anyway, Captain didn't check in with the sheriff now, and I figured he had his reasons.

Captain sent for brand inspector John J. Smith and the U.S. marshal. To Smith he said, "We captured a herd of cattle on Palo Alto prairie this morning. I want you to take possession of them. Find the brand owners if you can and sell the rest according to the law. I want a written report on it."

Marshal Joe O'Shaughnessy came a short time later. "My boys had a fight at Palo Alto this morning," Captain told him. "I want you to take charge of the plunder and turn it over to the court for disposition. You'll need a wagon. I also want you to bring in the bodies for identification. You'll need an army ambulance for that."

"How many bodies, Captain?"

"I don't know. Quite a few, maybe. Bring all of them in."

Captain was in a good mood, for he'd just come out on top in a whale of a battle against big odds. He gave orders like a general, and they were obeyed without question or hesitation. He told Lieutenant Wright to rush word up to Las Rucias for the rest of the Ranger company to come to our camp at Brownsville. He ordered all hands to be held at the ready, which meant he wasn't sure the fighting was over.

Major Anderson of Fort Brown loaned a wagon and army ambulance to the marshal, then called on Captain at the Miller. He told him he expected Cortina's men to come over in force if they had lost as many at Palo Alto as he'd heard in the first reports. Quite a few years back a couple of Cortina's men had been jailed in Brownsville, and he'd captured the town and shot the marshal. "I've got only half a company of infantry," the major said, "but that should be enough to throw back an invasion. Let me know your plans."

Captain told Rudd to bring four men to his headquarters. Many Rangers had flesh wounds but Josh and I hadn't even been scratched, so we were among the four. That gave us a chance to see and hear at least part of what was going on in town.

While we were sitting on the hotel porch waiting for orders I listened to the Mexican women who walked past us. They all wore black shawls over their heads, and none of them looked our way. Their talk was about the fight we'd had that morning, only from what they said you'd never have guessed it was the same scrap. The ole gals sounded like they'd gladly kill all of us and chop us up into mincemeat.

"The Captain is an assassin," one said, "a cold-blooded murderer. Those poor men held up a white flag. After they surrendered he ordered his men to kill them. That's what I heard."

"Those poor men had just bought some cattle," another said. "They only wanted to earn a little money for their families. They bothered nobody. Those gringo devils ambushed them when they weren't looking. They couldn't even defend themselves. Poor men," she said, crossing herself. I didn't see how we could have ambushed them when they were waving a white flag at us, but those women were angry and didn't worry about minor details.

One grim-looking señora spoke up. "Do not worry, sisters. Those gringo assassins will pay for this. If the sheriff does nothing to them for killing innocent men, Cheno Cortina will kill them all. You will see. He always avenges our people." That cheered them up some, I guess. I wondered if it might be true.

It seemed, from what I overheard, that we'd killed some of Browns-ville's leading citizens, and that there were others among the men who'd escaped. Those raiders had a lot of men on our side of the river working with them, and not only Mexicans. I explained to Josh what the women had said. "Seems that they're expecting Cortina to massacre us if the sheriff doesn't arrest us for killing all those innocent men after they surrendered."

Old Rock visited us at camp just after dark and talked to Sarge. Josh and I and some of the others moseyed up to listen. We told them what we'd overheard earlier. "They're all as innocent as angels, to hear 'em tell it," Rock said. "There're only about eighty Americans in Browns-ville, but they include some mighty shady characters wanted by the law in other states. You'll probably find a number of them in the book."

The wounded men had been taken to the fort, where the army doctor fixed them up. Only Jim Boyd didn't go, saying he was just scratched. Sonny Smith's body had already been taken to the chapel at the fort.

Marshal O'Shaughnessy and three soldiers who went with him re-turned with the army ambulance and the wagon piled high with guns and saddles. "We found the bodies," he told Captain. "Mostly they were around the *resaca* and the edge of the prairie. We looked over the prairie and found three more of them there. We may have missed a few, but I doubt it."

Captain pointed to a place in the plaza. "Stack the bodies there," he ordered, "out in the open." The soldiers stacked them like logs. Captain told Sarge to post an eight-man guard around the plaza and to arrest anyone who came to identify any of the bodies. I wasn't sure what he had in mind, but maybe he thought Cortina had some spies in Browns-ville and wanted to have a little talk with them. I asked Sarge Arm-strong about it. "My guess is that he's expecting Cortina to send some men to see who he lost," Sarge told me. "He's probably hopin' we'll have a big scrap and add some more bandits to the pile."

That night Captain and Major Anderson talked a bit, and then the major ordered the ferry tied up for the night and posted a guard at the river. No one was allowed to cross in either direction.

Everyone in Brownsville was expecting to see a big battle, and most of the people probably would have enjoyed seeing the Rangers get shot up good. We'd killed a bunch of their friends and relatives, so their feelings against us were understandable. The Cortina bunch had taken a beating, and Cortina was one who always avenged his men. They were eagerly waiting for him to take Brownsville again, like he did in '59 when some of his men were in the jail.

None of us worried much about what Cortina might do, for we felt pretty cocksure. We'd whipped more than twice our number and killed at least sixteen men, with the loss of only one of our own. Josh and I had a new feeling about ourselves, for at Palo Alto we had become men, little McNellys. We felt pretty proud, except when we remembered Sonny Smith.

Eight of us stood guard all night in the plaza. Those bodies were plain to see in the moonlight but no one came to take any of them. Captain checked on us and the soldier guard at the river once, then got a few hours sleep. Seems like that's as much as he ever slept.

The rest of our company loped into camp about daybreak, after rid-ing hard all night. They knew there'd been a big scrap at Palo Alto and that more fighting was brewing, so they'd hightailed it. We were glad they'd gotten to Brownsville before anything else happened.

Captain asked the major to send a squad of soldiers to the plaza to relieve us at about sunup, and then we headed for camp. After he sent a report to Austin over the army telegraph, Captain came to camp and had us line up. "Don't any of you go into Brownsville except when ordered," he said. "Stay close to camp at all times, ready for orders. We may have to move fast and on short notice."

One of the Rangers who'd just come in from Las Rucias asked, "Cap-tain, are you figuring on ordering us across the river?"

Captain walked down the line to him, and I felt the hair on the back of my neck trying to stand up. His eyes seemed to bore into the man, who looked down at his boots. "You want a discharge? Is that what you're driving at?"

"I ain't going to cross the river to fight."

"No, and you probably wouldn't fight worth a damn on this side. Fall out and wait at my tent. Anybody else want to quit?"

Six more men stepped forward. With a cold smile, almost a sneer, Captain wrote out their discharges. The reason he put on them was "Not needed."

"Our pay should come in a day or two," he told them.

"Can we stay in camp till it comes?" one of them wanted to know.

"If the others will let you." They looked at us and knew the answer, just as Captain had known it. Not one of them had been in a fight or fired a shot, and for that they'd draw a month's pay. They turned in their rifles and left.

A soldier marched up and saluted Captain, and then word was passed down the line that we were going to the fort for breakfast. That was the best news I'd heard since the carpetbaggers lost the election a couple of years before. I couldn't remember when we'd eaten last, and Josh and I almost ran to the fort. The smell of frying bacon and flapjacks led us straight to the mess hall.

We loaded and reloaded our plates and downed cup after cup of coffee. The old black cook watched and kept urging us to have more. "I sho' like to see hungry boys eat," he said. We put on a show that must have done his old heart good. The only Ranger who didn't come to the fort was Jim Boyd.

After breakfast Captain and Major Anderson made plans for burying Sonny Smith. Then the major loaned Captain a two-seat carriage and driver, and Orrill, Rudd, Josh, and I accompanied him back to the Miller. The other Rangers patted their stomachs and strolled back to camp.

The first thing Captain did was to send for the marshal and tell him to turn the bodies in the plaza over to Sheriff Green. "Identify as many as you can and let me have your report," he said.

Soldiers put Sonny Smith's coffin in a light wagon and covered it with an American flag. Captain and the Rangers followed on foot, and behind us were several squads of soldiers. We circled through the streets of Brownsville so everyone could get a good look at us and see that the Army was on our side. Then we headed for the military cemetery. A bugler played "Taps" and a squad of soldiers fired their rifles over the open grave. That playing of "Taps" put a big lump in my throat. I couldn't have talked to save my life.

After the funeral the marshal reported to Captain on what had been gathered at Palo Alto. There were twenty-two pistols, twelve rifles, and fourteen saddles. "Nine of the saddles are new," he said, "and they're dandies. Silver conchos and tapaderos and all. The name on them is Dick Heye, San Antonio."

"Let's have a look at 'em," said Captain. "Sounds like they're part of the loot from Tom Noakes' store in Nuecestown." And that's what they were beyond a doubt. "Have the judge send them to Tom Noakes," he ordered.

Captain was mighty pleased at all this, for the men using those saddles had been high up in Cortina's organization, not just ordinary rustlers. The marshal said that five of the dead men had been respected citizens of Brownsville, which shows how widespread the raiders' network was. What was bad was that the Brownsville men had gotten themselves killed at Palo Alto. Captain probably hadn't thought of that possibility when he had the soldiers stack the bodies in the plaza. He'd been trying to make Cortina's men angry enough to cross the river so we could make another stack. But the Brownsville relatives of the dead men considered Captain a heartless fiend, and the rumors about us grew and spread until a lot of people who should have known better believed them.

One rumor that never died was that the slain men had been on a cattle-buying trip, and that when the Rangers arrived the men held up a white flag and tried to surrender. Actually they'd started shooting at us when we were still out of range, which is a funny way of surrendering. The brand inspector's report also put the lie to that story, but didn't keep it from spreading or being believed.

He'd located the owners of some of the brands in the herd, and every one of them said that the rustlers had overpowered or killed their vaqueros and stolen the cattle. If we'd been Army troops instead of Rangers, the rustlers would have surrendered, for they'd done that many times. All the Army could do was turn them over to the sheriff. They always made bond and were back in business right away. Since there were lots of cattle on the range, finding men near a herd didn't prove they had stolen it. I guess that's why Captain preferred it when outlaws put up a fight. Then he didn't have to make arrests.

We did a lot of loafing around camp for a while, except when three or four us were sent to the Miller to carry messages or run errands. The Army gave us a box of lye soap and loaned us some horse clippers. We bathed well and washed our clothes, then took turns trimming each other's shaggy manes. When we got through at least we looked different. Not good, just different.

By now we were sort of a brotherhood and each of us was fiercely loyal to the Special Force. We were from all over the country, mostly the South. Corporal W. L. Rudd was a Londoner; Tom McGovern was from Ireland; and "Cow" McKay was a tall, powerful Scot. W. O. "Dutch" Reichel was a big, slow-moving German. Jesús was originally a Mexican, for when he was born the Strip was part of Mexico. Horace Rowe was small and looked delicate, but he held his own in any scrap. He'd been to the University at Waco and had published a book of poems. All of them, wherever they were from, however different they were from the others, made good Rangers. The reason was that each had the right stuff in him and Captain knew how to bring it out. The ones who didn't have it had already quit.

Most were in their twenties and about as carefree as they come, but a few were older and wiser. All of them slept on the ground and went without food or sleep just like Captain when he had us on the move. They accepted discipline because it came from the man they respected above all others, and because they could see that it paid off against the undisciplined crowds we faced. Rangers were almost always outnumbered unless they were fighting one on one, but odds didn't worry them.

We finally figured out that it was the discipline that made the Rangers different from the posses and armed bands they used to raise when Indian troubles were bad. When the Frontier Battalion and the Special Force were organized in 1874, the men chosen to head them—Major Jones and Captain McNelly—were both experienced in commanding troops. A third of the Rangers had been in the ranks before, so they were accustomed to discipline. Once Josh and I caught on we realized that was one of the things that made it possible for us to whip three times our number of bandits.

We hardly ever saw Captain those days, for most of the time he stayed in his room. The army doctor visited him often and had goat milk delivered to him every morning and evening, so we figured he wasn't doing well. Lieutenant Robinson was at the Miller all the time, and the only other people he let in to see Captain were Old Rock and Charley Stillman, who owned a big store. He was a great admirer of Captain, and he cashed our state scrip without discounting it like everybody else did.

Lieutenant Robinson sent word that anyone who went into Brownsville had to leave his pistol in camp. That meant no one went, for most of the Rangers would rather have gone without their pants than their pistols. It was Captain's order, of course, and we knew it made sense. A lot of people in Brownsville hated us, and it would have been easy to get into a shooting scrape. And the sheriff would have been on their side and glad for the chance.

Finally Lieutenant Robinson sent word that we could wear our guns if no more than three of us went and we were accompanied by a corporal. No one was to touch his pistol unless ordered to. We couldn't go into a cantina, and had to be back in camp by dark.

Josh and I went to town with Corporal Rudd. We both needed new duds, Josh most of all. He still wore the same old cracked farm boots and his father's floppy hat. We went to Stillman's store with our pay in our pockets, knowing it wouldn't go far. I bought a flannel shirt while Josh tried on good felt hats. He found one that fit him perfectly.

Charley Stillman came up about then and shook hands with us. Josh took off the hat. "Keep it on, son, if you like it," Stillman said. It was priced at more than a month's pay.

"No!" said Corporal Rudd.

"Half price," Stillman said.

"Come on," Rudd ordered. "We're leaving." Josh didn't get to buy anything that day. When we were outside, he put on his floppy hat.

"Shucks, Corporal," he said, and Rudd interrupted.

"You remember that Captain ordered us not to take even an ear of corn without paying for it? The same goes for hats and boots. Do you think Charley offered you the hat because he likes cotton-choppin' boys from Georgia?"

"No, I reckon it's because he likes Captain and knows I work for him."

All this made Josh feel reckless, for back in camp he got into a stud poker game with Jim Boyd and lost his whole month's pay. Parrott and Jim Wofford almost had a shootout over a shell game, so Sergeant Orrill ordered no more gambling in camp. That was a wise order, but too late to help Josh.

Letters for some of the men came on the San Antonio stage that day, and one was addressed to Sonny Smith. "I guess I better see what it says," Lieutenant Wright told us, "so Captain can tell whoever wrote him what happened." He opened the letter and read it aloud.

"Darling Sonny," it began, "I had an awful dream about you, that something terrible was happening. Please write and let me know . . ." Lieutenant Wright's voice got sounding strange. He folded the letter and cleared his throat. "I reckon I'd better let Captain read it," he mumbled. Josh and I just sat there, not saying anything for a long time. Thinking about Sonny made it hard to feel proud of ourselves.

VI

Knowing that Captain must be real sick worried us, for we rarely got to see him and imagined the worst. But one day when Corporal Rudd was on Captain's detail he took Josh along. They found Captain in an adobe house under some big cottonwoods where the army doctor had moved him. The doctor had also sent for Carrie McNelly, so she could feed Captain right and see to it he got plenty of rest. There wasn't much else you could do for anyone who had consumption but just give him good food and rest.

Lieutenant Robinson sent Josh with a note for Sheriff Green. When he got to the sheriff's office, Josh told me, the men there stopped talking and just stared at him. "I've got a paper for Sheriff Green," Josh said. A heavyset hombre reached for the note. "I'm the sheriff. What is it and who's it from?"

"Captain McNelly."

He looked Josh over as he unfolded the paper. "You one of his men?" Josh was proud to admit that he was.

"Where you from, boy?"

"Georgia."

"How old are you?"

Josh was getting tired of his questions. "Old enough," he said, but the questions kept coming.

"You got one of those books full of names?"

"Yes, sir."

"Can I borrow it?"

"No, sir."

"Can I look at it?"

"No, sir."

"A sassy kid," he said. "Does your captain know that most of that list is several years old? That lots of those men have married and settled down? Some are ranchers and others are public officials, some of our best citizens. Does he know that?"

"Better ask him."

The sheriff fumbled through the papers on his desk and handed one to Josh. "This is what he sent you for, the list of those we buried. I—"

"Much obliged," Josh said and left with the list. "I don't think he likes Rangers much," Josh told me. "He must be worried his name's in the book."

Josh handed the paper to Lieutenant Robinson. "You give it to Captain. He wants to see you," Robinson said. "But don't say one word about his being sick. Understand?"

Captain was propped up in bed when Josh entered his room. His cheeks had some color in them, and he looked pretty good. "Lieutenant Robinson told me to give this to you, sir."

"It's the list," Captain remarked, counting the names. "Only sixteen. I thought they'd likely find more than that."

"Maybe they missed some," Josh said, backing away. Captain stopped him. "I was in my first shooting skirmish when I was about your age, George. My captain gave me a pat on the back afterward and it helped a lot. I saw you out of the corner of my eye at Palo Alto, and you did all right. You learn fast and you came through in good style. Keep it up and you'll make a first-rate lawman. You can pass the same word along to Concho."

Josh was pleased and embarrassed. "I came mighty near not making it in, sir."

"Before we opened fire? Before the shooting started?"

"Yes, sir."

Captain smiled a little. "That's natural. That's human. Only being on the right side allows a man to hold his fire till he sees his target. Those on the wrong side have to hear shooting or they panic. You saw them."

Josh pondered that. "Supposing those wild shots had hit their target?"

"Fighting's a chancy business. Both sides have guns and both aim to win. A peace officer doing his sworn duty is in the right. He's protected until it's his time to go. That might be from an outlaw bullet, or a horse falling on him, or between bedsheets in his own home. The Scriptures say that a man's day and hour are set the moment he's born. I believe that. Remember that courage isn't absence of fear. Courage is controlling fear and not letting it control you."

Josh stayed for lunch with Captain that day. Afterward he went outside with Lieutenant Robinson. "Food like that and wages, too, just for loafing," Josh said.

"Go right ahead and take the money. You'll be earning it pretty quick now."

"You mean the outfit is going to be moving?"

"That's the general idea."

"When?"

"When Captain gives the order. Captain's sick, all right, no question about it. But he ain't through, like he wants some folks to think. He's had lung trouble a long time, and he has these spells when he's got to rest awhile. But he always gets back on his feet when the time comes. Right now he's lettin' things simmer. Since that first bunch quit us, word got around that lots of Rangers were quittin', and that Captain would head for home as soon as he's able to travel.

"Actually he's using this time to build up a spy system. A bunch of ranchers are helpin' out with money, lettin' Old Rock hire a few outlaws for spies. He gets reports every day, and he'll know about any raiders before they get back to the river. Ever since his war days in Louisiana Captain has been known as a chicken hawk kind of leader. He finds out what he needs to know, then sails in like a hawk and lands on 'em where he ain't expected."

Josh felt mighty pleased about his talks with Captain and Lieutenant Robinson, for it showed they both had confidence in him. He told me all they'd said, for he knew that I wouldn't repeat it.

We talked over what Captain had told him about fighting, and got it really set in our minds. We could see now why Captain was successful in battle. After seeing how Captain fought we weren't worried about following him against other bandits, whatever the odds. The cool way he headed straight for them and held his fire had scared them out of their wits. He knew things about men they didn't know about themselves. Naturally we were excited over Captain's words of approval. We knew for sure we were real McNellys, and nothing in the world could make us prouder.

Captain's son Rebel sneaked away from the house and came to the Ranger camp nearly every day, and he turned out to be a little terror. He got into everything, but he liked guns best. Some of the men unloaded their pistols and let him play with them, though that didn't prove to be a good idea. Holding a gun with both hands, he learned to draw the hammer back and then pull the trigger, yelling "Bang!" at the same time. At first we let him get away with anything because he was Captain's boy, but he went too far and got to be a pest.

Once Rudd, Parrott, Josh, and I got a bar of soap and headed for the river. Rebel tried to follow us, but we shooed him back a couple of times and thought we'd gotten rid of the little brute. We were splashing around and adding a bit of rich soil to the Rio Grande when Parrott shouted a warning.

Rebel had slipped up to where we'd left our clothes and grabbed someone's pistol. Rudd was off by himself, and he started circling around behind Rebel. The little monster pulled the hammer back, and a bullet whined over our heads as we ducked under the water. He got off two more shots before Rudd reached him and grabbed the gun. Those bullets had been too close for comfort, and I didn't feel sorry for him when Rudd warmed his britches and sent him squalling for home.

One morning Rudd, Rowe, Josh, and I were walking down to the plaza when a fancy carriage passed us and stopped. The driver held the team while a young lady stepped out holding a silver tray in her hands. She looked like a typical upper-class Spanish lady and her dress and the carriage both confirmed that. She held the tray toward us and lifted off the lacy cloth that was covering it. We took off our hats like they were full of hornets. The tray held *dulces* fresh from the oven and still warm. We each took one and nibbled on it.

I figured she had to be from one of the old families of Nuevo Santander. "My family lives on the old Rivera grant up-country," I told her in Spanish. "My grandmother inherited it." She looked at me, probably surprised to hear a Ranger speak Spanish.

"Ours is Las Rucias," she said. "I hope you brave men will make it possible for us to live there again." She smiled in that distant, impersonal way that only real Spanish ladies can, and held out the tray again. We each took another *dulce*.

"We aim to try," I assured her, "and now that we've seen you we'll try harder." She dimpled at that but immediately looked serious again. As she turned to leave Rudd thanked her and bowed, so the rest of us did the same, feeling like a bunch of schoolboys. But she'd made us feel good, for nobody else in Brownsville had acknowledged that we were human.

The days passed with us still loafing around camp or wandering into Brownsville, but most of the folks there still didn't smile when they saw us. One night we heard music and knew there was a dance not far away. Josh, Boyd, and a couple of others of us walked over there hoping to have a little fun. It was in a big room with benches down opposite sides for men and women, a typical Mexican *baile.* It was going strong until we walked in and lined up on the men's side. The music stopped abruptly, and everybody stared at us.

A big deputy sheriff with a gun on his hip pointed his thumb toward the door and said "Git." Josh and I headed for the door, remembering our orders to avoid fighting. Boyd took his time, and the deputy grabbed his arm and shoved him.

That was a mistake, even if we were uninvited and unwelcome. Boyd flattened him. Others got in the fight and we saw a knife flash and disappear into Boyd's heavy brush jacket. Then Boyd's knife flashed, and we heard a man groan and go down. Boyd followed us outside and we headed for camp.

He had a puncture under his ribs on his left side, but his brush jacket had saved him from worse. Dad Smith looked at the cut and told Boyd to go to the army doctor and get it swabbed out good and sewed up. Boyd told him to douse it with tequila and it would grow together, and that's all he did. Later he admitted that he'd killed an army officer in California, and the Army was still looking for him. That's why he never went to the fort.

One afternoon Wofford came to camp and called me. "Captain wants to see you right away," he said. "Didn't say why." That was like Captain. He said only what was necessary, nothing more. Like any Ranger who was told Captain wanted to see him I was mighty curious, but didn't let on. I headed for Captain's house like I was taking a stroll to town, only I didn't dawdle.

When I knocked softly on the door Carrie opened it. "Oh, Concho. Lee's resting. Come sit in the patio until he comes out." I followed her around to the back of the house and sat on a bench in the shade of the *ramada*. She sat opposite me, while I fiddled with my hat.

"I'm sure you must know how much Lee appreciates all of you," she said.

"Never gave it much thought, ma'am. We're mostly too busy bein' grateful for havin' him as our Captain. Bein' a little McNelly's the greatest thing that ever happened to Josh and me, and maybe most of the others. Captain doesn't say much about things like that. He doesn't talk much about anything, near as we can tell."

She smiled. "I know. Only Robinson, Armstrong, and the others who served with him in the war really know him. He tries not to show it, but he's got deep feelings about others. He once told me he'd rather be saving souls than sending bad men to . . . wherever they deserve to go. He wanted to be a minister, you know."

"Yes, ma'am. I heard that and I believe it."

She seemed thoughtful for a time. I was feeling kind of uncomfortable. To Josh and me, Captain was bigger than life, sort of a god, and it didn't seem right for anyone, not even Carrie, to talk about him like he was an ordinary human.

"Against bad men he has a charmed life," she said at last. "He has no fear that one of them will ever kill him, but . . ." She stopped again. "Do you know why I'm telling you these things?"

"No, ma'am." I couldn't think of anything more to say. I didn't even want to think about it.

"It's because I know how much he trusts you. I learned long ago that

I can talk to the ones he trusts most. You and Josh are young and you weren't in the war, like some of the others, so you may think that Lee is a cold-blooded killer because of the way he treats outlaws. Actually he's terribly tenderhearted. He suffers every time any man wastes his life. That's why he doesn't talk much—afraid he'll give himself away and seem unworthy to lead you. But he has strong feelings for good people who are abused by lawless men. Whenever he sees that it makes his blood boil and he becomes an avenging angel."

The back door opened and Captain came out. He looked a heap better than the last time I saw him, but he was pale and walked slow. I didn't have to glance at him twice to see that he wasn't quite ready for another Palo Alto scrape.

Carrie rose and I stood at attention. "I've got some things to do," she said. "Excuse me, gentlemen."

Captain waved me to my seat and sat opposite me. He got right to the point. "Concho," he said, "things are about to blow up in Matamoros. I've got to get word to a man who works for us there, and as quickly as possible. He's George Hall, Cortina's shipping agent. Word came from Washington that President Lerdo has ordered Cortina arrested because the U.S. State Department demanded it. I don't know if he'll be shot, but Porfirio Díaz is in Texas planning a revolution, and General Canales is a Díaz man. He's also Cortina's enemy. When Cortina is arrested Canales will undoubtedly kill off his key men, especially the Americans. No one will worry about what happens to gringos. George is in real danger and I've got to get him out fast. Troops are on their way by sea from Tampico and they'll arrest Cortina any moment now. There's no time to lose."

"Yes, sir."

He stopped like he didn't want to say more. I was beginning to get the idea that I was on my way into a bear's den, and it made my skin feel prickly. "By the way, George Hall is a sergeant in our company and a good man, one of the best. I can't sit here and risk him gettin' shot," Captain added. I squirmed a bit.

"Concho, you're the only one I know who can pull it off. Rock and Jesús would be recognized before they got off the ferry. But I'm not ordering you to go. I just want you to think it over and decide." He rose. "I've got to drink some more goat's milk and lie down for a bit. Doctor's orders. I'll be back."

I sat there not knowing what to think. If any of the kinfolk or friends of the men we'd killed at Palo Alto got word I was in Matamoros, they'd see to it I didn't get back in one piece. But this was something

Captain wanted done. While I was wrestling with it I hardly noticed Carrie return. She sat awhile, just looking at me.

"Lee wants you to do something terribly dangerous? Across the river?" she asked. I looked surprised.

"No, he didn't tell me," she said, "but he's been awfully quiet all day and I know the signs. Something serious is bothering him, like he must ask someone to risk his life. He's always this way when he has to do that."

"It's sorta like that," I said, squirming a little and wishing she wouldn't press me.

"Are you going to do it, whatever it is?"

"Do you think, ma'am, that I'd ever say no to Captain, no matter what it was he needed done?" She didn't answer but leaned over and patted my hand.

"I'm sure he'd rather go himself if he could," she said. "You know that, don't you?"

I nodded. We sat in silence until Captain returned. Carrie rose, smiled at him, and went into the house. I didn't let Captain ask me what I'd decided. "How do we go about it?" I asked.

Captain smiled, a little sadly, I thought, and drew a deep breath. "I've got a Mexican sombrero and a serape for you," he said. "Just in case. I'd be wearing them myself otherwise. Even though my Spanish isn't very good I'd have to give it a try."

He told me what he knew about the places to look for Hall. He and some of Cortina's men hung out at a cantina called La Golondrina that was on a side street or alley, but Captain didn't know in which part of town. Hall had one good friend there, José Benavides, who could be trusted. There might be several men in Matamoros who'd answer to that name, but at night he could usually be found at La Golondrina.

I asked a lot of questions while I had the chance. Cortina's number one enemy was General Canales, Captain reminded me. He'd betrayed Cortina earlier and would kill him or any of his men if he had the chance. Finding Hall was only part of the problem. We'd still have to get back across the river. If things blew up we shouldn't dare go near the ferry. I had to find Hall fast and get back to Texas. Otherwise . . .

Captain gave me a handful of coins in case I needed money. By now it was late afternoon. "Wait till dark," he said. "With the sombrero and serape you'll look like the rest of the passengers. I hope you can find him tonight, but if you can't and Cortina hasn't been arrested, look for him down by the river where they load cattle. While you're waiting for dark, Carrie will bring you something to eat."

"Tell her not to bother. I heard somewhere that men keep goin' longer on empty stomachs."

Captain laughed right out loud at that. "You'll do, Concho. Bring Hall here when you get back. Good luck."

I sat there until dark, doing a heap of thinking. When the sun finally set I waited a bit longer, then left my own hat on the bench. I sure hoped I'd be wearing it again soon. The sombrero was a bit tight, but it would do. I put the serape over my shoulder, drew a deep breath, then headed for the ferry landing. Brownsville's main street was dark now, except for the light from coal oil lamps near the windows of houses and cantinas.

I suddenly noticed that there were three men ahead of me, standing outside a cantina and smoking corn husk cigarettes. I sure wished I'd seen them in time to cross the street without being obvious about it. There was nothing to do but walk on past them, so I kept going. A faint light shone through the door as I went by, holding my breath like I was threading my way through a nest of rattlesnakes.

I looked straight ahead and kept walking, though my legs felt shaky. I could tell that they were staring at me. Out of the corner of my eye I saw that one was stocky and bearded, and I felt like I'd fallen into an icy stream. Blackie! I couldn't tell if he recognized me. I wanted to run, and the skin on my back seemed to be writhing, trying to crawl away, none of it wanting to be in the path of a bullet that might come at any moment. To throw them off I turned down a cross street instead of heading straight for the river. As I turned the corner I glanced at them. All three were watching me.

The ferry was nearly full when I got there, and the ferrymen were ready to push off. I handed one of them a coin and found a seat on one of the benches. The men already seated paid no attention to me, but in the moonlight I saw three figures on shore, apparently watching us as the ferrymen poled the boat toward the other bank. I wondered if they were Blackie and the other two I'd seen earlier, and if they'd follow me to Matamoros. Finding Hall and getting back to Texas would be hard enough without having to worry about Blackie.

VII

When we got off on the other side I lowered my head and followed the other passengers into town. I could see the glow of light in windows along the street. Captain had described George Hall, so when I passed lighted windows I glanced in, looking for a tall man with a dark brown beard. He hadn't been able to describe Benavides.

La Golondrina was on a side street, I knew, but I had no idea which one. I walked around for an hour, going up and down all of the side streets with no luck. By then I was wondering what to do next, for I figured I was running out of alleys to check. Failure was out of the question when you were working for Captain. Finally I turned a corner and saw what looked like a cantina, and in the dim light coming from it I saw a sign over the door that proclaimed it was La Golondrina, The Swallow. It didn't remind me of any swallow I'd ever seen, but maybe the name was for what men did there, not for a bird. At least I'd found it. I walked through the door to the bar, hoping I'd see George Hall.

"Aguardiente," I told the *mozo* behind the bar. He poured some in a glass and pushed it toward me. I held up the glass toward one of the coal oil lamps like I was an expert on *aguardiente,* and managed to get a quick look at each table. Hall wasn't there. I turned to the *mozo,* who was wiping the bar with a dirty rag. "I'm looking for José Benavides," I told him in Spanish.

"Friend of his?" I guess being nosy was part of his job.

"Never met him. My uncle in Camargo asked me to look him up." The *mozo* nodded toward a man sitting alone at a table in the corner, barely visible in the dim, smoky light. I took my glass and went to his table. He was short and heavyset and looked like he was in his thirties.

"I believe you're a friend of Jorge Hall," I said. "I've got to find him pronto. Tonight."

"Please be seated. Is it some kind of trouble?"

"Could be big trouble."

"Finish your drink and we'll find him. We must not seem in a hurry."

For the first time I took a sip of the dark stuff in my glass and nearly gasped. It reminded me of when I was a little shaver and wondered what coal oil tasted like. I figured if we stayed till I finished it the sun would be shining and my lights would be out. I worked at it some more, but it didn't get any better. "You've got to help me out," I told José. "I'm not used to this stuff. One glass of it would make a man fight a rattlesnake and give it the first bite."

José smiled broadly, showing his white teeth, and pushed his glass toward me. I poured all but a few swallows into it, feeling like I had a live coal in my stomach.

We finished our drinks about the same time. José picked up his sombrero and we headed for the door. I was sure relieved at finding him and knowing I'd soon see Hall. We walked down the dark street and turned the corner past a cantina. José glanced through the window and frowned. "There's something going on in there. Wait here out of sight." He went in, and I stepped into the dark corner of a doorway and waited for what seemed like ten minutes. Finally he came out and walked quickly up the street with me following.

"They say there're rumors something is going to blow up around here but they don't know what. There are three men from Brownsville looking for a man who came here tonight. They think he's a Ranger and asked if I'd seen him." Like all Mexicans, he called Rangers "Rinches." "I promised to watch for him and let them know if I spot him. Are you the one?"

I said I was. "Is one of those men stocky and mean-looking with a black beard?"

"He's the one looking for you. He looks like one bad hombre. They think maybe the Rinches are coming across the river, or something like that, and that you're a spy. You must know something about it, since you're looking for Señor Hall."

"The Army heard from Washington that President Lerdo has ordered Cortina arrested and asked the Rangers to watch for him if he escapes into Texas. Captain figures that the moment Cortina is arrested Canales will wipe out his *jefes*. He sent me to get Jorge Hall out of here tonight."

José whistled. "You know what this means. If they can, the men from Brownsville will kill you but not Señor Hall. The Canales men will try to kill Señor Hall but not you. That probably means that both sides will try to kill my favorite Mexican, José Benavides." He laughed and patted the pistol on his hip. "Good luck, hombres." Then he was serious. "We'd better get moving and find Señor Hall *muy pronto.*"

He led the way all over town, looking in every cantina. From time to time we knocked on the door of the little adobe house where Hall lived, but no one answered. My legs were aching and my feet felt blistered. I was feeling desperate, afraid they'd already gotten Hall. Finally José stopped abruptly.

"I'd forgotten his girlfriend. He must be with her." I followed him across town again, to where there were a few scattered houses. He pointed to one. The faint glow of candlelight shone through the window. José knocked on the door. I heard boots pound the clay floor, and then Hall opened the door, hand on his gun.

"Who's there?" he called. "Oh, it's you, José. What's goin' on this time of night?"

I stepped forward into the dim light. "Captain McNelly sent me to get you out of here tonight," I told him. "He got word from Washington that Lerdo is sending troops from Tampico to arrest Cortina, and he knows you won't be safe a minute after that happens. And it's likely to be tomorrow, maybe even tonight. We've no time to lose."

"I'll be damned," Hall said. "He's right enough about that. Wait a minute." He turned and spoke to someone, and a girl said "Adios. Go with God." Hall came out, putting on his hat.

"What you reckon we'd better do, José?"

"Señor Hall, the ferry is tied up for the night. Let me think." He did some figuring. "You're safe tonight, at least Señor Hall is. Both of you must be at the ferry when it makes its first crossing, around sunup. No one is looking for Señor Hall yet, so you will be safe at his *casa*. I will come and warn you if anything happens before morning."

We said adios to him, then headed for Hall's *casita*. He got out some bread and cheese and we washed it down with wine; then we stretched out on mats on the floor. Like a good Ranger, Hall was asleep right away, but I wasn't so lucky. We weren't back in Texas by a long shot and that live coal still burned in my stomach. We were both up before dawn, but I wasn't ready to face the day.

About daybreak someone knocked on the door, then José rushed in. "Señores, they just arrested Cortina, but few people know it yet. We must get to the ferry at once."

We hustled after him down the street toward the river, about a mile away. We were nearly there when we heard shouts behind us. A platoon of Mexican soldiers was coming. José led us into a courtyard, where we crouched behind the wall and watched. The troops marched past us in two columns, with a bearded, well-dressed, dignified-looking man walking along between them.

"Cortina," Hall whispered. "They've got him all right."

"Is that Cortina?" I couldn't believe it, for I'd heard him described as an ugly monster. "I thought . . ." Hall cut me off.

"You thought all those things you heard about him were true. If they'd let him come back to Texas when he asked for amnesty he'd be a good Texas citizen like his half-brother Cavazos. But he whipped that Brownsville crowd twice and they'll never forgive him. He's no bandit, though he does buy stolen stock—figures he's evening the score for all the cattle Anglos stole from Mexicans."

"Never mind Cortina," José said. "You've got your own necks to worry about. We'd better decide what to do now and we can't afford to make a mistake."

"I don't want to get you in trouble, amigo," Hall told him. "You'd better not be caught with either of us." With a wave of his hand José brushed that suggestion aside.

"There's a place you can hide not far from the river," he said. "Let's go before everybody's in the streets." When we got near the river we saw the soldiers putting Cortina on board a little steamer. Off to one side was an abandoned *jacale,* a little shack of poles with mud daubed over them. "No one ever comes near it," José told us. "Everyone knows ghosts live in it." We looked around to see if anyone was watching. No one was, so Hall and I headed for the tumbledown shack, ghosts or not. "I'll bring you some food when I can," José called after us, "and let you know when it's safe to leave. Watch out for the ghosts." He grinned and left us.

There were men swarming around the ferry landing all morning, so we didn't dare leave the shack. We stayed there all day without food or water. Whenever we heard voices, we peered through cracks where the mud had fallen off. One bunch of men was searching every possible hiding place.

"Canales' men," Hall said grimly, "looking for me." One headed straight toward the shack while we held our breath and drew our guns. The man slowed down and stopped about thirty paces away, like that was close enough. He looked a bit frightened, but he picked up a rock and threw it at what was left of the roof. A crow flew out, cawing loudly, sailing right over the man's head. "Mother of God!" he yelled and ran.

"That was a close one," Hall said. "I never knew ghosts could come in handy. We'd better take a couple when we leave."

"If we leave," I added.

We took turns watching after that. Once I saw three men snooping around, looking for someone, and I recognized Blackie and pointed him out to Hall. It was bad enough having Canales' men after us without having to worry about Blackie. He couldn't be sure it was me he'd seen, but he wasn't giving up the chase. The three men looked at the *jacale* but didn't come near it. By late afternoon we were thirsty as well as hungry, wishing it would get dark so José could come. But even after the sun set there was no sign of José.

"I hope they haven't got the little feller," Hall said after a few hours. "We ain't goin' to see him tonight, I guess, so we may as well catch a little shut-eye." We stretched out on the hard floor and listened to rats or mice playing games in the rafters. I'd thought the day would never end, but the night seemed even longer.

When I awoke it was just starting to get light. I was numb and sore from sleeping on that clay floor, but I stiffly arose and peered out.

"See anyone?"

"Someone's comin', maybe José." Hall was on his feet in a moment, groaning and stretching. He rubbed his eyes and stared out in the dim light.

"It's him, all right, and he's in a hurry."

José was almost trotting, looking back once in a while to see if he was being followed. He was breathing hard when he slipped into the shack. "Canales' men held me all night," he gasped. "This morning they let me go. I think they expected me to lead them to you. That's why I couldn't bring any food. It wasn't easy to give them the slip."

"Never mind about the food," Hall said. "How do we get out of here?"

"It would take a miracle, señor. I came to die by your side." That wasn't an attractive prospect, but I couldn't see any signs of miracles about to happen.

It was getting lighter, and the ferrymen arrived and prepared to make the first crossing. Looking toward town, I saw five men walking down to the river. I nudged José.

"Canales' men," he said. He watched them approach the ferry and say something to the man in charge. It must have been an order, for he nodded his head. As the five headed back toward town, Blackie and the two other Brownsville men approached the ferry and also spoke to the ferryman. When they left, José went to the door. "I know one of the ferrymen," he said. "I'll find out what they were talking about." He soon returned.

"The Canales men told them to watch for Señor Hall and when he comes to stall until they return. The other three hombres want them to do the same thing when you come," he told me. "They both have the same plan, and that is to kill you and dump you into the river on the way over. We've got to figure some way to disappoint them."

We all did some heavy thinking. Finally Hall spoke. "I've been tryin' to figure what Captain would do if he was here, and I think I've got it. He'd maneuver some way to get the drop on one man and make the others throw down their guns. Then he'd tell them that if anyone tried to rescue his prisoner he'd be the first to die. Only we've got two groups to deal with." We thought a bit more.

"One bunch is after you and one after me," I said. "That should give me a chance to get a drop on the ones after you, and you can do the same with Blackie." Hall agreed.

"Let's give it a try. It's our only hope, and maybe we can bring it off. José, you keep back out of sight and when they all show up, fire a shot. That'll make 'em turn and give us a chance to make our play. But keep out of sight so they won't be lookin' for you next." On that we both shook hands with José and headed for the ferry. It reminded me of that morning we had followed Captain across the *resaca* at Palo Alto.

I went first so they wouldn't know we were together. The boss of the ferrymen looked me over, to be sure I was one of those he was watching for. "When do you depart?" I asked in Spanish.

He shrugged eloquently. "Who knows, señor? We must wait for more passengers."

"Bueno, I'll wait." I sat on a stack of boxes off to one side.

Hall moseyed up a few minutes later, asked the same question, and got the same answer. He sat on an empty keg opposite me. The ferrymen glanced nervously at us from time to time and then at the road to town. One of them muttered something and the others looked up. I turned and saw the five Canales men coming, followed at a distance by Blackie and the Brownsville men. When they reached the ferry they ignored us and stood in two groups. One of the Canales men told the *jefe* he was ready. I figured he was the boss and the one I should go after. Hall and I stood up slowly, like we didn't suspect they were after us. We moved cautiously into position.

A shot rang out and we knew José was on the job. Only it wasn't José. It was more of Canales' men coming and signalling for the ferrymen to wait. I shoved my gun in the leader's back while Hall did the same to Blackie.

"Tell your men to drop their guns pronto or you're a dead man," I ordered, grabbing the man's pistol. He did as I said, and they all unbuckled their gunbelts and dropped them. "Now move away." They did. "Tell those men to stop where they are if you don't want to die." He called to them not to come closer. I shoved him toward the ferry, and Hall, having done the same, brought Blackie on board. But the Canales men kept coming. One raised his rifle.

We sat down in the ferry, but the ferrymen just stood there, glancing fearfully at the approaching men. I swung my pistol toward the boss. "Get moving if you want to go on living," I told him. "We're Texas

Rangers." That got fast action. We were moving into the stream when the Canales men got to within fifty yards of the river. The man with the rifle was trying to get a bead on one of us, but we used our prisoners for a shield. He fired a shot that hit the ferry and scattered splinters on us. The ferrymen stopped poling. In another minute or two the ferry would turn downstream and the man would have a better shot at us.

A pistol was fired from somewhere behind the Canales men, kicking up dirt alongside them. They scattered like hens when a hawk appears. I ordered the ferrymen to get moving. "Good ole José," Hall said. "I knew we could count on him when we needed him most."

That was the end of the trouble. We kept our cocked pistols on our prisoners until we reached the Brownsville side and hopped out. I paid the ferrymen for our passage, but they looked shaky and tried to refuse it. We let the Canales man go, and marched Blackie to the sheriff's office.

Sheriff Green wasn't there but his deputy Saldaña was. "Hold this man," Hall told him. "There are warrants for him in Missouri." Saldaña put Blackie in a cell.

"I ain't done with you, Carter," Blackie said to me. "Next time I see you I'll get you."

At Captain's house I knocked lightly on the door, for it was still early morning and they might not be awake. Carrie greeted us. "Oh, thank heaven you're here!" she said. "Lee, it's Concho and George. They're back!" She turned again to us. "Come in. Lee's been biting his nails ever since you left, Concho. When he heard Cortina was arrested yesterday morning I was afraid he would head for Matamoros."

"Tut, tut, Carrie. I knew they'd come. I never doubted it for a minute. But I've never been good at waiting. Did you have any trouble?"

"No, sir," Hall answered, "but we didn't miss it by much. You sent the right man for the job." It was my turn to blush, but I was proud to hear him say that to Captain. The main thing that little caper had taught me, and one I'd never forget, was what Hall had said about figuring what Captain would do if he'd been there. That was a lesson worth learning. Hall told him we'd turned Blackie over to the sheriff.

"I'll get John to arrange for shipping him back to Missouri," Captain said. We headed for camp.

"Where in the world have you been?" Josh asked me when Hall and I got to camp. I gave him a brief account of my visit to Matamoros. "At least we got rid of Blackie," I told him. Everyone wanted to know about Cortina's arrest.

"Does that mean the cattle-raidin' business is over?" Boyd asked.

"No," Hall replied. "As long as the Spanish army in Cuba is buying beef someone will find a way to supply it. General Flores up at Camargo has been workin' with Cortina, and I'm sure he'll keep things going. Cortina's absence won't make the slightest bit of difference. You'll see."

After hearing Cortina blamed for every crime in the Strip, the Rangers found it hard to believe he wasn't a real ogre. Some folks never forgave him for fighting back, and others believed whatever they heard.

Lieutenant Robinson came to camp about sundown. "I went to the sheriff to bring charges against Blackie," he told us. "He claimed there were no grounds for holding him and had to let him go." Josh and I just looked at each other. That was rotten news.

VIII

When Captain rode Segal into camp one evening, we knew we'd soon see action again. We fell in for roll call. Captain had a little Frenchman with him who looked like a real dandy. He carried a heavy riding whip, which I guess made him feel big.

"This feller's down in the book as Pete Marsele," Captain told us. "Scratch his name off and work with him. See to it he's not harmed."

I instinctively disliked the little dude, with his diamond stickpin and fringed doeskin jacket. The book had him down as a gambler and a killer, and none of us trusted him as far as we could have thrown him, but we figured Captain knew what he was doing. Just the same I decided to wait awhile before I scratched his name from the book.

We were told to be ready to leave in the morning, and that was good news. Loafing is all right for a couple of days, but after that it's downright boring. Jesús rode in with another hombre at sunup, and when we lined up Captain told us his name was in the book as Old Blas. Scratch him and work with him, he ordered. He was a crafty-looking old codger no one would want for an enemy. Or for a friend, either. According to the book he'd committed just about every kind of violent crime known.

When we got to Las Rucias late that afternoon we saw that it wasn't in ruins any more. The corrals had been rebuilt and were full of slick grain-fed cowponies, and a few vaqueros were looking after them. The ranchers had supplied them to help Captain, for they knew he was the only one who could make their herds safe. There was cattle-stealing along the Rio Grande for 150 miles, and Captain now had only twenty-nine men. But he'd organized a spy system, and that could make a big difference. If he got word about raiding parties in plenty of time, we could be waiting for them when they tried to cross back into Mexico with stolen stock and put them out of business.

Captain began sending out patrols, for the raiders were coming over in small groups at many places, and then meeting to gather herds. They pushed the cattle hard for crossings from below us to up around Las Cuevas and Camargo, about a hundred miles upriver. On one patrol Rudd, Parrott, Josh, Jesús, and I hid out about fifteen miles up the river at a spot Jesús had chosen. Our orders were to capture any little bunches of rustlers and bring them to Las Rucias for questioning.

In the light of a full moon we saw two men loping along the trail toward us, heading south. When they were close we stepped out and covered them with our rifles. They surrendered without any fuss. Both were well armed and one rode a Dick Heye saddle, so we knew we'd made a good haul.

Since they might be scouts for a raiding party, we turned them over to Jesús and told him to take them to camp while we hid and waited. Soon we heard a noise down by the river, like horses stomping and a man squalling. We figured the men must have jumped Jesús, so we mounted and loped after him. We weren't at all prepared for what we found.

Jesús wasn't in any trouble. He'd looped each man's rope around his neck and thrown it over a cottonwood tree limb and tied it. Then he'd slapped their horses on the rump and left the men swinging and kicking in the air. Jesús had thrown his hat down and was looking skyward, crossing himself repeatedly and muttering something we couldn't hear. It looked like foam was flying from his mouth, and his eyes were like burning coals. We pulled back fast, feeling plenty sick. It was an hour before my hair quit standing up.

"So that's Haysoose's prison camp," Josh said. "I see now why Captain goes to his tent when we turn over prisoners to Haysoose."

We hid till morning, but no one else came along the trail. Remembering what we'd seen, I was almost glad we hadn't caught any more. In the morning we came across fresh tracks only a few miles from where we'd hidden. When the scouts had failed to return, the raiders had taken a different trail with the cattle. There were plenty of men to take the scouts' places, and the raiders didn't worry if they lost a few.

We headed for Las Rucias feeling glum. We didn't have any captives to question, and a herd had crossed almost within hollering distance of us. From the pony tracks with the herd it looked like they had as many men as steers, and the four of us probably would have been wiped out if we'd attacked them. The main thing was that we'd failed, and in Captain's book there was no word for failure.

Captain was away, so we reported to Sarge Armstrong. Then we got the book and tried to find the names and descriptions of the two we'd caught. "Never mind the names," Sarge said. "Captain doesn't want to know, or he'll have to report them. Too much writing when there's work to be done. Parrott, Captain wants to see you when he gets back."

Parrott looked flustered, for Captain had never asked to see him before. He wondered what it was about, and so did we. When Captain returned Parrott reported to him, while we hung around out of curiosity. Right after he talked to Captain, Parrott went to the supply wagon and got out his camera and gear and packed it. All he told us was "I'm pulling out for Eagle Pass. Orders."

Sarge whistled and shook his head. "That there's King Fisher country. If we're going in there, somebody's liable to get hurt."

Captain was in the saddle every day, riding horses out of the remuda the ranchers had supplied, saving Segal. There were dozens of raiding parties, and in that big stretch of country we weren't catching many, though Captain's spies brought plenty of reports. Twenty-nine men couldn't watch 150 miles of river. The raiders had hundreds of men, and their spies were everywhere. The price of cattle was up to ten dollars a head, which made all the risks worthwhile for the raiders. We weren't surprised that Captain was getting frustrated and mad.

We were still sending scouts and patrols up and down the river five months after we'd arrived. The patrols found little bands of raiders now and then and shot a few, but that didn't slow them up for a minute. What we needed was another scrap like the one at Palo Alto, so we could kill a flock of them. Our patrols were always out for twenty-four hours at a stretch, and so we were all pretty lean.

Old Blas came and went, talking to Captain or Rock when in camp. We figured he was crossing the river and finding out where raids were planned. Lots of times after he'd been in camp we hid out and shot down little bunches of four or five men. But Captain wanted something bigger, something the raiders would feel.

One time after Old Blas came back to camp, Sarge Armstrong ordered fifteen of us to draw bullets and saddle up. We lit out fast, with Rock leading the way, passing the cavalry camp outside of the little settlement called Edinburg. We came across the trail of cattle headed for the river, and Old Rock spurred his horse into a run, with Captain and the rest of us hard after him.

The raiders were just pushing the herd across the river when we spotted them. They saw us coming and whipped the steers with their riatas. Captain had his pistol out but didn't fire a shot until he was on them. Most abandoned the last bunch of steers and headed for the other side, but four of them stayed and peppered away at us. They were four thieves who'd made their last raid, for we killed every one of them.

We watched where the others were heading with the stolen steers, toward a hill off to the right a few miles away across the river below Reynosa. Then we followed Captain to the cavalry camp. Captain Randlett was out on patrol, but Captain Farnsworth was there with twenty men.

Captain and Farnsworth talked some. I guess Captain asked him to cross the river with us and help get the cattle back, but I couldn't hear what was said. I saw Farnsworth shake his head and hold his hands palms up like he was explaining why he couldn't go with us.

Captain returned to us. "He won't cross the border," he told Sarge. "Says he'd be cashiered if he did."

When we got back to where the cattle had crossed the river, Rock pointed toward the hill. "They're probably holding them at the Sabinal ranch," he said. "It's two-three miles away, over beyond that hill."

Captain thought a bit. "Keep the men here and watch," he told Sarge. "If you see anyone tryin' to cut us off from this side, light into 'em. I'm goin' to find those cattle." He nodded to Josh and me to accompany him and Rock.

Our horses waded most of the way across the river, except for one place in the middle where they had to swim. Rock led the way, following the trail through the mesquite. I kept my hand near my gun, sure we'd run into some bushwhackers.

Rock must have sensed that a rider was coming, for he held up his hand and then he and Captain rode off the trail to the left. Josh and I turned our horses into the mesquite on the right. A few minutes later a young vaquero rode into sight. His pony smelled our horses, and its ears shot up. We all rode out with pistols levelled. The vaquero stopped his pony and held up his hands. He was unarmed.

"Ask him where the cattle went that just crossed the river," Captain told me. I asked him in Spanish.

"*¿Quien sabe?*" he replied.

Captain cocked his pistol, and we did the same. "Tell him he'd better remember fast."

The look in Captain's eye helped the vaquero's memory. "They took them to Reynosa, I think. There are many soldiers there."

Captain and Old Rock talked quietly for a minute or two. "You two take him back to where we crossed the river," Captain ordered. "Rock and I are goin' to have a look at the Sabinal ranch. We may have to come back here one day soon. Hold him till we get back, then let him go. He doesn't look like a cow thief."

Josh led the way to the river, with the vaquero following. I brought up the rear, keeping him covered. I told him we'd let him go when the others returned. He didn't seem to find that comforting. I figured he must be sure they wouldn't be coming back.

"Why do you work for the gringos?" he asked me. "Texans are all devils."

"Some are, some aren't. There're good ones and bad ones, same as with you. Why do you work for cow thieves?"

"They're just getting back our own cattle that the gringos stole."

"Maybe they were at first, but not any more. They're stealing other people's cattle. We were sent to stop it, and we'll kill anyone we catch with stolen stock. Don't go with them. I wouldn't want to kill you." He seemed to think some about that.

When we reached the river we rode to high ground and watched for Captain and Rock. It wasn't more than half an hour before we heard gunshots and saw a couple of riders coming on the run a mile or two away. We didn't have a clear view of them because of the mesquite. A minute or two later we saw a bunch of riders hard after them.

"You'd better get on down the river and keep out of sight," I told the vaquero, and he was gone. Josh and I dismounted, pulled our Sharps from the scabbards and rested them on mesquite limbs, and waited.

"What do you reckon we should do?" Josh asked.

"Good question. Whatever Captain would do. I figure he'd pick off the first two riders, and that would stop the rest long enough for him and Rock to get here and across the river."

We watched until we saw Captain and Rock appear. Rock's horse had slowed down and Captain was holding up Segal. Rock was waving at him to go on, but Captain stayed with him. The others soon appeared and were gaining fast.

"You take the first one and I'll take the second," Josh said. "For God's sake don't miss."

We took careful aim, resting our heavy rifles on the mesquite limbs, and we fired at about the same time. The first two horses spun around and the riders disappeared while we hastily reloaded. We took careful aim and fired again. The riders were bunched together and we must have hit someone. They all disappeared in a hurry whether wounded or not.

Captain looked back and saw they were no longer following. He slowed Segal to a trot, and the two of them rode up to us. We'd already mounted and were ready to visit Texas.

"We've got to go slow, boys," Captain said. "Rock's horse took a bullet. Won't kill him, but he's not in a hurry. Stay here till we get across, then hightail it over. We'll cover you."

We hopped down and got in the mesquite again. A few of the raiders had left the trail and were slipping through the brush toward us, but we couldn't see them most of the time. We heard Rock shout. They were across.

"Let's give 'em one more to slow them up and then run for it," I said. Josh nodded.

"Fire the first time you see anybody," he said. We both fired, and if we hit anything it was probably a mesquite, but the raiders turned back. Then we ran to our horses and crossed the river.

"Good work, boys," Captain said. "You saved our skins for sure."

"Amen, brother," Rock agreed. "After listening to those Winchesters and Henrys yapping at us, those buffalo guns sure sounded sweet to these old ears."

We rode back to the Army camp at Edinburg. "While you were gone General Escobedo paid us a visit," Farnsworth told Captain. "He's in command at Reynosa."

Captain called for Sergeant Hall and me. "You two go to Reynosa and hunt up the alcalde. Tell him I'd like to talk to him over on this side. If you see any steers try to get a look at the brands. I'm sure no one will bother you."

We rode back to the river and crossed it. There were corrals on the edge of town, and the steers in them bore Captain King's Running W and other Texas brands. We found the alcalde without any difficulty and I explained to him that Captain McNelly of the Texas Rangers wanted to talk to him. He seemed flattered and accompanied us willingly.

"A herd of stolen cattle was driven across the river this morning," Captain told him. "They're at Reynosa, and it's your duty to arrest the thieves and deliver them and the cattle to me."

"Si, señor," the alcalde replied. "I will return the cattle and punish the thieves."

"No, deliver the thieves to me."

The alcalde thought it over. "*Bueno*, señor . . . but the thieves will have to be sent over at night, in secret. Otherwise my life won't be worth much." He returned to Reynosa.

"Do you think he'll do what he says?" I asked Hall later.

"He may want to and try to, but I don't think there's a chance in the world he can do it. Captain is just setting things up. When he decides to go in and bring back a herd by force there'll be a lot of squawking. Then he can remind them that he asked politely for assistance from Mexican officials and they failed to cooperate." That made sense, but the prospect of us going over there and trying to recover a stolen herd sounded like a good way to get us all killed.

Pete Marsele, the little Frenchman, came to camp occasionally after this, and Captain kept him well supplied with *dinero*. He always had his flunky with him, and the way Pete ordered us around would have gotten him shot if Captain hadn't warned us not to harm him. When he wanted something he slapped his leg with his heavy riding whip or whistled through his teeth at us. "Back in Georgia that's the way we called our hounds," Josh said. We hated the sight of Pete.

One day in September Pete came to camp when Captain was away on a scout. He ignored us, like we weren't fit to speak to, but when Captain returned they went into his tent and stayed quite a while. When Pete left he was smirking, like he'd done something smart. Sarge told us to get ready. We didn't move that day, but all patrols were kept in camp.

Lieutenant Robinson was with Captain most of the time, but he couldn't tell us anything. "Only the Good Lord, the Captain, and his spies know what's goin' on," he said. "He doesn't tell me any more than he tells you. But something's on the fire for sure. We'll know when it's cooked and ready to eat."

Late the next night Pete and Old Blas rode in and joined Captain and Rock. Right away Lieutenant Wright told us to saddle up and draw all the shells we could carry. Then we rode out in single file, with Rock in the lead and Captain next on Segal. Rock kept his horse in an easy lope as usual, and we covered a lot of ground.

About midnight we stopped for a breather and to water our horses. Then we crossed the Arroyo Colorado and moved slowly and cautiously to the north, with scouts out ahead. We crossed the Taylor trail near the Laguna Madre. We didn't see any cattle tracks, and guessed the raiders were still farther up the coast, if Captain's spies had told him right.

There was a big motte of oaks, the Amargosa Don Juan, on the edge of the Big Sands, and Captain pulled us in there. He signalled for us to gather around him. "Boys," he said, "a good many bands of outlaws have crossed below Brownsville in the last week or two and they're gathering a big herd above us. They'll be coming along any time now, and we ought to get every blasted one, even though there may be a hundred of 'em." It was a good hiding place, for we could see clear to the coast.

About sundown the wind rose and thick clouds formed. Many of the gusts slapped us with cold drizzle that got heavier by the minute. Corporal Rudd walked out in the open, rubbing his hands. "Chaps, there's a Norther coming," he said. "It could be tougher than a two-bit steak. We ain't got the right clothes for a wet Norther."

Captain and Rock made a scout but saw no sign of a herd. Both wore old army overcoats—Captain's was Confederate gray and Old Rock's was Yankee blue. That didn't matter, for we weren't thinking Civil War just then. Our nearest enemy was the cold, and even a Yankee coat was a lifesaver. Some of the men had extra clothes and put on everything they'd brought. A few had yellow slickers from their cattle-trailing days.

I had on long johns and a heavy shirt as well as a brush jacket, but poor Josh had only what he'd worn from Georgia and a brush jacket he'd bought from Charley Stillman. He'd wanted to buy some long johns but had run out of money. "It's your fault I'm out here without long underwear or warm clothes," he said to Jim Boyd. "You and your damn poker."

"Take it easy, son," Boyd said. "You young lads have to learn the facts of life the hard way. Never bet all your pay on fillin' a bobtail straight."

Standing guard that night was brutal. First there would be a gust of wet wind, then it would die down and a blast of icy air would follow. They took turns making our lives miserable all night. We used to laugh about the way a Yankee had described a Blue Norther up around Fort Worth. "First it rained, then it snew, then it frizz, then it thew, then it rained some more." That night it didn't seem funny, for it was colder than an outhouse in January.

In the morning the clouds were still heavy, but the wind had died down some. We huddled near our ponies, except for Captain. He was lying on a blanket, resting his head on his saddle, with his coat pulled tight around him and his eyes closed. One of the Rangers had covered him with a saddle blanket. He looked tired and weak, and whenever any of us looked at him we shook our heads. This weather and no food could kill him. None of us had eaten for two nights and a day, and it was worse for him. We fed our horses mesquite beans, though not enough to founder them, and they found a little grass. "Wonder when we'll get to eat," Josh said.

"That's easy," Sergeant Orrill answered, "when we get back to Las Rucias." That place was about half a day's ride away.

"No funnin', Sarge. How much longer do you think we'll be nested up here?"

"You recollect what Captain brought us here for?"

"To catch some bandits."

"Correct. And you know Captain. He'll stay holed up till the bastards come within shooting distance."

"Supposin' they never come?"

"Then the buzzards will have a feast, and many years from now some folks will come here looking for historical souvenirs. They'll put together some bones and say, hanged if this don't look like the bones of that long, hungry boy from Georgia."

That's the way old Orrill was. He was from Mississippi, one of those long-necked piney woods boys. Josh had taken a real liking to Orrill, who was a wise old owl and a first-rate Ranger.

Nothing happened all that miserable day, except that we were cold and wet to the skin. The Norther kept alternating between a drizzle and a gusting dry wind. Captain and Rock rode out on a scout for five or six hours, but saw no signs of cattle trails. Captain was so weak when he returned that he let one of the Rangers unsaddle Segal for him, something he'd never done before. He had no business being out in the cold or going without food for days. We all worried plenty about him, and that made us half-forget how cold and hungry we were.

That night was as miserable as the others, and in the morning Captain looked unconscious. His cough was bad and getting worse. Around midday Jesús rode in from the north. He'd been gone since yesterday morning and his horse was worn down, for he'd ridden clear to the Santa Gertrudis. He'd learned that a big raid, one of the biggest ever, had gone clear into Nueces County. There weren't any vigilantes or posses after the raiders, for Captain had ordered them to disband. They'd swept the country clean, knowing where we were.

When he heard that news Captain was about as whipped as a man could be and still live. Pete Marsele had tricked him—had gotten him to hide us here out of the way while hundreds of raiders had crossed the river from the Las Cuevas ranch and made a big sweep. They'd done some looting and burning along the way and made it back to Mexico with about eight hundred head of prime steers.

Captain motioned for us to come around him. He could only whisper. "I'm finished," he said hoarsely. "I've put you boys through this for nothing. Even if my lungs were good I wouldn't be fit to lead. I'm turning command over to Lieutenant Robinson, then I'm going home." His last words to Robinson were "Put Pete Marsele back in the book."

Rock helped Captain get on Segal, then mounted his own horse. As Captain headed into the Norther, Rock rode after him. "I don't want you to come," Captain said, pointing back.

"I don't give a damn what you want. I'm going to see you put to bed," Old Rock answered. Silently each of us thanked him for that.

Josh and I walked over to our horses, pretending we had something we needed to do, for our eyes were flowing and we were too choked up to speak. When I finally turned my red eyes toward the others, I noticed that they'd all gotten busy doing something that required them to turn their backs and to be away by themselves. There was a lot of throat-clearing going on.

Then I got to thinking about Pete Marsele, and my face was hot with rage. Right then I made a vow. If it cost me my life, I'd even scores with that two-faced little bastard for what he'd done to Captain. He'd done it to us, too, but that wasn't important. Captain was going home to die, thanks to Pete's trickery. I hoped I could get the job done in time to tell Captain, but it didn't look like he could even make it home.

IX

We straggled back to Las Rucias like we were heading for our own funerals. Nobody spoke, and I guess most of them were also wondering if Captain would make it home alive. With Captain gone we wouldn't be the same outfit. According to what we'd heard in Brownsville, a lot of folks were urging the governor to disband the company. With Captain gone they might as well send the rest of us packing anyway.

There'd been many complaints about Captain's not taking prisoners and a lot of things that were made up, like the charge that he paid no attention to the law. The lies about the Palo Alto fight were still going around, for the ones who got hurt kept them alive. Only the ranchers, who were still losing cattle to raiders, supported the Rangers. The charge that Captain ignored the law was a lie, though when he fought outlaws it was kill or be killed. There wasn't any other way to deal with them. But he was strict about upholding the law and protecting law-abiding people. I wondered if the governor and the legislature believed the lies.

By the time we reached Las Rucias we were too numb to feel hunger any more. We unsaddled our horses and turned them loose, then walked stiffly to the chuck wagon, where Dad Smith dished out frijoles and biscuits. I'd forgotten what such things tasted like. We hadn't eaten since we left Las Rucias four days earlier, and we hadn't accomplished one damn thing.

Josh and I filled our bellies and stretched out on our bedrolls to do some thinking. "We'll never see Captain again," Josh said. "What do you reckon we oughta do? Look for another job?"

"We're still drawin' pay, I guess. Why don't we see what the others aim to do. Find out what some of the older hands think."

Josh ambled over to Sarge Orrill and asked what he'd do now.

"Me? Well, son, I'm goin' to do just what I've been doin'. That's whatever I'm ordered to do."

"You mean you're stayin' in the outfit?"

"Ain't you?"

"Well, with Captain gone, I—" Josh began, but old Sarge cut him off.

"What the hell's that got to do with it? Captain's gone now, but he ain't dead by a long shot."

"He looked awful weak last we saw of him. Didn't look like he'd ever recover. He surely can't come back."

Sarge put his big hand on Josh's shoulder. "You've known Captain about six months? Right? I've known him since he was your age. He had consumption then—that's why he come to Texas before the war. If he hadn't taken sick he'd be a preacher back in Virginia right now. He left preacher school to come out here and get well. He just hasn't ever had a chance to rest."

"People always die of consumption, I've heard."

"Mebbe. But I was with Captain in Louisiana and he served four years without one day of sick leave. Most folks have a way of dyin' of something sooner or later; if it's not consumption, it's a bullet. But if you knew Captain you'd know he ain't going to die till he evens things up for what happened and scratches Pete's name off the list of the livin'. Captain can't die with those things on his mind. I know him. He'll be back."

That made us feel better, and although we didn't quite believe him we decided to stay on as long as Orrill did.

Word of Captain's leaving spread up and down the Rio Grande, and it made a lot of hombres smile. The way they told it made it sound like Captain was all right when he was on top, but when he was losing he sold out and claimed he was sick. That made them feel pretty good, for they were all afraid to meet Captain face to face.

Things weren't the same without Captain. Lieutenant Robinson didn't want to take over, and he spent most of the time in Captain's tent by himself. He didn't send us on any patrols or anything else for a while. We began feeling guilty about taking the state's money, for we weren't earning even part of it.

We all hoped that Rock would come by and tell us he got Captain home all right, but he didn't. Old Jesús had vanished and no one knew where to find him, for he didn't sleep in the same place two nights in a row. We heard about the raids from ranchers who came by Las Rucias and told us the news. Some of them got together one time and followed a big bunch of raiders. They killed three of them but lost two of their own as well as the herd. That's the way it was for ten days or maybe two weeks before Lieutenant Robinson sent us out on patrols again.

His orders were different from Captain's, for Robinson went by the rules laid down in Austin. For example, if we ran across raiders we couldn't cut loose on them unless they shot first. We had to tell them we were Rangers and then ask would they kindly surrender.

Five of us were out with Sarge Armstrong once when we saw a couple of riders coming, and we were sure they were scouts for a party of rustlers. Sarge was a real McNelly Ranger and he did things the way Captain did when he was leading us. When the two riders got near he stepped out with his Sharps levelled. "We're Texas Rangers. Get your hands up." They surrendered willingly. "How many with you?" Sarge asked.

"Just the two of us," one answered. Sarge rammed the muzzle of his Sharps in the man's belly, almost lifting him over the cantle of his saddle.

"Try again."

"Sixteen," the hombre gasped, trying to get his breath.

Sarge told us to hold one of the men. "Go back to your party and bring four of 'em to surrender," he ordered the other. "Do it or this man dies. Bring four of 'em and tell the others not to try anything or all prisoners will be shot." He wasn't fooling and they knew it. It made us feel almost like Captain was still with us. In less than an hour the whole party rode up with a herd of stolen cattle. We made them leave the herd, but now we had sixteen prisoners on our hands and no idea what to do with them.

Lieutenant Robinson looked shocked when we arrived at camp. "You said fetch in some prisoners. Here's sixteen of them," Sarge said.

Robinson was mighty puzzled, for what to do with prisoners except turn them over to Jesús was something he hadn't learned from Captain. "What do you reckon we best do with 'em?" he asked.

"Let's get a law book and read it to 'em. Maybe they're just poor ignorant cutthroats who don't know Texas has laws against stealing cattle. Let's start us a sort of law school for 'em."

Robinson ignored this sarcasm, and wrote down the names the prisoners gave. Then he ordered Sarge to deliver them to the sheriff in Brownsville to hold for trial. Any of us who wanted to could go along, though the prisoners didn't need to be guarded. We'd disarmed them— most had two pistols and a Winchester or Henry rifle—and we packed their arsenal on a horse. They went along meekly enough, which made it pretty clear they weren't worried about being arrested.

Armstrong handed the list to Sheriff Green. "Here's sixteen prisoners to hold for trial."

The sheriff looked at the prisoners. "On what charge?"

"Cattle stealing."

"What cattle? What brands? How many head?"

Sarge said, "Hell, we caught them headin' for the river with cattle. They let the cattle go."

"Did they resist?"

"No."

"You ain't got anything for me to hold these men on. If they had cattle, could have been some they bought. The brand owners would have to say different. I can't sign this receipt and take custody of these men just on your say-so. We run our affairs according to Texas law—not the way your Captain McNelly did when he was here. His ideas ain't law, and besides, he ain't around any more. Ran out on you, didn't he?"

That would have gotten the sheriff killed a while back, but Sarge just swallowed hard and changed color a few times. Then he tore up the list. When he turned to leave, the sheriff stopped him. "Where are these citizens' guns?" Sarge told us to bring them in and give them to the sheriff. I knew where I would like to give them to him.

As if he hadn't insulted us enough, he yelled after us as we rode away, "Don't any of you get drunk and try to raise hell around here or I'll throw every damn one of you in jail." This sorry business was the sum total of our activities in October.

We didn't have regular patrols but just went out in groups of two or three or on our own, not taking any prisoners but not killing many bandits. I guess Robinson was just trying to hold us together till he heard from Captain or they ordered us to disband. Once when I was riding alone near the river I saw Old Rock. He told me that he'd gotten Captain to Santa Gertrudis, where they fed him good and let him rest. Then Captain King had one of his men take him home in a spring wagon.

"Where can I find Pete Marsele?" I asked him.

"Probably at Flores' Rancho Las Cuevas. He works with the spies who come over to keep track of the troops and Rangers. I think every other week he rides down to Matamoros. Why?"

"I want to find him and fetch him over here. I'd like you and Jesús to be around in case I need help."

Rock whistled. "I'll get word to Jesús, and find out when Pete's expected in Matamoros. Meet me back here same time next week."

I waited a week, then found Lieutenant Robinson alone in Captain's tent. I asked if I could come in and he nodded, so I squatted in the opening.

"What's on your mind, Concho? You look like you're havin' big thoughts. You ain't thinkin' of leavin' the outfit before Captain returns, are you?"

"I sure want to be here if, I mean *when* he comes back, but I've got some business to tend to. It's sort of Ranger business—across the Rio Grande."

He looked at me, eyes wide open. "May I ask what sort of business takes you there? It's damn risky business, you know, whatever it is."

"I aim to get Pete Marsele one way or another. Rock's findin' out where I'll have the best shot at it."

He stared at me as he thought about it. "I can't give you permission, but your name'll stay on the roll. They'll kill you if they catch you, but you speak Spanish like a native, and you just might be able to swing it. Don't tell anyone, not a soul. If that bastard of a sheriff ever gets wind of it we're all in big trouble. I suspect he's in cahoots with the raider bunch. Good luck."

I turned in my Sharps at the supply wagon, for the bandits knew the Rangers used them. "Leavin'?" Dad Smith looked surprised.

"Just temporary. I'll be back for it."

I'd been riding horses from the remuda, so my mustang was rested and ready to go. I slipped out of camp without having to make excuses, but crossed trails with Josh as he was returning with Deaf Rector from a scout. Josh stopped but Rector rode on to camp. "Where you headed?" Josh asked.

"On a little manhunt south of the river."

"Who?"

"Pete."

"Kill the son of a bitch!" He paused to think about it. "Let me go with you."

"No. They'd recognize you as an Anglo a mile away. Don't say anythin' to anyone, or someone might tip off the sheriff. I'll tell you about it when I get back." He shook my hand and nearly crushed it.

"Captain will . . ." he started to say, but his voice got choky. I turned my pony and loped away.

I met Rock and Jesús. "Here's what I learned," Rock said. "Tomorrow he'll be ridin' down the road to Matamoros. Probably won't be alone; his flunky usually goes with him, and there could be others. They should be opposite us by about mid-morning. I'll watch and cover you if you get in trouble. Jesús better keep his eyes peeled for hombres coming toward the river on this side. He ain't very popular over there."

That night I didn't sleep much, thinking about what might happen. None of us had much to say in the morning, but those light blue eyes of old Jesús were throwing off sparks as I mounted. *"Buena suerte,"* he said. "Good luck." My pony waded most of the way across, for the river was low. I had to ride three or four miles toward Las Cuevas to find a place where I could hide and watch the road in both directions. My skin tingled; the palms of my hands were wet but my throat was dry.

Several groups of riders came along heading west, but it seemed like hours before I saw two men approaching from my left. My hand trembled and my legs felt weak. I spun the cylinder in my pistol for about the fiftieth time and mounted my pony, still keeping out of sight. One of the riders was Pete, no doubt about that, and the other was his hired man. Both were armed, and I knew Pete was a killer. They were also well mounted, probably on stolen horses.

After they passed me I rode up to them at a trot. "Hombres," I called in Spanish, "you are going to Matamoros? *Bueno,* I'll accompany you."

Pete didn't seem glad to have company, and hardly looked at me at first. But as we rode I noticed him glancing sideways at me a few times. "Where have I seen you before?" he asked.

"Maybe at Rancho Las Cuevas. Or Matamoros."

"I think not on this side of the river." He flicked his heavy riding whip and signalled with his eyes to his flunky, who tried to swing his horse behind me. I pulled my gun and told them to get their hands up, then lifted the flunky's pistol from its holster and dropped it. I ordered him to take Pete's pistol out and drop it. The fool tried to turn it on me, but I hit him across the side of the head with my gun and knocked him out of his saddle. Pete put the spurs to his horse and galloped off. I followed him, and though he was well mounted my mustang didn't let him get far ahead.

Flunky came to after a few minutes and picked up his pistol and followed, shooting at me from well out of rifle range. After about a mile and a half of hard running both of their horses slowed down. Pete whipped and spurred, but I drew steadily closer. As my pony overtook him I saw a cloud of dust and a party of horsemen coming toward us, maybe a mile away. I fired a shot near Pete's head and told him to stop. He did.

"Head for the river," I told him, and whacked his horse with the end of my reins. He tried to slow it down until his flunky or the riders could catch us, for they were coming on the run. "If anyone tries to rescue you, you're a dead man," I told him, jabbing him in the ribs with my gun. "Move!" He headed his horse into the water and we crossed. As we rode up the bank the riders arrived and fired a few shots at us, but we got over a ridge and out of their sight. I looked for Rock and Jesús, but they were probably a mile or more away.

Some of the riders crossed the river after us, and I heard their horses clattering up the bank. The moment I turned to look, I felt Pete's heavy riding whip crash against my temple and then I went down. Dimly I heard shots and somehow knew that I'd failed.

When I came to I looked up and saw Old Rock squatting by me. "I heard them comin' and took my eyes off him for a moment," I said, gingerly feeling the lump on my head and cursing myself for letting Pete escape. "That's how I let the bastard get away. I'll never be able to face Captain now. I ain't fit to be a McNelly."

Rock laughed. "That wasn't them coming," he said. "That was me and Haysoose. We knocked a couple of them out of their saddles and the others cleared out. Pete didn't get away."

"Where is he?"

"Jesús took him dancin'. Here, give this to Captain." He handed me Pete's diamond stickpin. "It's a little souvenir Pete don't need any more."

When I got to camp at Las Rucias, Lieutenant Robinson walked up as I was unsaddling. He had an inquisitive expression and was looking at my black-and-blue temple. I pulled out Pete's stickpin and showed him. "Hot damn," he said, and then mumbled something that I figured had to do with Pete's character, ancestors, and personal habits.

I told Josh about it, and had to make him wipe the silly grin off his face before the others saw him and started asking questions. Life in camp now was about like it had been before, with patrols going out and shooting a few bandits but not taking any prisoners. Still no word from Captain. Josh got restless and discouraged again.

"I think I'll quit and get me a job on some ranch," he said. "We're just wasting our time here, not doin' any good at all. At least I could be learnin' how to handle cattle. Then maybe Captain King would hire me."

"Why don't you talk to Sarge Orrill first?" I urged him. "He's got a level head at the end of that skinny neck."

Josh hunted up Orrill again and told him he was thinking of quitting and hiring on with a rancher.

"You could probably get a job working stock," Orrill agreed, "but it's hard work and poor pay for a green hand. Or you might start drifting and think of using your pistol for a livin'. Boys like you get queer notions when they're on their own. You thought of that?" Josh said he had.

"Well, I guess that's natural for a restless young feller, but I'd hate to see you strike out on your own just yet. Captain saw what he figured was some promise in you. He likes you, even if he hasn't had much chance to show it."

"But he's gone. He won't be back."

"Mebbe, but I ain't give up on him. Why not wait till they muster us out or till after Christmas? If nothin' happens and we don't hear from Captain, I'll pull out too and we'll team up. How about that?" Josh agreed.

We stayed on, going through the motions of being Rangers, but we didn't accomplish anything and our hearts weren't in it. We knew that hiding out in the Norther had almost killed Captain, and no matter what old Orrill said there was no way Captain could recover enough to come back. So we glumly kept going, waiting for the governor to order the company to disband.

About mid-November one of Captain Randlett's soldiers rode into camp with a message that had come over the military wire for Lieutenant Robinson. It was from Captain, and it ordered us to meet him at Ringgold Barracks outside Rio Grande City right away. As Robinson read the order, we watched his expression change to surprise and then delight. He threw his hat in the air and put two bullet holes in it before it hit the ground. He let out a Rebel yell that roused the whole camp. "Load up with bullets and be ready to ride in five minutes." We whooped and hollered, but we were ready to hit the trail three minutes early.

X

We rode hard to Rio Grande City, covering the fifty-five miles to Ring-gold Barracks by moonlight in about six hours. We turned our winded horses loose when we got there, knowing they wouldn't wander far. Captain was waiting for us. He was starched and ironed like an army officer and looked great to those of us who thought we'd never see him again. He'd fixed up a cotton wagon with a canvas cover, and he brought Carrie along. That way he'd get to sleep on a featherbed and eat good food most every day, at least when we were in camp. When we saw him, Josh and I wondered why we'd ever doubted he'd be back. Now we knew he'd keep coming back as long as he was needed.

When Captain got to Ringgold Barracks the day before, he learned that Major Clendenin's troops had just missed stopping a stolen herd that same day. They got to the river in time to watch bandits drive the cattle up the bank on the other side. The rustlers fired a few shots at them but didn't hit anyone. I knew how those soldiers felt; they wanted to follow those rustlers and empty their saddles.

Captain wired Austin over the Army telegraph line that a party of raiders had crossed over at Las Cuevas with stolen cattle and had fired on Major Clendenin's troops. "He refuses to cross without further or-ders," Captain said in his message. "I have ordered my men up and shall cross if I can get any support."

Sarge Armstrong lined us up and Captain paced back and forth in the moonlight. "Men, Las Cuevas bandits crossed with two hundred and fifty beeves yesterday. I aim to bring those cattle back to Texas. Pete's holed up there, too, and I'm going to kill him." He paced some more, chewing his unlit cigar.

"I can't order you to go with me, for you were hired to fight in Texas and nowhere else. I can't order you, but I sure need your help, every one of you who'll volunteer to cross over with me.

"Remember, we'll probably be on our own, and I can't guarantee any of us will make it back. All I can guarantee is one danged good scrap. If you don't volunteer it won't be held against you or show in your record. Take your time making up your minds. Any of you who decide to go, take two paces forward." Most of us needed a minute or two before we could digest it all. I remembered when we'd crossed below Reynosa, and Captain and Rock had had to run for it. Las Cuevas was raider head-quarters, so it would be well defended.

The first to step forward was Deaf Rector, followed by Charley Nich-ols, who loved a good scrap, Armstrong, Orrill, and Lieutenant Wright. Then every man remaining took two steps—all twenty-nine of us were ready to go. In the moonlight I saw Captain trying to check a smile. It's hard to describe my feelings, but I was both thrilled at the men's re-sponse and scared of what lay ahead. When we were dismissed I waited until I could catch Captain alone.

"You won't have to kill Pete, sir," I said, handing him the stickpin. "I brought him across the river, but he knocked me out with his riding whip. When I came to, Rock had already handed him over to Jesús. Rock sent you the pin for a souvenir."

Captain frowned at first, for I guess he was disappointed that he couldn't even scores with Pete personally. Then he thought about the way Jesús took care of prisoners, and half smiled. "Thanks, Concho," he whispered, and put the pin in his jacket pocket. "You can scratch him out of the book for sure."

We'd loaded up with cartridges from the supply wagon before leaving Las Rucias, so our belts and pockets and saddlebags were bulging. We walked down to the river before daybreak, and in the half-light saw a small rowboat tied up to the opposite bank. The daredevil Matt Flem-ing took off his clothes, swam over, and rowed it back. It carried only a couple of men at a time, so it took a while to get everyone over.

While we were waiting our turn, Josh and I did a little pondering about Las Cuevas. From what we'd heard there were two or three hun-dred men there when they weren't away on raids. Maybe more. And there were just thirty of us.

Captain was talking to Captain Randlett, who kept the telegraph line busy asking for permission to accompany us with troops. He told us that someone in Washington had wired our consul in Matamoros to demand that the cattle be returned. The demand had been forwarded to our agent at Camargo, so he could deliver it to General Juan Flores Salinas. Flores owned Las Cuevas ranch and was also the alcalde of Camargo. He and Cortina had sort of been partners. At least Flores had kept him supplied with choice Texas steers.

"If you wait until they receive a reply to this demand," Randlett told Captain, "they might let us support you if it's refused and you have to invade."

"Do you really believe that?"

"No, but Colonel Potter ordered me to tell you that, and he got his orders from General Ord in San Antonio. Ord gets his instructions straight from Washington. I've got to report to him soon—can't stall too long—and when I do they may order me to prevent you from crossing. You're fixing to violate two laws, you know. One's against mounting an armed invasion off of American soil, and the other's against committing suicide. That's illegal, by the way. But we'll try to recover the bodies and bury you on this side. We'll stay here and help you back across if you're in trouble. Unofficially, of course," he added.

Captain was the last one to be rowed over, and there was old Jesús sitting beside him. How he'd learned of this campaign and found us in the nick of time we never knew, but we suspected he had some kind of mystical power. Maybe Captain had gotten a message to him somehow. When our eyes met, his flashed for a moment, but his expression didn't change and he said nothing.

He led the way through the thick fog, with Captain right behind him and the rest of us following in single file. When we got away from the river Captain called us together. "Form a skirmish line. Keep the line in sight and move quietly. Las Cuevas is two or three miles from the river." None of us was in the mood to make any noise as we moved through willows and blackjacks in the spooky fog.

We'd gone about a mile or more, I guess, when Jesús came to a new fence right across the trail. That seemed to rattle him some, for he hadn't expected it. He followed it and found a pole gate, but it was so foggy we couldn't tell if it led to a corral or a pasture. The only way we could distinguish a man from a fence post was when he moved.

Somehow Captain signalled Sarge Armstrong, and he moved ahead. There was thick brush in the way now. Sarge took a couple of men and probed the brush without finding anyone. The fog was thinning a bit, so our line spread out and kept moving. Pretty soon we saw what looked like sheds or stables.

Sarge and his scouts stepped out into the open. Someone fired a rifle at him and barely missed. Captain sprang forward and shot the sentry with his pistol. A flock of men came running out of the shed with guns in hand, looking every which way but not seeing us. We opened up on them, dropping ten or twelve, then we crouched in the brush and remained silent. There was a little *jacal* farther on, and men ran out the door and raced for the brush. Some of them wore Mexican Army uniforms.

The fog was nearly gone, and we could see a woman in the *jacal* patting out tortillas, not paying any attention to the shooting. I slipped up and asked her what this place was. It was Las Cachutas, she said, a line camp of Las Cuevas, which was farther on. She showed me where the trail branched, saying the left fork went to the ranch. All the time she was talking she kept on making tortillas, like something bad would happen if she stopped. I wondered who'd be around to eat them.

Captain had been aiming to surprise the men at ranch headquarters, but by bad luck we'd hit the new line camp. That ended any chance of a surprise attack on Las Cuevas. Some of us figured that we might as well head back to Texas, but Captain had come to kill bandits and recover stolen cattle. Half crouching, he trotted down the trail to Las Cuevas. We ran after him, holding our Sharps ready.

We went at a good clip for about half a mile, when Jesús crossed over a little rise and raised his hand. We slowed down and inched forward. Below in a sort of basin was the main ranch and village, surrounded by a wooden stockade. On the slopes around the house were *jacales* where vaqueros lived.

Half an hour had passed since we hit the line camp, and we expected to see lots of action, but there wasn't much. Men were catching horses and saddling them, but they didn't seem in a hurry. Soon a party formed and rode out through the stockade gate and then stopped while four of them scouted through the brush. There were still patches of fog, and they didn't spot us.

We all picked targets and waited for Captain. When he shot one of the scouts we got the other three, then opened up on the bunch that was milling around. They were out of range of Winchesters but not of Sharps, and our opening fire emptied a lot of saddles and brought down a few horses. Those who hadn't been hit hurried back inside the stockade. We were strung out in a long line and had good cover.

Our shooting really got them moving, but they seemed to have neither plans nor leaders. They galloped around in all directions, apparently looking for mounted men. None of them had seen us. They rode right back into range of our guns, and when Captain fired we cut loose on them again. Retreating for the second time, they seemed completely befuddled.

If Captain Randlett had gotten permission to cross over when we got in trouble, Captain planned for us to take one of the ranch buildings and hold them off until the troops came. At least that's what Sarge Hall told us. We didn't take them by surprise at Las Cuevas, so there was no chance of doing that. And even if we had, the troops wouldn't have come anyway because higher-ups had ordered them to stay in Texas. Captain knew that, so he gave up the plan before we crossed into Mexico. If we could have done that and the troops had come we could have put the raiders out of business.

A big group of mounted men galloped up from the direction of Camargo, led by a man on a blooded horse. Captain looked at him through his binoculars and said he was General Flores. He soon had a hundred or more armed men around him, and he showed right off that he knew how to fight. He split them into two groups and both headed toward the river on opposite sides of us, aiming to cut us off from the river and then finish us.

Captain crouched low and took off on the run, with us right behind him. "Break for the river," he yelled, "or we'll be cut off. Keep low and don't shoot unless they overtake you. Each man make his own way."

We didn't need any urging. Luckily there was thick brush between us and the river, and they still didn't know how few of us there were, so they weren't eager to come into the brush after us. All they knew was that every time they'd gotten near it the air was thick with bullets. They probably weren't sure whether there were men or ghosts in that deadly brush, for they still hadn't seen us.

Over at Ringgold they heard all the shooting. Lieutenant Guy Carleton, who manned the telegraph, reported that we were surrounded and being wiped out. Our consul at Matamoros got that report and wired his man at Camargo to hurry to Captain and tell him to surrender.

Captain had us giving way ahead of them in the brush but not firing a shot. The fact that we didn't shoot convinced them we were trying to draw them into an ambush, so they held back. That probably saved our lives, for we were all running low on Sharps cartridges. If we'd made a stand, we wouldn't have lasted long.

As they gained on us Captain signalled everyone back into a skirmish line. General Flores really knew what he was doing, and his men began pressing us as we neared the river. Captain ordered us to fire one round and then fall back, and that slowed them up. They kept coming but they were mighty cautious, still not sure we weren't drawing them into our main force. When we didn't spring a trap on them they moved faster, to outflank us and cut us off from the river, still three or four hundred yards away. We were fighting the kind of war Captain knew best, and even though they were well-led and capable fighters, his tactics worked.

We came to a cattle trail through the brush to the river, and raced down it, until something slowed everybody up. Big Dutch Reichel was lumbering along in the lead, and he couldn't run worth a damn. Josh was breathing down the back of his neck. "Git movin' or git outa the way," Josh yelled in his ear. That got him galloping a bit faster, and we made it to the river ahead of Flores' men.

We crouched behind the river bank, with pistols or rifles levelled over it. In front of us was Captain, walking back and forth, watching the enemy. Seeing him fearlessly expose himself to their fire must have given the Flores men something to think about, like maybe he wasn't human. I don't know how many times they shot at him, but somehow he wasn't even scratched by all the flying lead. I wished he'd take cover and not risk his life unnecessarily, but, as usual, he knew what he was doing. They outnumbered us at least three to one, and all of us were now out of rifle bullets. If they played it right, sooner or later we'd be out of pistol bullets, too, and they could finish us off. If we tried to swim to the other side they could line up on the bank and have a little target practice. Flores and about thirty men were on our right; a larger number was on our left, and they were slowly closing in.

Across the river Captain Randlett and a company of the 24th Infantry were watching. Off to one side, Sergeant Leahy and a squad of soldiers manned a Gatling gun. When the enemy closed in and shot at us, some of their bullets hit near Leahy's men. At least that's what he claimed later, and it was probably true. Leahy opened up with the Gatling and his men fired their rifles. General Flores and many of those with him fell. As soon as the soldiers started shooting we climbed up the bank and shot the rest of the crowd with Flores. Those on the other side of us pulled back fast.

Some of the soldiers slipped off their uniforms and swam over to help us, for the Cuevas bunch was coming back with more men. One of those who joined us, we learned later, was Captain Young. All of them were eager to even some scores with the bandits, and they did some good shooting with their rifles. Finally the firing stopped, for the Cuevas men pulled back out of range. Over at Ringgold Barracks an excited Lieutenant Carleton sent word over the wire that our first bunch had been wiped out and the rest of us were surrounded and asking for terms. That news went across the country, and must have sounded like the Alamo all over again.

Captain had never taken cover, and when the firing stopped he called us up out of the water and told us to take off our boots and dry our socks. We obeyed, but some of us were looking to see if the Cuevas bunch was coming back. Captain noticed our worried looks.

"They've broken off the fight," he told us. "They won't come back except under a flag of truce to pick up their dead and wounded." We looked again, wondering how he could be so sure, and why he didn't send us back to Texas. By then I'd enjoyed Mexico about as much as I could stand. In the excitement I guess I forgot we'd come after a herd of cattle.

In about an hour Major Alexander took command from Captain Randlett on the opposite river bank. He was rowed across to us, and asked for Captain McNelly. We crowded around while he read Captain a telegram he'd received from Colonel Potter at Fort Brown.

"Advise Captain McNelly to return at once to this side of the river. Inform him that you are directed not to support him in any way while he remains on Mexican territory. If McNelly is attacked by Mexican forces on Mexican soil do not render him any assistance. Let me know if McNelly acts on this advice."

Major Alexander handed Captain the telegram and waited while Captain read it for himself. "What shall I tell the Colonel?"

"The answer is no."

"Anything else?"

"No. Just no." Captain smiled. "Sorry, Major."

"Colonel won't like that."

"The answer is still no."

As the major turned to go, Captain said, "My men set out this morning before breakfast after riding half the night, and we haven't had time to cook a meal all day. They're sort of used up, and so am I. If I go back with you, could you let your cook fix up some bread and stew meat for us?"

The major smiled. "My orders are not to help while you remain in Mexico, but Colonel didn't say anything about not letting you have some food. I'll chance doing that."

Captain called Lieutenant Robinson. "I'm going across to look after these wires and rustle up some food for us. Sit tight where you are unless they move in on you. Just hold what we've got. Set up an outpost and let the boys rest." Captain and the major were rowed across, and I sure hoped he wouldn't get far away. I'd have been glad to row the boat for him right then.

Things were quiet for an hour or longer, and then three riders appeared holding a white flag tied to a rifle barrel. A letter was under the flag.

"A truce party, or at least it looks like one," Robinson said. "We'll see what they want." He sent Sergeant Hall over to tell Captain.

When the truce party got within a hundred yards, Lieutenant Robinson took Sarge Armstrong, Boyd, Josh, and me out to parley with them. The leader was Doc Headly, or at least that was the name he was listed under in the book. He was an American renegade and one of the main leaders of the border gangs. He was replenishing his courage from a bottle of mescal.

"You're not McNelly," he said thickly.

"Let me see the letter," Lieutenant Robinson replied.

Doc Headly took another pull on his mescal bottle, to keep his nerve up, I guess. He had a long white beard that looked like a horse's tail. His face was the color of raw meat, so he must have had a couple of bottles already to get him this far. "This here letter's from the Chief Justice of the state of Tamaulipas, and it's addressed to the commander of the Texas and United States forces that have invaded Mexico. You ain't the commander."

"Hand me the letter," Lieutenant Robinson said. His voice had a steely ring I hadn't heard before.

"How many men you got?"

"Enough to go to Mexico City if we decide to. I want that letter."

"You have invaded Mexico and killed the alcalde of Camargo and eighty other citizens."

"It'll be eighty-four if you don't hand over that letter." He nodded to us and lifted his pistol. We drew ours and covered the three of them.

Doc Headly started to say something, but Jim Boyd interrupted. "If I get the first slug into that drunk windbag can I have those fancy pistols and the gun belt?" he asked Lieutenant Robinson.

The lieutenant nodded.

"If I get the second slug in can I have the saddle?" Sarge Armstrong asked. Lieutenant Robinson nodded again.

Old Doc seemed to sober up a little, at least enough to know that the Rangers were dead serious. The letter was under the hammer of his rifle, which he held upright with the butt resting on his saddle horn. He handed the rifle to Lieutenant Robinson butt forward.

While we were jawing with Headly, one of our men yelled, "They're movin' in on the other side!"

"The first shot fired and you're a dead man," Robinson told Headly, cocking his pistol. Headly's red face turned white.

"Can I send 'em a message? Can I send one of these men?"

"He'd better be quick about it," Robinson said, aiming his gun at Headly's midriff. One of the men galloped round to the other side and we heard him shouting orders. The men there withdrew in a hurry.

Captain returned just then and took charge. He opened the letter and read it aloud. It was from the Chief Justice, as Doc had said. They wanted all Rangers and soldiers to leave Mexico and then they'd talk about any Texas complaints. Captain told us to put up our pistols, and handed Doc Headly his rifle. "We'll negotiate when we get those stolen cattle. We'll stay here until they're delivered."

Doc Headly talked with the other two in his party, then turned again to Captain. "Let's suspend fighting for tonight and tomorrow. It's Sunday. Then we'll deliver the cattle."

"We suspend nothing. The only way to stop fighting is for you to keep out of our range. That's final."

"Those cattle are penned at Camargo," Doc told him.

"You write an order for them and sign it. Then we'll see."

Captain wrote the order himself and handed it to Doc. "Sign it," he said, and Doc did as he was told. Then Captain dismissed them and they left.

The Army brought over a big pot of stew and a dozen or more loaves of bread. We didn't have any knives or forks, so we broke off chunks of bread and sopped up stew as fast as we could eat it. By now it was late afternoon, and we were all famished, for we hadn't eaten since we left Las Rucias. We didn't even slow down when a soldier brought Captain a telegram. He licked the stew off his fingers before reaching for it.

It was from Colonel Potter to Major Alexander. Captain read it out loud. "Secretary of War Belknap orders you to demand McNelly return at once to Texas. Do not support him in any manner. Inform the Secretary if McNelly acts on these orders and returns to Texas."

Captain must have been feeling pretty uppity. He tore a leaf from his notebook and wrote his reply. "I shall remain in Mexico with my Rangers and cross back at my discretion. Give my compliments to the Secretary of War and tell him and his United States soldiers to go to hell." I guess Captain remembered when he used to fight those soldiers in Louisiana not many years before.

We had just finished demolishing the bread and stew when another white flag appeared, and with it came a party of men and several wagons. Captain talked to them. We couldn't hear what was said, but we saw him hand one of them the order Doc Headly had signed. When he returned he told us to get ready to cross the river. It was dark by the time all of us got rowed over in that little boat.

It had been at least twenty-four hours since we'd saddled up and left Las Rucias, and now that we'd eaten we were ready for some serious sleeping. We'd ridden more than fifty miles in the night and then spent the day fighting and running. We didn't worry about earning our pay that day.

XI

Captain wasn't ready for a rest yet. The soldiers had brought in and fed our horses, and Captain ordered us to saddle up. My bones and muscles protested, but reluctantly obeyed.

"I want to be across from Camargo at daybreak to receive the cattle. Those hombres may change their minds. I don't trust 'em," Captain said.

Sergeant Hall, who had plenty of experience with raiders, told us "They ain't going to deliver those cattle. They've taken a big licking and lost their *jefe* and a lot of men. They'll be forted up at Camargo, be sure of that." I didn't find that news consoling.

The ride to Rio Grande City didn't take long, so when we got there we stretched out on the ground and used our saddles for pillows. Sleepy as I was, I couldn't help worrying. So much had happened that day it was hard to remember everything. All I could think of was that we'd been lucky to get out of Mexico alive. I couldn't help wondering how our luck, or maybe Captain's luck, could last through another day like that one.

When I opened my eyes the sun was rising. Captain and some of the Rangers had already ridden the half-mile down to the ferry that ran between Rio Grande City and Camargo. Captain had sent a message to Diego García, the number two man in Camargo, saying he was ready to receive the cattle and ordering him to send them over pronto.

The messenger came back from García, who said he was busy and would send the cattle tomorrow.

"Tell him we want them today, like Headly agreed to yesterday," Captain ordered. "They were to be delivered this morning. Tell him the commanding officer of the U.S. Army demands them now and will take military action if the truce agreement is violated." Back went the messenger.

Sergeant Hall was listening to all this. "Captain's wasting his time," he told us. "Those *bandidos* have spies and they know all about the telegrams to him yesterday. They know the Army ain't going to support him."

The messenger, who must have been getting tired from all the legwork, brought word that García had ordered the cattle delivered at three o'clock. This time the messenger was extra polite to Captain, way too polite. Sergeant Hall shook his head. "Smells like a trap," he said. All this wasn't the most reassuring talk Josh and I had heard.

We could see a corral full of cattle across the river, and near as many armed men as cattle. "Sergeant," I asked Hall, "do you reckon Captain will try to take 'em by force if they don't deliver 'em?"

"Only the Good Lord and Captain know what he might do or try to do. They're just stallin' for time while they get ready. Captain's trying to do something that ain't ever been done before. We'll soon know, won't we?"

"I reckon he'll try," I said, but looked again at all those armed men and figured more must be on the way. It didn't seem at all promising, even for a man like Captain who was used to doing the impossible. This time I figured Captain's luck had played out. There was no way we could get those cattle without help from the Army, and we knew the Army couldn't cross the river.

Captain was chewing his cigar and pacing back and forth, like he was trying to make up his mind about something. I knew that sign, and I was starting to feel scared even before I knew what was coming. I wasn't at all prepared for his next order. He told Sarge Armstrong to pull us back to Rio Grande City.

We loped the half-mile to Rio Grande City and stopped in front of a little cafe. We dismounted and threw our reins over the hitching rack, then followed Captain inside. He bought us all the coffee and *pan dulce* we could hold. Then we ambled around like passengers waiting for the next boat to Brownsville. Word got around that the Rangers were in town, and a crowd gathered to look us over. They'd heard about the Cuevas battle, and I guess they wanted to see if we had horns and forked tails. They asked some questions, like where were we going next. We shrugged our shoulders. We couldn't have answered that if we'd wanted to, for Captain hadn't told us where we were heading or what we'd be doing.

A little before three o'clock Sarge ordered us to mount and ride back to the ferry landing. Across the river in Camargo we saw a few men around the customs shack. A quarter of a mile from the river a big bunch of armed men were riding around the corral.

Captain stepped onto the ferry and smiled at the old Mexican who poled the ferry back and forth across the river. The old man smiled back, but it was forced. "Cut me off ten men from the head of the line," Captain ordered Sarge Armstrong. "Come on board with them and have the rest pull back a little and wait." He wasn't taking a picked crew; he figured any Ranger was good enough to handle what he had in mind.

Josh and I were in the first ten, and we weren't at all proud to be that near the head of the class just then. I thought of our first scrap and crossing that half mile of water at Palo Alto. That had seemed to take forever. Crossing the Rio Grande didn't take near long enough. I'd been half scared to death at Palo Alto. Now I was working on the other half. Those of us who went with Captain were ordinary Rangers except for Lieutenant Robinson, Sergeants Hall and Armstrong, and Corporal Rudd. One of us was the jokester Bob Pitts, who called us the "Death Squad."

"If you don't get back, Josh," one of those staying behind called, "who gets your horse?"

"Who wants him?" Josh asked, trying to make his voice sound carefree, and almost succeeding.

"Not me," the solemn Ranger Hardy said. "I rode him once and I'd rather walk."

That's the way the Rangers were. Most of us had been together a little over six months, and we'd been through a lot. We joked about anything and everything, only right then nothing seemed funny. I put on a smile, but it was kind of sickly.

Captain signalled to the old man to pole us over. He was in a good mood, and chatted some with the ferryman, while I translated for him. Captain asked how many kids he had and if he'd been to church yet, for it was Sunday. "Si, señor," the old man said, crossing himself a couple of extra times, maybe just to make sure.

When the ferry hit the bank Captain hopped out and snubbed it, then dusted his hands on his pants legs and looked up at the customs shack. The customs *jefe* was the man who'd been carrying messages between Captain and García, but now he had on his official coat and cap. Four of his men stood by his side, all of them armed.

We walked up to the shack and Captain shook the *jefe*'s hand like he was really glad to see him again. I explained in Spanish that it was now three o'clock and we'd come for the cattle. He was a match for Captain in politeness. He was so sorry that it hurt, he said, placing his hand over his heart, but he'd forgotten today was Sunday. It was against their religion to do business on Sunday. In the morning, real early in the morning, he'd deliver the herd. A thousand pardons.

We'd formed a skirmish line behind Captain without being told, for that was now second nature to us. We were ready for something to happen, but it was so quick we barely had time to draw our guns. The customs men all reached for their pistols. Captain drew his gun and leaped on the *jefe* like a panther, hitting him on the head with his pistol barrel and giving him a knee in the gut as he fell, knocking the wind out of him. The customs men were bunched together, to their disadvantage. Bob Pitts drilled the first one who got his gun out. The other three dropped their pistols and reached as high as they could. It looked like they got on tiptoe just so they could reach higher. We gestured to them to back away from their guns, and they seemed eager to oblige us. The mounted men at the corrals stopped their horses and watched. Then a dozen of them walked their horses toward us.

The *jefe* was stunned but still conscious. He rolled against the dead man and scrambled to his knees, scared out of his wits. Captain grabbed him by the collar and jerked him to his feet. The mounted men checked their horses and watched.

"Tell this man he's going across the river with us," Captain commanded me. "Tell him to order those cattle delivered in one hour or he's a dead man. If anyone tries to rescue him I'll shoot him between the eyes." I told him. He nodded hard, like he understood and believed every word. He was mighty pale as he gave orders to his men. He told them, "Do not fail, for the love of God."

We shoved him onto the ferry. The old ferryman was so scared he dropped the pole twice and had trouble poling us across. He kept looking fearfully at Captain, like he thought Captain might shoot him just for fun. The rest of our outfit back onshore was nearly as shocked as the customs people, or the ten of us, for that matter. None of us, except maybe Robinson and Armstrong, had had any idea of what was coming and it was over so quickly we could barely take it all in. The only one who was cool and relaxed was Captain. It had been his show all the way. We were just decorations.

We saw someone open the corral gate and let the cattle out. Riders headed them for the river just like that was what they'd intended to do all along. Pretty soon the herd was back in Texas, where the Rangers drove them out to the prairie. Then Captain told Sergeant Hall to take the *jefe* to the ferry and let him go. I figured the first thing he'd do was go home and change his underwear.

Captain taught the Rangers a good lesson for lawmen that day. When you have a crowd to handle, grab the leader but don't kill him. Do it in a way that doesn't leave any doubts in his mind about who's boss. That way a couple of peace officers can handle a mob without much shooting. The way Captain had handled it was certainly unexpected by them and by us, and it worked like magic.

The herd they'd delivered turned out to be more than the 250 steers we were after. It was closer to 400—everything they had in the corrals.

There was one cow following the steers. Captain had us drive her to the river to give to the ferryman. We herded the steers along to Retama and set up camp. Dad Smith arrived the next day with the supply wagon, and Captain brought Carrie and his covered wagon to the new camp.

Old Rock showed up about this time, and Captain sent him to locate the brand owners so they could send cowboys for their stock. About every brand in the Nueces Strip was represented, from Captain King's Running W to Hale and Parker's Half-Moon from down near the coast. They were all prime steers, for the raiders had killed the cows and scrub stock for their hides.

We loafed around camp some, for there wasn't much to do right then. The raiders must have had second thoughts about crossing the Rio Grande, for they'd lost their big *jefe*, General Flores, and almost ninety others. For something to do, we began delivering cattle to their owners. A couple of us took steers to a ranch near the Nueces and had a good meal before we headed back. Josh stayed in camp, though I tried to persuade him to go with me.

He hung around, hoping to deliver Captain King's steers; he wanted to see Miss Caroline again. Sarge Armstrong was in charge, and I heard later that when he was picking the men to go to Santa Gertrudis, Josh was at his elbow. He said he'd sure like some more of that good coffee. Then he mentioned the old farm horse he'd left there—it had been with the family a long time, and someday he'd have to tell them what had happened to it. Sarge just smiled.

"Sure you don't just want to see that young lady?"

Josh turned red. "No, but she sure makes good coffee."

"All right," Sarge said. "Corporal Rudd can take you and couple of men from his squad." Rudd took Josh, Bill Callicott, a lanky man from Tennessee, and Bob Pitts to deliver the steers, about thirty-five of them, to the Santa Gertrudis, about a hundred miles away.

Captain King was amazed when they rode up with the steers. "Boys, I am glad to see you. From the reports we heard there didn't seem any hope that a single one of you would make it back to Texas. How many men did Captain McNelly take with him into Mexico?"

"Thirty."

"What! Invaded Mexico with thirty men? And on foot?"

"Yes, sir."

"And you attacked Las Cuchatas and Las Cuevas both! Those are the two worst ranches in Mexico—headquarters for all the bandits who steal cattle over here. I know all about Las Cuevas. It belongs to General Flores."

"Not any more, sir. The General was killed when he attacked us." Then Rudd told him all about the fight.

"Well," Captain King said, "I'm delighted that you got back alive. We heard you were surrounded and wiped out. There isn't another man who could have done it. Captain McNelly is the first man who ever got stolen cattle back from Mexico. Of the thousands I've lost these are the only ones I ever got back and I think more of them than any five hundred I own." He gave orders that not one of these steers was ever to be sold.

Captain King invited them into the house, Josh said. It was nearing Christmas and Caroline and the two King daughters were home from school. "None of us has had a chance to bathe or change clothes for ten days," Rudd told King. "We're simply not fit to be in the presence of ladies." Instead they went to a bunkhouse. There was a huge supper for them in the mess hall, and they gorged themselves. The ladies made a cake big enough for the whole Ranger company and brought it to the mess hall. On the cake they'd written, "Compliments of the King women to the McNelly Rangers."

Josh heard them coming and was ashamed for Caroline to see him in his shabby and outgrown clothes, so he hid behind the big stove. When Caroline asked where the other Ranger was, Josh said he blushed up a storm but stayed put. The others said he'd stepped outside.

"It's no disgrace to be poor," Rudd assured Josh later.

"No, but it's damned inconvenient," he said.

They bedded down for the night, and about midnight Josh had a nightmare. He jumped up, pistol in hand, shouting, "Shoot, boys! Here they are, shoot!" The others managed to disarm him in the dark and hide his gun till morning. When they left Captain King offered them fresh horses and money for food, but they refused. He loaded them up with enough grub to last them three or four days.

"Someday I'm going back there dressed decent," Josh told me, "and ask Captain King for a job. From now on I'm savin' my pay." He didn't add what else was on his mind, but he didn't need to.

XII

While we were camped at Retama a big batch of mail came from Ranger headquarters. The wire that Lieutenant Carleton had sent while we were in Mexico made it sound like we'd been massacred, and he hadn't corrected it when we returned without a loss. Relatives of Rangers wrote from all over the country asking that whatever was left of their relatives' bodies be gathered up and shipped home for decent burial.

Some of Josh's kinfolk in the Carolinas had written to say they'd pay his freight back to Georgia. I guess they figured his mother couldn't afford it. And someone in the East named Rockefeller wanted to know if our scout had been killed. That's how we found out Old Rock's real name, for he'd never told us. Captain said for everyone to write his folks and tell them not to pay attention to crazy stories off the telegraph.

There was also a dressing-down for Captain from Ranger headquarters because he hadn't ever reported on what happened at Las Cuevas. All they'd gotten from him was the wire saying he was crossing into Mexico. Had consul Tom Wilson arranged his surrender? What terms had he made, and what had he promised?

Captain was miffed, for he'd rather be poked in the eye with a stick than write a report, but he was even madder about the questions. He should have reported immediately, of course, for that silly wire had made it sound like we'd gotten into a real disaster in Mexico. I'd thought that we had for sure, which only means that I'd underestimated Captain's fighting ability.

"What makes you think I'd make terms with outlaws?" Captain wrote Adjutant General Steele. "Why would a Texas peace officer ever have to beg for terms from bandits?" He went on to say that he hadn't gone to the Strip to write reports but to bring law and order where there was none. Other Ranger companies and the U.S. Army had written lots of reports, but you can't stop bandits with ink. A well-placed Sharps bullet did more for law and order than a whole stack of reports, Captain told the adjutant general.

What Captain had done so far in the Strip had earned him the admi-
ᴛ and support of all law-abiding cowmen in the area, Mexicans as
as Anglos. Headquarters sent us some shiny new badges, and Cap-

tain had us pin them on our shirts. Wherever we went now, folks would know who we were. If they were law-abiding, they'd know we were on their side. If they were the other sort, they weren't likely to wait around to shake hands. And all of this was because Captain, being the kind of man he was, had been given a free hand by the governor.

Our camp at Retama was in a grove of big Spanish oaks by a stream, not far from a number of Tejano and Anglo families. They were all good people, and when word got out that Captain needed goat's milk he soon had more than he could handle. Some of those folks butchered a yearling every week, and they kept us supplied with steaks and stew meat. It was easy living. We got paid, and Josh finally bought a shirt and pants that fitted him. He was beaming when he put them on.

"It's the first time I ever had clothes someone else hadn't already worn out," he said.

Things were quiet all along the border for a while, and we rode patrols for days without seeing anyone who might be a rustler. There were still a few raiders slipping over and trying to steal small bunches, but the ranchers and their hands took care of them, now they knew it could be done. After Captain came to the Strip and showed the way, cowmen took heart and refused to allow themselves to be robbed without fighting back.

One bunch of raiders was killing and skinning cattle just below San Diego in Duval County. Cowmen in the area got together and went after them, killing every last one. It gradually got to be known on both sides of the border that stealing cattle was no longer safe and profitable. Captain McNelly had taken the fun out of rustling.

Josh and I were on one patrol that went all the way to our old campground at Las Rucias. We took our time, staying a few miles back from the river and scouting the area as we rode. The people we saw weren't worrying about bandits all the time like they used to, and the way they felt about Captain would have made him blush. They'd heard about him going over and making the bandits return stolen cattle, which was like performing a miracle. If we'd told them Captain had won the battle of San Jacinto and captured Santy Anny single-handed they'd have believed us.

We camped at Las Rucias a few days for old time's sake. I thought of the young lady who was hoping we'd make it safe for her and her people to return, and wondered how much longer they'd have to wait. While we were there old Blas rode into camp. Captain hadn't changed the order to scratch his name from the book or we'd have arrested him like he deserved. Somehow the old rascal knew just about everything that went on in the lower Strip country. He stayed with us until we left, and we learned everything there was to know about what people were doing.

Porfirio Díaz was in Brownsville getting ready to start a revolution against President Lerdo, Blas told us. Old-time ranger captain Rip Ford, who was working for a paper in Galveston, had visited Díaz and learned that he needed money to start his revolution. Díaz asked Ford if Texans would lend him money. Ford reminded him of the trouble the raiders were causing in Texas. Lerdo still held Cortina in Mexico City, but that hadn't stopped the raids. If Díaz would promise to keep Cortina away from the border and stop the raiding, Ford said, he was sure Texans would lend him the money he needed.

Díaz agreed, Blas said, and the money was coming in. One of those who contributed was rancher Sabas Cavazos, Cortina's half-brother. Blas thought he'd loaned Díaz $50,000.

One of the men asked Blas if Pete Marsele had been at Las Cuevas during the fight. He wasn't there, Blas said, but he should have been. His man said an Americano had captured him and took him across the river. He paused and stared at each one of us separately, to see if he could detect any knowledge of Pete's fate in our eyes or expressions. *Bandidos* had found what looked like Pete's body dangling from a cottonwood limb. They suspected the Rangers of doing it, but Pete had lots of enemies, Blas admitted, and any of them might have done it. Josh and I kept still, but the other Rangers expressed their delight at the news. Each wished he'd been there to pull on the rope.

In camp Captain left his lieutenants in charge while he mostly rested. His beard and the hair at his temples were turning gray, and he walked slow and sort of bent over. Some time in January he rode over to Ringgold Barracks with Wright and Armstrong. From what Armstrong told us he'd sent a telegram from there to Washington, asking for an 8th Cavalry troop under Captain Farnsworth and two companies of the 24th Infantry to accompany him into Mexico. With them, he said, he could clean out all of the bandits on both sides of the river.

Captain went back to Ringgold a week or two later to see what the response was. The answer was no. Major Clendenin told him that Sergeant Leahy, who'd fired the Gatling gun at the Mexicans across the river, had been busted to private for it. The Army was also preparing charges against Captain Young for swimming over to join us.

That news really got Captain chewing on his cigar. He figured telegrams wouldn't do any good, for they'd likely ignore them. The only way to set things right was for him to go to Washington. About the middle of February he rode to Galveston and caught a ship for the East Coast at his own expense. He was gone about six weeks, and he never told us what went on. But Major Clendenin said that Sergeant Leahy got his stripes back and the charges against Captain Young were dropped.

We had little to do except ride on long patrols and be sure there weren't any raiders crossing over. The cowmen in the Strip were gathering steers to put in trail herds over on the Atascosa. The money from those herds was helping the little cowtowns hire lawmen to keep the peace. The Strip was changing, but the rustling wasn't over. The raids were by four or five men who tried to find a few steers near the river. They didn't go far inland. There were also plenty of Anglo thieves inside the country, for steers were bringing good prices up in Kansas.

When Captain returned from the East he looked worn down, and he did a lot more resting. Early in April a wagon arrived from the Santa Gertrudis, bringing thirty new Winchester 44.40 rifles and cases of cartridges. These were a gift from Captain King, his way of saying thanks to the McNelly Rangers. Most of us were glad to turn in our heavy Sharps cannons for those light repeating rifles.

About the same time Parrott rode into camp and handed Captain two saddlebags full of photographs. He wouldn't tell us anything about where he'd been or whose pictures he'd taken, but we soon knew that Captain had been waiting for them. We broke camp the next day and headed north, with Parrott in the lead. We remembered that Parrott had said he was heading for Eagle Pass when he'd pulled out.

Captain rode in his wagon, and didn't seem to be in a hurry to get wherever it was we were going, and Josh and I wondered if he was really in shape for another ruckus. We rarely saw him, but when we did he looked all right, though he moved slowly and wasn't chewing on a cigar. It was the middle of May when we got to Laredo, just over a year since we'd signed up with the Special Force outside Burton. To me it seemed more like two years.

When we got to Laredo some of the men and scouts from the lower country asked to be discharged, and headed for more familiar territory. We'd had turnovers occasionally since the beginning, so it was nothing new. About forty-five men had been with the company at one time or another, but we still numbered only thirty most of the time.

At Laredo Captain signed on a young Easterner named Jennings, partly to write reports. I guess he didn't figure on getting chewed out again for failing to get them in on time. Jennings was a writer; later he sold a lot of stories to magazines about Captain and himself, and then put them in a book. In these stories Captain was almost as good a fighting man as Jennings. He even wrote about the fight at Las Cuevas as if he'd been there. We played a lot of tricks on him because he was gullible, and when Jim Boyd learned that Jennings got checks from home he taught him to play draw poker.

We camped near Laredo for a few days, while Captain and Carrie stayed at a hotel. I guess he got a lot of reports and letters written, for Jennings went there every day. Captain also lined up some scouts who knew the country, and he signed up Gregorio Gonzales to take charge of them. Gregorio had been city marshal at Laredo and county sheriff, and he was a real lawman. Josh and I asked him where he was taking us.

"We're heading for King Fisher country," he told us. That didn't mean as much to Josh as it did to me. King Fisher was the ruler of a big area of the upper Strip, and according to what folks said he had a hundred or more outlaws organized into bands. Their business was stealing cattle and horses and robbing and killing travelers. They had camps in many counties and did a regular business of driving stolen stock far away for sale. They'd sell a herd of stolen horses in East Texas or up along the Red River, and then they'd steal another herd before they left, to sell somewhere else.

For some reason King Fisher's name wasn't in the book, and he'd never even been indicted for any crime. He was only twenty-two years old, but he was already well known all over that part of Texas, from Goliad to the upper Nueces.

He'd gotten to know Doc White and Charley Vivian and their people, who'd pulled out from Goliad for the Pendencia region across the Nueces. King Fisher had followed them when he was seventeen. This was empty country at the time, but raiders soon made off with most of their stock. They elected Doc justice of the peace and told him to get some law and order around there.

Doc White appointed King Fisher marshal, and the raiders soon learned to steer clear of the Pendencia. But Anglo outlaws discovered that King treated them right, so men on the run flocked to the country around the Pendencia, knowing they'd be safe from the law there. According to accounts, King had killed twenty-six men, mostly Republicans. He was one of the few who could shoot straight with either hand.

King Fisher was said to be a cold-blooded killer and surrounded by outlaws who did his bidding. One story I heard was that eight Mexicans had delivered a herd of "wet" stock, cattle or horses stolen in Mexico and driven across the Rio Grande. King refused to pay them what he'd promised, and they argued awhile. Finally he paid them and they left, but they hadn't ridden ten miles before his men ambushed them and took their lives as well as their money. Another story was that a rancher and his son had followed the tracks of their missing horses to a corral. A man who was there met them in a friendly manner and invited them to dismount. While they were stepping down off their horses he shot both of them in the back. Thereafter, when anyone who wasn't a friend of King Fisher discovered his stock missing he didn't go looking for it. Going into his country seemed every bit as risky as the raid on Las Cuevas. Maybe more so.

XIII

We rode into the little settlement at Carrizo Springs, which Parrott said was only about ten miles southeast of King Fisher's headquarters on the Pendencia. His place was just west of Lake Espantoso, an old channel of the Nueces that was about half a mile wide and ten miles long. It was full of alligator gar that devoured the bodies of people who were thrown into it. That's why it was named Espantoso, meaning Ghost. It probably had more ghosts per gallon than any lake in the world.

The wagon road from San Antonio to Chihuahua went right by the lake. According to stories, many travelers who'd left San Antonio or who were headed there disappeared on this stretch of road and were never seen again. They'd been killed and thrown into the lake by some of the King Fisher crew. Where the trail from the Pendencia hit the road to Eagle Pass we saw King Fisher's sign. It said, "This is King Fisher's road. Take the other."

Captain talked to old Levi English, who had a general store at Carrizo and who'd had his troubles with outlaws. Captain got a lot of information about the King Fisher crowd, but he didn't share it. Parrott introduced him to a tall lad named Drew Taylor, who knew how to get to King Fisher's Pendencia settlement without following the road. He also told Captain that King was there with part of his crew.

Captain left a few hands to guard our camp and took about twenty-five of us with him. With Drew Taylor showing the way, we rode west until we crossed the Pendencia. Then we headed north through open country until we crossed the stream again and came to brush. Captain stopped and told us we were near King Fisher's headquarters.

"There may be some women there," he said, "so don't shoot unless we're shot at. We'll have to give them a chance to surrender." Naturally, from what we'd heard about them, none of us expected them to do that. We figured we'd have a real scrap, and some of us would surely be killed.

We rode in a skirmish line until Captain saw the ranch house in the midst of a cottonwood grove. The whole place was surrounded by brush, so we were able to get real close without being seen. We saw men playing cards in the saddle shed behind the house, so we spread out and closed in from all sides. When Captain raised his hand and gave Segal his head, we all hit the brush at once and came out facing a rock-and-rail fence we hadn't spotted. Despite the surprise our horses all cleared it, and we surrounded the house.

We hit the ground with Winchesters in hand, expecting to be shot at from all sides. Josh was paired up with Parrott and I was with Jim Boyd. One of the men who'd been playing cards in the saddle shed came out to see who'd arrived, and there I was face to face with my old friend Blackie. I pointed my rifle at his chest. "Get your hands up or I'll drop you," I ordered. He raised them in a hurry.

"Damn you, Carter, I ain't done with you yet. One of these days I'll get the drop on you and there'll be one less greaser in Texas."

"Shut up and stand over there facing the wall." I pulled his gun from the holster and threw it behind me. Some of the Rangers covered the rest of the men in the saddle shed. So far not a shot had been fired. I couldn't believe, after all we'd heard about the King Fisher outfit, that they'd surrender without a shot.

About that time a man Parrott knew as Frank Porter came around the corner of the house with a cocked Winchester in his hands. Parrott's rifle was also cocked.

"You're that damned picture man," Porter said, raising his gun and aiming at Parrott's chest. Parrott raised his rifle.

"Drop it," Parrott ordered. "We're McNelly Rangers."

Porter raised his rifle two more times, then held it over his head with both hands and threw it down. Cursing savagely, he surrendered. According to the book he'd often boasted that he'd never be taken alive. He'd have had the first shot, but neither could have failed to kill the other, and Porter's nerve left him. Later he alibied, saying he was surrounded and outnumbered. Captain and a bunch of us were watching, but no one interfered with another Ranger in a man-to-man showdown. Parrott would have been plenty mad if someone had tried to help him.

Later I asked him how he'd stayed so cool and steady with a killer pointing a gun at him a few yards away. The trick, he said, was to catch the other man's eye and hold it. "If he's facing you and you have his eye, he can't shoot." Captain had said much the same thing, and after watching Parrott face Porter I knew it had to be true.

Eight men surrendered without firing a shot, and all of them were in the book. These were Blackie and the others in the shed. We still didn't know who might be in the house with King Fisher. Captain walked to the door just as King Fisher opened it. The two best pistol shots in Texas stood face to face, but neither had drawn his gun.

"I'm Lee McNelly, Texas Rangers," Captain said. "Lock your hands behind your head and come out." King did.

"Turn around. Back up and don't move your hands." Captain took King's two gold-inlaid pistols and handed them to Sarge. "Turn around."

King turned, smiling, like being arrested by Rangers happened every few days and was fun. Captain frowned. "Why in hell did you give up so easy?" He wasn't used to taking prisoners. Then he noticed King's wife standing in the door. "Excuse my language, ma'am," he said.

"What are you doing to my husband?"

"He's under arrest. We're Texas Rangers."

"What are you arresting him for? He hasn't done anything."

"Let me handle this, Sarah," King told her, motioning her back into the house. He turned to Captain. "Shucks, Captain, I knew who you were the minute you told me to give up. That's why I did. I'm a law-abiding man."

"Shut up. You're going to jail."

"On what charge?"

Captain didn't have an answer, and he felt pretty uncomfortable with a flock of prisoners on his hands. King's name wasn't even in the book, though everyone knew he ran the biggest rustling and horse-stealing operation in the West. There was nothing else to do but take the flock of them to Eagle Pass.

While we were rounding up the men outside, Josh disarmed one who called himself Bill Templeton. He'd signed on with us under a different name at Burton, and he was one of the ones who'd quit in Brownsville. "I reckon you know me, Josh," he said, meek as a lamb.

"I know you, all right. You ran out on us in Brownsville."

"Reckon I could speak to Captain?"

"Anybody who knows how to talk can speak to him."

"Captain, what are you going to do with us?"

"Make a break for the brush and I'll be glad to show you."

"You remember me, Captain?"

"I never forget a damn coward."

Captain was figuring what to do next, with nine prisoners on his hands. "Call out your wife," he ordered King Fisher. "I want to speak to her."

She came to the door, looking like one of those pretty little Irish gals from down around San Patricio—black hair rolled up into a ball and dressed like it was Sunday and she was going to town.

"Lady, I'm taking these men to Eagle Pass. They're under arrest. I want you to pass along this warning—if anyone tries to rescue them they'll all die on the spot."

Her face darkened and her eyes flashed. "So that's your law. We've heard all about how you make your own laws, but let me tell you, if you kill my husband I—"

King interrupted her. "That's enough, Sarah. Do as he says. If you happen to see any of my friends get the word to them. Let the Rangers have their way right now. I'll be home before you know it."

Captain ordered Lieutenant Wright to take six of us and start for Eagle Pass with the prisoners. "I'll be along tomorrow," he said. He didn't say so, but we knew he wasn't up to going on horseback. Those four days we'd hidden out in the Norther without food had left their mark on him. He'd bounced back some after a rest, but he wasn't the same man we'd signed on with in Burton.

It was about thirty miles to Eagle Pass. We took our time, so Captain wouldn't have to hurry, and got there around noon the next day. Captain arrived in his wagon about an hour later. We took the prisoners to the sheriff's office, and for a bunch of cutthroats facing trial for their crimes, they were mighty relaxed. But this time, I was sure, Blackie wouldn't get off so easy.

King Fisher's lawyer was waiting in the sheriff's office, impatiently tapping on the desk with a pencil. I couldn't tell if he did regular work for King or had gotten word of his arrest and saw a chance to make some money. I didn't see much about him to admire.

Captain went into the sheriff's office, and we stepped up to the door to listen. "My name's McNelly. I'm a Texas Ranger, and I have nine prisoners to deliver to you to hold for trial."

The man behind the desk got up and shook hands with Captain. "Jim Vale, chief deputy of Maverick County. I'm happy to meet you, Captain. You are Captain McNelly of the Rangers, aren't you?"

"That's right."

"And you have some prisoners you want me to hold?"

"Correct. Nine of them."

"Very well. I see you have Mr. Fisher."

"I've got King Fisher, yes."

"On what charge, Captain?"

"He can't be a stranger to you. He's a thief and a killer. You know that as well as I do."

The lawyer spoke up then. "That's an opinion, Captain, not a charge under Texas law. You must name any victims and produce them as witnesses. You must also produce the bodies of any homicide victims, with proper witnesses."

Captain's head was sinking on his chest, and it reminded me of the time he learned that Pete had tricked him. It sounded like Captain was having trouble breathing, and those of us around the door were fingering our guns. At least I was.

"Up here," that putty-faced lawyer was saying, "we go by Texas law as it comes from the courts, not the jungle law of some Ranger Captain wearing a two-bit star." I grabbed my pistol instinctively, not knowing what I was doing, but Josh took two or three long strides forward and slapped that lawyer across his pasty face. He spun around a couple of times as he flew across the room and bounced off the wall. I let go of my gun handle; maybe Josh had just saved that mealymouthed bastard's life. He got up spitting blood. "You and those lawless killers of yours," he said, dabbing his lips with his handkerchief.

"I'm sorry," Captain said. "It won't happen again unless you keep asking for it. We're peace officers and we know the law." He turned to Josh, frowned, and pointed to the door. "Out, Josh. Never do that again." Josh walked out upright and proud, for he knew he'd done what all the rest of us were bustin' to do.

Captain told Deputy Vale that "Kansas has felony warrants for two of the prisoners—Frank Porter and Wes Bruton. Missouri's got felony warrants for three—"

"Do you have warrants, Captain?"

Captain pulled a copy of the book out of his jacket pocket. "Their names are in here, and this book is a blanket warrant."

"Do you know of any court decisions that say that, Captain? What have the courts done with men turned over to them under the warrants you claim? Has the book stood up in court?"

"No." Captain's voice was barely audible.

"If I hold these men under that blanket warrant, can you guarantee that Kansas and the other states will send for them in the regular manner and pay for their keep and expenses?"

"No."

Captain gave up. He turned to Lieutenant Wright. "Give these men their guns and release them." He walked outside and leaned weakly against the wall. King Fisher picked up his gold-inlaid pistols and holstered them. Then he looked at Captain.

"Much obliged, Captain."

"You've won, King," Captain said. "I'm licked." He looked King Fisher over for a minute. "You're a young man. You've won every bout with the law up to now. You may be lucky and win some more, but one day you'll lose, and that one will be for keeps, at least if you lose it to Rangers. We don't fight draws and dogfalls. When we lose, we lose.

When we win, we win. No in-betweens. And when we win once, that's enough. The law may lose now and then like we just did, but the law always wins the last round. We represent the law and we'll win in the end."

"I'm a law-abiding man, Captain, like I told you."

"Make damn sure you stay law-abiding, King. You've got a nice wife. You could make a good citizen. You'd also make a nice corpse. All outlaws look good when they're dead."

"But I'm no outlaw, Captain. Nobody can prove—"

"Meaning I didn't prove it this time, which is correct. But look at it this way—anything that walks like a duck, looks like a duck, and runs with ducks is most likely a duck. I only aimed to tell you to get out of this outlaw business. The next time the Rangers come we just might leave you where we overhaul you. You could make a better life for yourself. It's up to you." King looked like he was going to ask Captain something, then shook his head and left.

Blackie gave me an ugly look as he walked past. "We ain't through, Carter. I'll see you again one of these days."

The rest of the Rangers had rounded up eight hundred cattle of many brands and brought them to Eagle Pass, but the brand inspector refused to look at them. "I've got a wife and kids," he explained. Mexican ranchers in the area owned some of the brands in the herd, but they were afraid to claim their animals, for they knew King Fisher's men would kill them. The Rangers finally turned the cattle loose. "That tells you somethin' about King Fisher," Sarge Armstrong said. "He's got everybody here buffaloed, even the brand inspector. Half are his friends and the rest are afraid for their lives. But the law will come here one day, and he'll get what's comin' to him."

Captain sent us back to camp near Carrizo and said he'd be along in a few days. "Captain ain't feeling well," Lieutenant Wright told us. "There's a doc here he wants to see."

We stopped to see Jim Wofford, who was driving Captain's wagon. He said Captain was coughing up blood, and Carrie was really worried and discouraged. She'd heard of a doctor in San Antonio who had some medicine that thickened the blood and thought maybe that would help. She aimed to take Captain there.

There was a lot of gloating back in Carrizo and around the Pendencia, for everyone had been wondering what would happen if Captain McNelly brought his terrible Rangers to King Fisher country. All of those who were wanted by the law breathed easier now that they knew they wouldn't be forced to pay for their crimes, at least this time.

King Fisher was riding so high we couldn't tell if King was his name or his title.

One reason King had never been indicted for any crime was that anyone who stood up to him was sure to be killed. No one in the whole region dared to testify against him, and nobody worried about what happened to travelers who disappeared. King Fisher's word was law, and because he seldom touched liquor, Carrizo had no saloon. He didn't allow it, and smuggling whiskey there was likely to be a fatal error.

They held a big rodeo and fiesta at Carrizo Springs, but the Rangers weren't invited. We did catch sight of King Fisher when it started, for the rodeo arena wasn't far from our camp. He rode a big dapple gray horse that had a lot of thoroughbred in him. The brand had obviously been worked over by a running iron artist and made into a 7D, King's brand.

The saddle was about as fancy as they came, covered with silver. King wore a beaver hat, a silk shirt, and tiger skin chaps. According to what folks told us, his friend Ben Thompson, who'd killed many a man, had seen a tiger in a circus in North Texas. When the circus people wouldn't sell him the tiger he shot it and then bought the skin. He had it tanned and made into a pair of chaps. "You can paint a rattlesnake all over with gold," Sarge said when he saw King's finery, "but underneath he's still a snake."

About the time the festivities were starting Captain arrived from Eagle Pass. In the morning he turned the company over to Lieutenant Robinson and told him to set up camp in Oakville, county seat of Live Oak County; then he and Carrie headed for San Antonio. Lieutenant Wright turned in his badge and left at the same time. He'd had medical training and figured on going into doctoring.

XIV

We left Carrizo feeling down and out, for we'd been done in by thieves. We rode to Oakville and set up camp about half a mile from town. It wasn't much of a community, just a dozen houses and some shacks in the brush, a couple of saloons, a courthouse and jail, and a general store. It was famous for two things—bad water and killings. The water tasted so awful we had to make coffee extra strong to be able to swallow it.

In the past ten years at least forty men had been killed in and around Oakville, but in all that time only two men had been arrested for serious crimes, and those had been committed in other counties. While the two were in jail someone had slipped up to the window with a shotgun and executed them without benefit of jury. There were some big oaks in front of the jail, and folks told us they'd been used for private hangings.

Oakville became quiet and peaceable soon after word spread that the McNelly Rangers were there. We made a few arrests and took the prisoners to other counties for trial. Most of the outlaws slipped into the brush and avoided Oakville for as long as we camped there. Later the town was renamed George West after a tightfisted rancher who owned half the county.

Captain wrote for Corporal Rudd to bring three men to San Antonio for duty, and he took Spencer Adams, Josh, and me. We cut across country and rode all day and all night, reaching San Antonio before dark the next day. We left our tired horses at Staacke's Stable and walked to the Menger Hotel. "You wait for me here," Corporal Rudd told us when we reached the hotel lobby. "Captain's probably in bed. I'll tell him we're here and see what he wants."

It was nearly an hour before he returned, and we spent the time wondering what dangerous mission Captain had for us this time. "Captain has to stay in bed most of the time," Rudd said. "He's in bad shape. The first thing he wants us to do is get new clothes. Don't go around town in work clothes. He'll be real pleased if all of us get suits and wear 'em while we're here. We also need to get barbershop haircuts and have our boots shined. Josh, you need new boots. He didn't order us to do it, just said he'd be mighty pleased if we did all that."

Josh and Adams and I must have looked a bit puzzled. "There's a lot of talk going around that the Rangers are a bunch of killers who shoot men after they surrender, and worse. They blame it on Captain, and on Governor Coke for giving him a free rein in the Strip. People are always ready to believe anything bad about officials. Some are even pleased that King Fisher came out on top against us, even though they know he's a thief and a killer.

"Anyway, if we dress up and show ourselves around town they'll see that Rangers don't all have forked tails and pitchforks. Maybe they'll doubt that the stories they hear about us are true. So that's why we're here. We ain't here to fight, so don't get in the least bit of trouble or you'll ruin it for Captain. You'll be through as a Ranger, too."

Josh and I had been saving our money and had collected a share of several rewards. He'd won back his first month's pay from Jim Boyd, or maybe Jim gave it to him because it wasn't sporting to take money off kids. So he, Adams, and I went to Pancoast, the tailor who made uniforms for Army officers, and had him make us pants and coats. Then we went to Lucchese and got measured for boots. We got new hats, shirts, and even a necktie apiece, though we had to get the fellow in the store to show us how to tie them. While we waited for our clothes to be made we went to a barber shop and left enough hair to make a mattress. Everything was ready in three days.

When we were all decked out in our new finery we went to the Menger as usual to report to Rudd. "Unless you knowed our faces," Josh said proudly, "you couldn't tell us from store clerks." Adams and I stayed off to one side and watched. Josh sat in the lobby along with the drummers and cowmen. Rudd glanced at him as he walked past without recognizing him and went outside. Josh followed.

He put his hand on Rudd's shoulder. "Mister," he said, "can I interest you in a carload of barbed wire?" Rudd turned, prepared to say no, then looked amazed.

"Josh, is that really you?" He walked around Josh, looking up and down that big frame. "Dadburn," he said. "You sure don't look like a drifter now. You look great. How'd you like to go up and see Captain? He'll be mighty tickled to see you, and it may make him feel better."

They went upstairs; Adams and I followed. At the end of the hall Rudd tapped softly on Captain's door. Carrie opened it a little. "He's not awake yet," she told us.

"Yes I am. Who is it? Let him come in."

Josh took off his new hat and entered the room, which was lighted by the morning sun. We stood at the door. Josh walked up to the bed to see

Captain. His face was about as white as the pillow, but he raised up on his elbows and stared.

"Is that you, Josh? Carrie, just look at him. By doggies he looks like he's on his way to get married. You're a good lad, Josh, and you've made a real Ranger."

Josh blushed. "Thanks, Captain."

"Don't throw away the rest of your money, son. Save all you got left. You probably won't have a job with the state much longer."

"On account of something I done?"

Captain smiled a little. "I'm afraid so. You carried out my orders, and I carried out Governor Coke's orders. Now they say he had no right to give me those orders. I expect they'll throw him out in the election, and if he goes we go, too." Captain started coughing. Rudd took Josh's arm.

"Let's go." Josh stood there looking at Captain for a moment. I guess he was thinking about the man who'd led us at Palo Alto and Las Cuevas. Then he backed out.

Carrie followed them to the door. "When he gets back on his feet I'll take him home to rest," she said. "He's only thirty-two—too young to die." Josh brushed something off his cheek that might have been a tear, and strode ahead of us down the hall, like he had important business that couldn't wait. My throat felt knotted up, and I hoped I wouldn't have to talk for awhile.

We didn't have any orders except to keep out of trouble. The three of us walked around and talked to anyone who'd listen. We didn't do any bragging, just quietly answered questions and tried to act like decent humans. Mostly they asked us about Las Cuevas and getting the steers back at Camargo. Rudd stayed at the Menger every day in case Captain needed something.

The Silver Dollar Saloon and Jack Harris' Vaudeville gambling hall were where most of the men hung out. We ambled through both places from time to time, but we didn't spend any money at either one. We listened to the talk, and there were three things the men talked about most—women, crime, and the coming election. The bank at Gonzales had been robbed and the stagecoach to Austin had been held up a few days earlier. There was a lot of horse-stealing and rustling, and we heard King Fisher's name mentioned. Every cowman knew what went on at the Pendencia.

We read in the paper one day that Cortina had escaped from Mexico City when Díaz defeated Lerdo's army and that he was already back on the border. His enemy, General Canales, was now military governor of the state of Tamaulipas, with his headquarters in Matamoros. We read that Rip Ford had sent a man with a message warning Cortina that

Canales would arrest him. "Don't trust yourself in Matamoros," Ford advised him. "Sell off everything you have that can't be removed."

Ford's messenger said that Cortina had laughed at that. "That old white-haired Texan thinks he knows Mexicans better than I do," he said. He rode into Matamoros anyway, and Canales immediately arrested him and had him tried by court martial. The paper didn't say what the charges were, but they probably didn't matter. The court obligingly found him guilty and ordered him shot by a firing squad.

Rip Ford had fought Cortina earlier and helped drive him into Mexico. During the Civil War Ford had spent some time in Matamoros, and the two men had gotten acquainted. Ford saw that Cortina treated Texans courteously even though he favored the Union side. Ford came to respect him, realizing that he was no common *bandido*. When he learned of Cortina's arrest Ford headed for Matamoros and called on Canales.

"General Canales," he said, "it is known to everyone that you and General Cortina are deadly enemies. If you allow him to be shot it will stain your memory forever. Send him to President Díaz and let him decide. If he orders Cortina executed your hands won't be blood-stained." Canales followed this advice and sent Cortina to Díaz, who kept him in Mexico City.

One day Rudd told us to pack our war bags and get our horses. Captain was sending us back to Oakville with orders for Lieutenant Robinson to round up the King Fisher crew again. "Captain figures the only way to handle him is to keep arresting him," Rudd told us. "Eventually he'll either fight or quit the outlaw business." We packed our new duds and headed for camp, glad to be on the move. Loafing around town wasn't what we were paid for, and we'd gotten tired of it.

A day or two after we got to camp, redheaded Lee Hall arrived from Austin with orders naming him second lieutenant in Wright's place. We'd heard of him some, for he'd been an effective marshal up in North Texas, where they said he always got his man. Then he served as sergeant-at-arms for the Texas Senate, and I guess the legislature was confident he'd play by their rules. We all suspected that he'd been picked to replace Captain, and we felt that either Lieutenant Robinson or Sarge Armstrong should take Captain's place whenever he was too sick to serve. As a result we didn't greet Lieutenant Hall with much enthusiasm. We soon learned he was a good Ranger, however, and he seemed to understand our feelings. Since Rudd was "Colorado Chico," we called Hall "Colorado Grande."

Lieutenant Robinson ordered Sarge Armstrong to take twenty-five men and scout the Pendencia country again, like Captain had said. He'd received many reports of stolen horses and cattle moving through King Fisher country, and that was what the Rangers were supposed to stop.

Sarge was still McNelly's bulldog, and he ran the show exactly like Captain would if he'd been there. He gave us ten minutes to load our belts and pockets with cartridges and saddle up. We pulled out after dark and rode all night, then hid during the day. A few nights later we reached Carrizo.

It was like the lower Strip all over again, for our orders were to bring in everyone we saw. By afternoon we had five men in tow. Four of them were cowboys on some of the ranches, but Noley Key looked like a King Fisher hand. We employed the methods Jesús had used to unlimber tongues, and after we hoisted and dropped him a few times he was glad to talk.

King wasn't at his ranch, Key said; he'd left with some cattle to sell in West Texas. Six or seven men were holding a herd of horses from East Texas on the west side of Lake Espantoso. They were going to deliver them to some men with trail herds who needed remudas for their crews. Key didn't say so, but we knew that both the steers and the horses were stolen. He agreed to show us where the horses were held.

That night Sarge left some men in camp to guard the prisoners, then sent Sergeant Wright and several others to check out the lower end of the lake. Josh and I accompanied Sarge, along with old hands Evans, Devine, Boyd, and Parrott. Noley Key pointed out where the horse camp was, about half a mile away, he said. Sarge left Evans and Devine holding Key and our horses. A half-moon was shining, so the light was fair.

We ran smack into their camp before we'd gone far, for Key had lied about where it was, hoping we'd stumble into it and they'd gun us down. They had a lookout posted, and he shot at Sarge, clipping a limb off a mesquite right by his head. Sarge shot him with his Winchester, and the fight was on. They had a big fire going, which gave us an advantage—we could see them a lot better than they could see us.

There were seven men around the fire, and when the lookout shot at Sarge we cut loose on them with our rifles. They leaped to their feet, firing wildly as they ran for cover. We came in fast in a skirmish line and didn't give them any time to get organized or to escape. By the time we got into the circle of firelight, only three of them were still on their feet. The rest were down for good.

At the left end of our line Jim Boyd tangled with a huge outlaw named One-Eyed John Martin who was wanted by the law in Kansas and several other states. He'd emptied his pistol, so he threw it down and moved toward Boyd with a Bowie knife in his hand. By this time the other two men were down.

Boyd's Winchester jammed, so he dropped it and jumped back as the outlaw's knife ripped the air where he'd been standing. Martin kept after Boyd, who backed away fast while he drew his own knife. He should have used his pistol, but I guess he forgot it when he saw Martin's blade.

Boyd was quick as a cat, but he got cut several times before he sank his knife in Martin and they went down together. Boyd got loose and scrambled away, but Martin stayed where he fell. Boyd was pretty shaky and bleeding a lot, so Sarge had Parrott take him to the doctor at Carrizo. We found four of the outlaws in the book. Noley Key was also dead. He'd acted pretty nervous, and when the shooting started he'd made a break for the brush, but Evans dropped him. During the fight the stolen horses had hightailed it, and we couldn't find any of them.

Sarge sent word of the fight to Justice of the Peace Doc White in Carrizo Springs so he could send someone after the bodies. We made a sweep through the brush, and by the time it was through we had twenty-two prisoners. Sarge ordered them tied together in twos and put on bareback horses for the trip to Eagle Pass. He figured that King's lawyer would probably get them out, but they wouldn't forget that thirty-five mile ride, and it might make them repent their sins. When we got them there they didn't even want to see a lawyer. They just wanted to go to jail, they said.

While we were in Eagle Pass, Jennings slipped away and wired a report of the fight to the San Antonio *Express*. He'd no business doing that, and he made it sound like the Rangers still didn't take prisoners, because of the eight men killed. It was more ammunition for those who were trying to get Captain fired and the Rangers disbanded, and Governor Coke's political enemies made good use of it.

XV

Lieutenant Robinson left the company soon after Lee Hall arrived. We'd gotten a sack of mail the day before, and he had one letter. As he read it his expression didn't change, but his face turned white, then red. Next morning after breakfast he had us fall in.

"Boys," he said, "I'm turning command over to Lieutenant Hall, and I know you'll be in good hands. Do your best for him. I've got some personal business to attend to and don't know when I'll be back." Then he mounted and rode off, looking straight ahead. He sat upright in his saddle until he was nearly out of sight, when I saw his shoulders slump forward.

"Maybe he heard Captain ain't comin' back," Parrott said, "and he doesn't want to go on. They were pretty close." There was a lot of speculating, like maybe he'd learned the company would be disbanded.

Sarge Armstrong stepped in front of the line. "Lieutenant Robinson's headin' home to Virginia," he told us. "He's got pressin' family business to attend to on account of his sister. I think he's goin' to shoot some skunk. That's all you need to know, and I don't want to hear any mention of it again."

Even though Lieutenant Robinson had left us, Josh and I were still sure that Captain would show up like he'd always done. He was sure to get to feeling better, and the next time there was big trouble and we needed him, he'd be back. Word that Captain was laid up had spread fast, and we soon heard of big raids from across the river.

Late in August Lieutenant Hall got a call for help from Goliad—a bunch of men had robbed the bank and were terrorizing the town. The men were known, and they'd recently moved up from rustling cattle to robbing banks. One of them was Bill Taylor from DeWitt County. The sheriff was either afraid or in cahoots with them, for he refused to make an arrest. Leaving Armstrong in charge, Hall took eleven men and set out for Goliad.

On the way Hall signed up another Ranger, George Washington Talley, a half-Choctaw cowboy from up in the Nations. Hall sent him to Armstrong for training. Talley hit it off with Josh and me right away, for he was about our age. He was a crack shot with rifle and pistol, and a real daredevil. We knew he'd make a first-rate McNelly Ranger.

Before Lieutenant Robinson left he'd asked Sheriff Walton at Beeville to send him a man who knew the *Brasada*, for it was easy to get lost in the brush country. When Walton's deputy, John Young, arrived, Lieutenant Hall had just taken command, and he'd been told not to enlist anyone under twenty-one as a Ranger. Young was twenty, and he didn't care to lie about his age. There weren't any rules about scouts or guides, so Hall had signed him on as a guide at the same pay as the Rangers.

Young had been a brush-popper, and anyone who hunted wild Longhorns in the brush had to know the country. No one was more at home in the *Brasada* than Young, and while serving as a deputy in Beeville he'd helped round up some pretty hard cases. Hunting outlaws in the brush was in a way like hunting mossyhorn steers: both were dangerous and tricky. There were lots of wanted men hiding in the area in camps of from five to twenty, and they kept a lookout for lawmen.

Sheriff Ed Garner of San Patricio had been shot down as he was leaving church, and Sarge was determined to round up his killers. They were members of a band of eight or ten outlaws headed by a man called Johnson, who was wanted for a long list of crimes. Hall got word the band was camped near a certain spring in the western part of San Patricio County. Young knew where to find them.

Sarge ordered Parrott, Boyd, Josh, Talley, and me to load up with rifle and pistol shells; we waited until dark and then set out, keeping off the trails. If any outlaws spotted us, word would spread fast, and Johnson and his men would be on their way to Mexico. We hid in the brush all the next morning; in the afternoon Young and Talley rode out to locate the camp. Talley had grown up with his mother's Choctaw people, and he was a natural scout.

They rejoined us a little after dark. "They'd moved camp before we got there," Young told Sarge, "to another spring about five miles south of where they'd been. Must have a string of camps and move every few days. Talley counted the tracks of ten horses and one mule. We saw where they stopped, and Talley smelled smoke from their fire, so at least some of them are there. We can surround 'em before sunup."

We waited until the moon was up; then we followed Young and Talley in single file, moving slowly through the brush. We scared a few mustangs and heard a panther screech. Finally Young stopped at a corral that mustangers had once used. We loosened cinches, removed bridles, and turned our ponies into the corral. It hadn't been used for several years, so it had a good stand of grass. Taking our Winchesters—except for Talley, who had a Sharps—we went forward on foot. Young pointed to a clump of oaks we could barely see in the moonlight.

"They're camped next to those oaks," he said. "Their ponies are hobbled and in a clearing by the spring. While you're gettin' located around the camp, Talley and I'll unhobble the ponies and scatter 'em so they can't make a run."

Sarge placed us among the trees around the sleeping men. "Don't anybody shoot until I order 'em to surrender," he said. "If they refuse, shoot to kill."

It wouldn't be light for a couple of hours, so I sat with my back against an oak and half-dozed. When it started to get light in the east I stood behind the tree and rested my rifle on a limb. Soon I could see the men rolled up in their blankets. Just as the sun rose, Sarge stepped into the open, rifle half-raised.

"Texas Rangers," he yelled. "Stand up and raise your hands."

There was a wild scramble as they rolled out of their blankets, cursing like mule skinners. "Get the horses," I heard Johnson say. He fired a shot at Sarge and then ducked into the trees. Sarge shot at him but missed. The rest of us opened up from all sides, and only six of them made it into the trees. The one who'd gone for the horses came back on the run. "They ain't there," he shouted. He headed for the trees where the others were forted up, but Talley dropped him.

We stayed under cover and fired any time we had a target. They were desperate men, and they put a lot of lead into that oak tree where I was hiding. As the sun rose higher their return fire fell off. Soon only two were shooting at us.

"Keep low and move in," Sarge shouted. I crouched low and left the shelter of the oak. I hadn't gone far when Johnson yelled, "Hold your fire. We surrender."

"Come out with your hands up," Sarge ordered, and we walked toward them. Johnson and another ugly outlaw came out, hands in the air. They stood by the trees.

"Keep comin'," Sarge told them. Johnson glanced behind him, then slowly walked toward Sarge.

"There're a couple of wounded men yonder," he said.

Talley and Young hadn't joined the rest of us, but had quietly slipped into the trees on the far side. Both fired their pistols and then came on through the trees.

"There were two of 'em with rifles aimed your way," Young said. "That was a trap."

"I ought to string you up right here," Sarge told Johnson, "but I'll let the court do it proper."

Josh and I went for our horses, then rounded up the outlaws' animals. We packed the dead men on them and headed for Refugio. Sarge turned them and the prisoners over to the sheriff.

"Good work," the sheriff said. "I've had warrants for these men for a long time. We'll take care of 'em."

We had a square meal of steak and beans, then camped outside town. Next day we rode back to Oakville. Things were quiet for a while, and all we did was go out on patrols. Then one day a cowboy galloped into camp to tell us a dozen raiders had made off with a herd.

Sarge ordered Parrott, Boyd, Josh, Talley, and me to load up with rifle and pistol cartridges and be ready to ride in five minutes. When the cowboy told Young where the herd was headed, Young said he'd get us in front of it. We followed him at a fast lope for a few hours, when we crossed another trail. "The cattle will come this way in an hour or two," Young said.

Sarge spread us out in a half-circle on both sides of the trail and told us to keep out of sight until he fired a shot. "Then surround the herd and don't let anyone escape. We don't want any prisoners. We'll cut loose on 'em and they'll have to fight." That suited us. It was almost like having Captain back.

As Young had figured, the herd came along in about an hour. We were all in position with our rifles ready. When the lead man was about fifty yards from where he was hiding, Sarge rode out with his rifle half raised. The man took a hasty shot at Sarge, who fired a couple of times and knocked him out of his saddle.

We raced to surround the others. I didn't have time to count them but there were at least ten, maybe more, for some of them made it to the brush and didn't wait to see what happened. The others headed for a clump of trees on high ground. They dismounted in a hurry and peppered away at us.

All of us hit the ground and walked toward them, crouching low while their bullets whined over our heads. When we got about a hundred yards from them we hunkered down and crawled through the tall grass. None of us Rangers could see any of the others, but we knew what to do—keep moving and hold our fire, like Captain had taught us.

When we were fifty yards from the trees, Talley rose to his feet and charged them with his pistol blazing. They panicked and ran for their horses. We got to our feet and cut loose at them. One or two made it to their horses and got away, probably carrying lead. When the firing stopped we approached cautiously. Five of them lay in the grass. We caught their horses, took off the gear, and then turned them loose.

Except for the Mexican scout that Sarge had shot, they were all

American renegades, and a few were in the book. Sarge was pleased with the day's work. Those who'd escaped would spread the word that the McNelly Rangers were back. Sarge reported to the sheriff in Oakville, and told him where he could find the bodies.

Spencer Adams and four more Rangers returned from Goliad a few days after our brush with the raiders. Goliad was like a ghost town when they got there, Adams told us, for everyone but the robbers had taken cover. They'd caught one, and he named the others, who left town in a hurry. Lieutenant Hall had bucked up the law-abiding folks and they booted the sheriff out. Until they elected another, Hall had Horace Maben take over as sheriff.

Rancher posses from other counties were roaming around Goliad, but they weren't looking for bank robbers. They were running off squatters, and they'd killed a couple who refused to leave. Lieutenant Hall ordered the posses to clear out and disband or be treated like outlaws. They saw he meant business and did like he said.

Some Rangers took the trail of the bank robbers heading for Mexico. A few of the other outlaws were said to be in Karnes and Gonzales Counties, so Hall and a couple of men went after them. He arrested all he could find and turned them over to sheriffs, then came back to camp.

One thing I'd learned since Hall had joined us and we'd rounded up several hundred men wanted for murder, horse stealing, and rustling, was that slick lawyers had gotten the majority of them either released on bond or acquitted. They did this even though it was well known that most of those men deserved hanging. It was all done by manipulating the law. They always managed to get the juries to include friends or accomplices of the culprits, or they'd get the trials delayed until the witnesses had disappeared. I could never understand it. We risked our lives to arrest the men who killed and stole, and then slick lawyers defended them, and juries let them go to kill and steal some more. Much as I disliked the thought, I came to the conclusion that with most of those outlaws it was best for everyone if the Rangers reported "killed while resisting arrest."

When Hall returned there was a letter waiting for him from Captain. Judge Henry Clay Pleasants of DeWitt County had asked Captain to bring his Rangers to Clinton as soon as possible. Captain ordered Hall to take six men and go there at once. The Taylor-Sutton feud had taken an ugly turn, for a bunch of men had murdered Dr. Philip Brazell and his oldest son. The judge hadn't been able to hold court for years because witnesses were run off or shot. The cold-blooded killing of the Brazells was too much to swallow, and so he had finally called on the

Rangers. He especially wanted Captain McNelly, but Captain was still ailing in San Antonio.

The Suttons had gotten their men in as sheriffs and deputies in De-Witt and other counties in the area, and they naturally wouldn't serve warrants on their own people. It was this same Sutton crowd who'd murdered the Brazells.

Corporal Rudd had told us that the Special Force had been set up in part to restore peace in DeWitt and surrounding counties, where the Taylor-Sutton feud had made life unsafe. Its other duty was to put a stop to cattle stealing in the Strip, which had gotten so bad that Captain had tackled that job first. Now it was time to cool off the feuding.

The feud was probably the bloodiest ever in Texas, Rudd said, even worse than the Horrell-Higgins standoff in Lampasas County. It had started in 1868, he told us, when Buck Taylor took a herd of horses to East Texas. Several ranchers had given him horses to sell, but Bill Sutton had stolen the ones he put in the herd. That got Buck Taylor into a heap of trouble.

He was still fuming when he returned, and he told anyone who would listen that Bill Sutton was a no-good horse thief. I guess Sutton was sensitive about being called what he was, for one day he ran across Buck Taylor and Jack Chisholm and killed them. John Wesley Hardin, a cousin of the Taylors, rode over from Gonzales. They say he was a Methodist preacher's son, but he didn't come to pray for Buck Taylor. He killed Sutton and a couple of black state policemen who tried to arrest him. By then, killing folks had gotten to be a habit with Hardin.

After that, Taylors had killed Suttons and Suttons killed Taylors until there were few of either left alive. Other men in DeWitt and adjoining counties got into the feud, and the killings were no longer limited to Taylors and Suttons. It was more like a free-for-all, Rudd said.

"In July of '74 Governor Coke asked Captain to raise forty men and try to bring the leaders of both sides together and make peace," Rudd explained. "Young Bill Sutton and his wife had decided to quit feudin' and leave Texas, and a chap named Gabe Slaughter accompanied them to Indianola. Somehow Buck Taylor's sons Jim and Bill got wind of it and followed them. Slaughter had never been involved in the feud, but the Taylors gunned down both men after they'd boarded a ship. Then they had a big party to celebrate it."

The Sutton crowd lynched Buck's nephew Scrap Taylor and two other cowboys for no reason except that they couldn't lay hands on Jim and Bill. The governor received frantic calls to send Rangers, for there were by then about 150 men on each side and they were getting ready

for war, Rudd said. Bill Taylor had been arrested and taken to Indianola for trial. His friends were talking about rescuing him and the other
side wanted to lynch him.

Captain'd had Rudd live for a time at the home of Joe Tumlinson,
head of the Sutton faction. By then there weren't any Suttons left in
the county, but the feud was still spreading. Then Rudd had stayed
with Bolivar Pridgen, state senator from Victoria and a Taylor leader.
"The more we learned about them the clearer it was that there could be
no truce," Rudd admitted.

The law-abiding folks had been glad to see the Rangers and hoped
they could end the deadly feud. A young reporter from the Austin
Statesman who called himself "Pidge" accompanied the Rangers. "He
was a real character," Rudd told us. Pidge was short for pigeon, and he
joked a lot about his timidity and fear of guns. "The Captain said he
would shoot the first man who ran from a fight," Pidge wrote, "and I
look upon my death warrant as already signed and sealed. Every man
here carries his coat tied behind his saddle, and in its folds is a peace
preserver of the Smith and Wesson persuasion."

Joe Tumlinson and the rest of the Sutton crowd wanted to kill old
John Taylor, another member of the Taylor crowd, and Bolivar Pridgen
to prevent them from testifying. A flock of cases against Sutton men
were on the docket for the coming court term. Pridgen had left the
county but Taylor owned a big horse ranch and couldn't leave it. He'd
come to the Ranger camp for protection. On foot, Pidge wrote, Taylor
was an old sun-dried bucket about to fall to pieces, but on horseback his
powers of endurance were incredible.

Taylor had accompanied Sergeant Middleton and a squad of Rangers
to Yorktown to bring back a witness against Tumlinson. On the return
they were attacked by Tumlinson and fifteen others who tried to kill the
witness. The Rangers fought them off but the witness escaped. "They
are all alike, Taylor and Sutton," Captain wrote the governor, "equally
turbulent, treacherous, and reckless." He said he could handle the Tumlinson crowd with the men he had, but that was only half of the problem. The others had been so accustomed to ignoring law officers that he
would need a large force to overawe all of them.

No one would arrest Tumlinson, although his trial was to start soon.
He and his men had camped near the courthouse and the sheriff fur-
nished them with food under the pretense that they were prisoners.
"Captain told the district judge and attorney for the state that he
would gladly receive and execute orders to arrest Tumlinson and his
men," Rudd said. "Instead they postponed the trial. This emboldened
Tumlinson's men so they circulated a letter to the effect that they were

going to Indianola to see that Bill Taylor got justice. Obviously they intended to kill him before the trial ended. There were also rumors that John Wesley Hardin and Jim Taylor were coming back to rescue Bill Taylor. Captain swore he'd have them both dead or alive if they showed up."

Bill Taylor's lawyer had asked for a postponement, Rudd continued. "That was their favorite tactic—it gave the culprit's friends more time to kill or intimidate witnesses. As usual, the judge granted it."

"Joe Tumlinson has just sent to the Rangers for a guard to keep the Taylors off," Pidge wrote. "A guard is now also at the Taylors to keep the Suttons off, and we have to mount one in our camp to keep them all off." Later Pidge wrote that he'd gone to the church in Clinton, but "not a silver head could be seen, and I suppose that old people never come to DeWitt. If they are not killed they hide out in country above here called 'the brush,' where words of the gospel will never reach them unless used as wads for a double-barrelled shotgun."

About this time Tumlinson had gotten religion and died. The district court finally met, and the session was the quietest in years. That didn't help much, Rudd added, for the district attorney was drunk most of the time, and was of no earthly account when sober. It was impossible to stop the feuding. The Rangers' enlistments had ended and they'd left, knowing that the only thing they'd accomplished was to delay the next round of killings. In the spring and summer things had been relatively quiet in DeWitt County. "That's why Captain tackled the border raiders first," Rudd added. "They were out of hand at the time, as you know."

"What happened to Bill Taylor?" Josh asked.

"During the hurricane that destroyed Indianola the prisoners were released to help rescue families. Bill Taylor saved so many women and children from drowning, no one there would convict him of anything. He just borrowed a horse and headed for Goliad, and I guess he's still there. No one knows where Jim Taylor is."

Going to DeWitt County didn't look like it would be a picnic. From what Rudd said it sounded like trying to end the feuding would be a big job for the whole Ranger company, but Captain had told Hall to take just six men.

XVI

There had been plenty of killings of both Taylor and Sutton men, but
the grand jury had never gotten up the nerve to indict anyone for
murder. The killing of Dr. Brazell and his son was another matter en-
tirely, and it caused a lot of excitement and anger.

Dr. Brazell hadn't taken sides in the feuding and he'd treated
wounded men without asking questions. Killing him made no sense. We
soon learned more about the Brazell killings. A posseman had knocked
on the Brazells' door late one night and Dr. Brazell opened it. The man
told him they were a posse from Gonzales County and were looking for
William Humphrey, a neighbor of the Brazells. The other possemen
stood in the shadows, and some had bandanas over their faces. One of
them shouted, "Come out, old man, come out." Then they ordered
everyone out, and a man they called "Sheriff" searched the house.
George Brazell, who was twelve, recognized the men and whispered
their names to his mother. They let Mrs. Brazell and the three girls and
two youngest boys return to the house.

A few minutes later Mrs. Brazell heard shouting and gunshots, but
she knew no one had a reason to kill her husband. About midnight she
heard a knock on the door, and while she lighted the lamp her sons
Sylvanus and Theodore came in followed by neighbor William Humphrey.

"Bad news, ma'am," Humphrey said. "They killed the doctor and
George."

Sylvanus and Theodore had run and hidden. They saw David Augustine shoot their father and Bill Meador shoot George. After the men
left, the boys had run to Humphrey's house.

At the inquest Sylvanus was afraid to tell what he knew, and it was
then that Judge Pleasants had decided to send for the Rangers. Lieutenant Hall and six of us rode to Clinton. Our arrival caused a stir; everyone wanted to know if Captain was with us. "The sheriff wasn't very
glad to see us," Hall said. "In fact, he looked like he might take sick."
He was a Sutton man.

We kept one or two Rangers with the judge day and night, but he
showed no sign of fear. He was a Virginia gentleman, well qualified and

impartial, determined to carry out his sworn duty, and he carried a double-barrelled shotgun. "You do your part, Lieutenant, and I'll see that the court deals out justice. Together we can bring order out of chaos," he said, and he didn't mean maybe. On December 11 the district court opened session.

Judge Pleasants asked Lieutenant Hall to round up witnesses and to bring in the grand jury whether or not they were willing. We brought them in one by one, practically under arrest. Only three witnesses, all women, were still in the county, for the men who could testify had left. Mrs. Brazell got several letters warning her that she'd be killed and her house burned if she took the stand. Lieutenant Hall let it be known that she wasn't to be harmed. We rounded up some of the male witnesses from nearby counties and kept them at our camp. We promised all of them protection if they'd return and testify, and we didn't let anyone even speak to them.

"It's clear the sheriff won't serve any warrants on Sutton men," Hall told us. "We'll have to do it, and we've got our work cut out for us. Sutton men are defendants in most of the felony cases on the docket, and thirty-one of them are for murder. I'd guess about half of the county is so mixed up in this they don't dare let any of the brotherhood stand trial for fear they'll be indicted along with him." There were only seven of us in Clinton, but it sounded like we needed at least a hundred.

"I'm sending for a dozen men along with some new repeaters and a few breech-loading, double-barrelled shotguns," Hall said. I looked at Josh. We both felt some better, but I wondered why Hall didn't send for the whole company and maybe more.

"Don't count on any help from the people around here," Hall continued. "They've been so terrorized and trampled on they're afraid to move. We're completely on our own, so don't trust anyone but the judge and don't take unnecessary chances. Stay in pairs and keep your eyes open." We thought about that a bit.

"The judge is determined to make this a law-abiding county and we're here to help," Hall added. "He wishes Captain McNelly could come and so do I. But Captain sent us to do the job for him and we'll do it just like he was in charge. There's been enough blood-lettin' already, so this is one time I hope we can avoid addin' to it. But if anyone points a gun in your direction, shoot to kill. I don't want to lose a single one of you."

We were sure glad to see the twelve Rangers Hall had sent for, but we could have used more. On December 22 the court reached the criminal docket, and we'd gathered enough evidence to indict Bill Meador, David Augustine, Joe Sitterlie, Jacob Ryan, Bill Cox, Charles Heissig, and Frank Heister for the Brazell murders. The grand jury showed more backbone than it had in years and handed down indictments on them. The judge gave Lieutenant Hall arrest warrants for those men late one afternoon. Meador was deputy sheriff and city marshal of Cuero, and Joe Sitterlie was deputy sheriff of DeWitt County, but they weren't what you'd call real lawmen.

Lieutenant Hall rode to camp in a cold rain, and at sundown he ordered us to saddle up. Two Rangers were guarding the judge and jury, but sixteen of us were available. That night was a perfect time for rounding up the whole bunch, Hall told us, for Joe Sitterlie had just gotten married at his bride's home near Cuero. All of them would attend the wedding party at Anderson's double-log cabin a few miles from Clinton, because it was big enough for a large party. The house was lighted up when we got there, and we could hear fiddles. Lieutenant Hall ordered us to surround the house and not let anyone leave.

When he stepped through the door the music abruptly stopped. "We're Rangers," he said in a voice all could hear. "Joe Sitterlie, you're under arrest. Come with me."

I was standing behind Hall and a little to one side, so I had a good view of the room. There must have been fifty people there, men and women. When Hall spoke they all had the same shocked expression on their faces, like they couldn't believe their ears, like if they blinked their eyes we would go away. The fiddlers looked around for someplace to hide when the shooting started. Then Sitterlie recovered from his surprise.

"Go to hell, Ranger. This is my weddin' party. I ain't goin' anywhere. If you've got men enough, come get me."

"I've got all I need. I also have warrants for Bill Meador, Bill Cox, Jake Ryan, David Augustine, Charles Heissig, and Frank Heister. If you want a scrap we'll be glad to oblige. Clear out the women and children." He turned and called to us. "You Rangers with shotguns spray the porches when I give the word. All of you shoot to kill. They're gettin' the women and children out of the way."

I thought the women would run out screaming and fainting, but they were tough sisters and didn't panic. One old gal walked up to Lieutenant Hall. "Mr. Big Texas Ranger, is it all right if we women stand along the wall and watch you get wiped out?"

"Lady, you can do as you like. I'm here for these men and I aim to take them one way or another. It's up to them."

"What kind of papers you got, Ranger?" Meador asked.

"I've got warrants signed by Judge Pleasants charging you with the murder of Dr. Brazell. All seven of you."

Meador guffawed. "They're saying it took seven of us to kill one ole country doctor. We must be mighty bad shots. Seven to kill one ole doctor. Ha!"

"And a twelve-year-old boy," Lieutenant Hall said, his face turning as red as his hair. Meador's smile faded fast. Hall beckoned for us to come into the room. Only the two deputies, Meador and Sitterlie, wore guns. The others had left theirs on the porch, as was customary at such shindigs. We cocked our rifles and shotguns.

"Start shootin' whenever you want," Lieutenant Hall told them. "If you don't surrender pronto, we'll start." They'd all been drinking a lot, but seeing us with cocked guns must have been a sobering sight. Meador and Sitterlie glumly handed Lieutenant Hall their pistols.

A woman walked up to Lieutenant Hall. "Look here, Ranger, why not let the party go on? There's food and whiskey enough for all. These men haven't done anything, and they won't run. In the morning they'll go with you and make bond. They're not law-breakers, any of them, so they have nothing to fear." If you ruled out murder, horse-stealing, and a few lesser crimes, the lady may have been right.

Newlywed Joe Sitterlie asked, "How about it, Ranger?" Lieutenant Hall thought it over. "I'll guarantee that every one of them'll be here at sunup," Sitterlie added.

"I might agree to that. Bring 'em all here. I want a few words with them." Sitterlie rounded them up and brought them to Hall. They were a mean-looking bunch of killers; most of them deserved hanging for their looks alone.

Lieutenant Hall read off their names again. "Everybody here? Good. Then I'm placing you under arrest. I'll let all but one of you go until sunup. I'll hold one under guard. If you run out or try to break him loose he'll be the first to die. Understand?"

They nodded. "All right, then, I'll hold you, Sitterlie."

"Hell, this is my weddin' party. Can't you hold Meador instead of me?"

"I can, but remember, all of you, if anyone tries to break him out he dies on the spot. That's Ranger law."

We took turns guarding Meador, and the party went on until morning. We ate some and a few Rangers had a drink or two, but not enough to keep them from playing with a full deck if anything happened.

When it got light outside, Meador said, "All right, Ranger. How much bond do you want us to make? We got friends and can make any amount you say."

"You're goin' to our camp. If the judge lets you out on bond that's up to him." We took all seven of them with us, and they grouched and complained the whole time. When we got to camp Lieutenant Hall wrote on each warrant, "Under arrest," and had Jim Boyd take them to the judge.

The weather was pretty cold that morning, and some of them didn't have coats. "When do we make bond?" Sitterlie wanted to know. "I'm a law officer, and I know we have the right to make bond."

"If you're a law officer you know that only a judge can set bond. You'll have a hearing when he says so."

Boyd returned with a message from Judge Pleasants. Meador and the other prisoners rose, ready to head for court and freedom. "Well, Ranger," Meador said. "How about it? Let's get movin'."

Lieutenant Hall read the judge's message: "The prisoners are to remain in the custody of the Texas Rangers without bond." They squawked and squalled over that, but they stayed with us.

The rest of the Sutton clan also raised a howl. About mid-morning twenty or thirty of them rode toward our camp, each man holding a rifle across his saddle horn. They stopped about a hundred yards away and scowled at us. One Ranger sat with a gun aimed at each of the prisoners, and the rest of us held our Winchesters ready. The Sutton men glowered at us awhile, cursed us good, then rode away without coming closer.

Judge Pleasants was threatened so often Lieutenant had three men stay with him at all times, and he remained out of sight as much as possible. He got several letters saying he'd be killed if he didn't release the prisoners on bond. He knew he had to give them a hearing in open court, and that would be like stirring up a volcano. The Suttons were used to having their way. But as Hall told us, if these men were brought to justice it was likely DeWitt County could be made safe for decent people. We still had a way to go before that happened.

The judge probably figured we could handle a big gunfight, but he knew there'd be lots of funerals afterward, and he wanted to avoid that as much as we did. He knew only one man he was absolutely certain could keep the lid on that crowd and prevent a shootout. Secretly he sent a man in a buggy to San Antonio to fetch Captain as fast as possible. We didn't know about it until after Captain and Carrie arrived, but word that he'd come sure spread fast. For all of us Rangers, including Lieutenant Hall, it was like the sun coming out after a bad storm. For the other side it meant a lot of cursing and a heap of hesitation. Captain's coming made them reconsider what they'd do. They'd been boasting for all to hear that their friends would never stand trial. We ignored them, for we had our own ideas about that. The bragging stopped when they heard that Captain McNelly was in town for the hearing. They hadn't even seen him; just the rumor that he was in Clinton cooled them off fast. There wasn't another name in Texas that would have done that. There was only one Captain McNelly.

The Sutton faction had sent for a couple of lawyers who knew their lawbooks, and they demanded an open court hearing for setting bond. The judge set the hearing for January 2, the day after Captain arrived. He and Carrie stayed in the judge's home, and only the guards there even caught a glimpse of Captain. Josh and I were sure anxious to see him.

The morning of the hearing we took the shackled prisoners to the courthouse and marched them upstairs to the courtroom. There were seventeen of us Rangers, and after we stood the prisoners in front of the judge's bench, Lieutenant Hall stationed us around the room with our backs to the walls.

A big crowd of Sutton men followed us, a lot more than could fit into the courtroom. They and the prisoners joked about what they'd do as soon as bond was set, and they kidded Sitterlie about running out on his wife on his wedding night. But their holsters were empty, for Boyd and Parrott had made them lay their guns on a table before climbing the stairs. Some probably had guns hidden on them, but we weren't worried about them.

Captain walked through a door at the back of the room and stood at the end of the judge's bench, holding a cocked pistol. You could feel the shiver that ran through the crowd, and the muttering stopped.

It was the first time most of us had seen Captain since he arrived, and he looked a lot better than the last time I'd seen him in San Antonio. Having him there sure made me feel good. Lieutenant Hall was as capable and fearless as they come, but he wasn't Captain and he knew it. He was as glad as we were.

As soon as it was quiet, Captain announced in his soft, steely voice, "This court is now open for regular business. Any man who interferes will die." He stood there for a minute or two that seemed more like half an hour, then turned and nodded his head. Judge Pleasants came through the door. I gripped my pistol and held my breath.

It seemed like no one was breathing, for there wasn't a sound as the judge walked deliberately to the bench and looked over that stony-faced crowd of Sutton men. "The time has come for me to announce my decision in this case," he said. "I shall do so without fear or favor, solely upon the evidence as it has been presented. This county has been for years a reproach on the fair name of the state of Texas.

"Over it have roamed bands of lawless men, committing outrages with impunity, murdering whom they pleased, cravenly shooting down men from ambush. Here in this very room are murderers who long ago should have been hanged. I am not speaking only of the prisoners at the bar, but also of you who are yet free. You are murderers, bushwhackers, and midnight assassins."

I glanced at the seven prisoners standing before him. Their smiles were gone now, replaced by the sallow look of fear. I guess they weren't used to meeting their foes face to face. The crowd of Sutton men in the courtroom looked like they couldn't believe what they'd heard.

The judge pulled some envelopes from his coat pocket and threw them on the bench. "I have here letters from some of you threatening my life," he said. "Naturally they're unsigned—cowards always fear to sign their names. Some of you accuse the sheriff of calling in the Rangers. *I* asked the governor to send them and he agreed to keep them here until this county is as peaceful as any in Texas. I tell you now, beware: The day of reckoning is at hand. When you deal with the Texas Rangers, you're dealing with men who are fearless in the discharge of their duty, and they've been sent here to arrest outlaws or kill those who resist. Your time is coming!" Then he banged on the bench with his gavel, and men jumped as if they'd been shot. "This court is now in session. Any person having business before this court come forward."

A lawyer walked up and stood in front of the bench. "Your honor," he said, "I represent Joe Sitterlie."

The judge looked through the papers in front of him and held up one. "Joe Sitterlie, you are charged by indictment with the murder of Dr. Philip Brazell on or about September 19, 1876. How do you plead, guilty or not guilty?"

"My client pleads not guilty, your honor."

Judge Pleasants laid the warrant down and glanced at Captain, who slowly raised his pistol. We did the same. The judge picked up the warrant and wrote on it. There wasn't a sound until he spoke. "It is the order of this court, Joe Sitterlie, that you be held without bond pending trial for murder. You are remanded to the custody of the Texas Rangers."

It sounded like everyone in the room had been holding his breath and all let it out with a whoosh. Then men started cursing the judge, calling him every ugly name they knew. He ignored them, and the proceedings continued. Each of the prisoners had his hearing, and in about an hour every one of them had been ordered back in our custody. After the last one, the judge said, "I shall send these men at the bar to jail to await trial for as wicked and cowardly a murder as has ever disgraced this state. Others of you will soon follow them. Rule by the lawless in De-Witt County is at an end."

There was a lot more cursing and growling, and the Sutton men looked at one another as if waiting for someone to make the first move. "Captain McNelly," the judge said, "clear the courtroom." Captain raised his pistol and we raised ours. The Sutton men scrambled for the door, still cursing.

"Captain McNelly," the judge ordered, "take the prisoners to Galveston to be held in a secure jail pending trial." The prisoners had stood shackled in front of the judge's bench the whole time. At first, when the lawyer had presented Joe Sitterlie's plea, they'd elbowed each other and giggled like schoolboys playing a prank on the teacher. Now Sitterlie looked like he'd seen the hangman, for he'd just gotten married and he knew that if justice was done he'd swing at the end of a rope before he ever had a chance to bed his bride. I might have felt sorry for her if I hadn't heard how her parents had warned her he was no good and begged her not to marry him. I guess it was remembering Sonny Smith that made me feel sorry for her at all. But that was different, another story.

XVII

After the courtroom was cleared, Lieutenant Hall walked over to Captain. "What's your wish? Will you take charge of 'em or do you want me to?"

"I'll do it," Captain replied, "but I want you along. I know you've work to do here, but the most important thing right now is getting these murderers behind bars. If they escape or their friends get 'em away from us there'll be hell to pay."

"Let's take twelve men for the first day or two," Hall suggested. "Then if we see we don't need 'em all we can send some back here and let 'em get to work servin' warrants." Captain agreed.

When we left the courtroom with the shackled prisoners, a crowd of Sutton men was standing outside the courthouse. Captain walked up to them and stared at their scowling faces for a moment before speaking. "I want you to understand that if any of you try to rescue these men they'll be the first to die. You'll be next."

We got a couple of wagons and loaded the prisoners and some grub in them, then headed down the road to Galveston. Scouts were out in front and on both sides. Lieutenant Hall led the way, and behind him was Captain in his buggy. Four Rangers rode in front of the wagons, and four of us followed them. As we left town I looked back and saw a big crowd of Sutton men riding after us at a safe distance. Josh also turned his head. "I see we've got company," he said.

The Sutton crowd stayed on our trail all day, but by late afternoon there weren't as many as there had been in the morning. Whenever we stopped they stopped, and they never came close to us. The prisoners kept looking back at them, and it was easy to guess what they were thinking. When we made camp that night Sarge Armstrong lined us up away from the prisoners, and Captain came up.

"I expect them to try something tonight," he said softly, so the prisoners couldn't hear. "They may stampede our horses and while we're chasing them try to grab the prisoners. Those men are all outlaws, and they know that when these killers testify there'll be a flock of new indictments handed down with their names on 'em. So if they can't get them away from us they'd as soon have us kill them. Either way they'll figure they're off the hook." He paused while we mulled this over.

"I told 'em we'd shoot the prisoners if they tried to rescue 'em," Captain continued, "but we won't. That would be playin' into their hands. When they show up Lieutenant Hall will yell 'Shoot the prisoners!' When he does that, fire your guns a few times but not at them. When the Sutton bunch hears that they'll likely clear out, figurin' they're safe. Understood?"

"Yes, sir," we answered.

"If any of the Sutton crowd comes anywhere near you, let him have it and shoot to kill," Captain added. He left us.

"We'll have four guards posted all night," Sarge told us. "That means each of you will have to stand guard for three hours—nine to twelve, twelve to three, and three to six." He divided the twelve of us into three groups and told us when our turns would be. He waited until after dark before showing us where to stand, so neither the prisoners nor their friends would know where the guards were.

Our horses were all tethered on good grass. I was on the second guard, posted where I could be sure no one sneaked in and cut the tie ropes. By midnight, when I went on guard, the moon had set, but I could see the dark forms of a few of the horses and hear them cropping grass.

About an hour later I heard my dun mustang give a warning snort and I knew he'd heard or smelled someone. I crouched and listened, and thought I heard a faint rustling, like someone crawling through the grass toward me. I strained my eyes but could see nothing in the dark. I heard the sound again, and something that might be two men whispering. I cocked my pistol, and it made a loud click.

"Let's get outa here," someone said not far from me, and I heard two men rise to their feet and start running. I fired a couple of shots in their general direction, and one of them fired wildly at me. I shot again, aiming at the spot where his pistol had flashed, and I heard a man yell. All of this happened within seconds.

"Shoot the prisoners!" Lieutenant Hall roared, and there was a clatter of gunfire mixed with cries of "Please don't shoot me!" from the terrified prisoners. We could hear cursing men running away in all directions, so we knew they'd been all around the camp.

Things got quiet pretty quick after the shooting stopped. Then I heard Sarge calling softly, "Concho, hold your fire. I'm coming."

I told him what had happened. "Good!" he said. "I hope you winged a couple of 'em. By now they're probably hightailin' it for Cuero."

In the morning we looked around but didn't see any bodies. Four of us made a scout and found where the Sutton bunch had camped. No one was there, and their horses' tracks showed that they'd pulled out like the Comanches were after them. Sarge'd figured right.

We traveled on toward Galveston without seeing any sign of the enemy. When we made camp that night Captain called for Sarge. "We've got just a few more days on the road," he told him, "and we won't see any more of that crowd. They're back in town holdin' a wake for their friends and thankin' us for killin' them. So leave six men with us and take the rest back to Clinton. If you keep out of sight when you get there, you should be able to catch some of those outlaws who think they're safe now with us gone and the prisoners dead."

Josh and I were hobbling our horses when Sarge walked up. "Do you two want to head back with me tomorrow or stay with Captain?" He didn't have to give us a choice; all he needed to do was tell us to go or stay and we'd do it. But he knew how we felt about Captain.

"We'd sure like to stick with Captain as long as we can," Josh said. "Don't blame you."

We thanked him. In the morning he and six Rangers headed back to Clinton while the rest of us rode on to Galveston with Captain and Lieutenant Hall and the Brazell killers. They'd sure gotten to be a quiet bunch. Just sat in the wagons looking glum.

When we reached Galveston a few days later, the sheriff wasn't real glad to see us. He accepted the prisoners, "but only temporary," he told Captain. "We got too many prisoners already. If I crowd in this bunch of killers for long we're liable to have a jailbreak."

Captain and Hall talked it over, then wired Ranger headquarters in Austin that the prisoners would have to be moved again. Orders were to wait in Galveston until other arrangements could be made.

Captain looked pretty peaked, and it probably would take at least a week to move the prisoners to a different jail. Like us, Lieutenant Hall was worried about Captain. "I can deliver the prisoners anywhere in the state with four men," he said. "No use wastin' your time waitin' around here, Captain. I'm sending Josh and Concho back to Clinton, and you all can ride along together."

Captain didn't protest, so we knew he was feeling as poorly as he looked. I thought of the way he'd been after we were in a Norther without food for four days. That time he'd ordered Rock not to go with him even though he was too weak to mount his horse. He could surely see what Hall was doing, and if he'd been well he'd have told him he didn't need a couple of nursemaids. But he didn't say a word. It really gave me a lump in the throat to see how different he was from the Captain we'd known.

We headed out on the Austin road, which passed through Burton. Captain slept most of the day and his driver didn't push the team, seeing Captain wasn't up to hard travel. Josh and I rode along behind the buggy and hardly said a word the whole day. When we made camp the two of us fixed the grub while Captain stretched out on his blankets.

Food and coffee seemed to perk him up a bit, and when the sun went down and the air was cooler he even got talkative, at least for him.

"I remember my first year in the Army as a private," he began. "My first service was in General Sibley's New Mexico campaign. I was seventeen when the war started, but I just had to get in it. It wasn't easy persuadin' Captain Campbell to let me enlist in his company, but I kept after him till he gave in. His company was in Colonel Green's regiment of Texas Mounted Volunteers.

"We marched to New Mexico, and my first action was at Valverde. Captain Sayers commanded our artillery battery, and he wanted to know where the federal troops were concentrated so he could send 'em his callin' card. Bein' a brash youngster I offered to find out for him. I rode out in the open between the lines, back and forth a few times, and let the feds shoot at me. Right then I discovered that I either had a charmed life or I didn't make a target big enough for a bullet to find. I also challenged their sentries and a few things like that. When Captain Sayers had figured out their main positions he ordered his artillerymen to open fire. Then we charged and drove 'em across the Rio Grande.

"The campaign started out good but turned into a disaster. We captured the feds' stores in Albuquerque and General Sibley ordered them destroyed. I never understood why he did that. We marched for Fort Union, but in Glorieta Pass the Colorado volunteers captured our camp and provisions. We straggled back to Texas with damn little to eat, losing five hundred men along the way. That was the end of Sibley's career, but Colonel Green was ordered to recover Galveston Island from the Yankees. We whipped 'em and got the island back, so they promoted Colonel Green to general. He'd taken a liking to me, so when he was sent to Louisiana I went along as a captain on his staff." He drank some coffee and stared at the fire.

"When I asked General Green to let me raise a scout company he didn't cotton to the idea at first. I pointed out that we could get behind enemy lines, capture couriers, knock off patrols, and things like that, so he agreed to let me pick a hundred men and see what we could do."

"I guess that's when Pap joined up with you," Josh said. Captain nodded.

"I had a good bunch of men from all over the South," he continued. "When General Green saw what we could do he was mighty pleased.

'Best idea I ever had,' he said, with a big grin. We captured a lot of Yankees and tricked others into surrendering. General Green swore our company killed or captured more Yankees than any regiment in Louisiana, but I never saw the figures and don't know if it was true or not . . . Well, time to turn in before I talk all night."

The next day Captain had his driver trot the team along a bit faster, so we knew he was feeling better. That night after we ate we could hardly wait for him to tell us more of his experiences. "I heard you were commander of the State Police for a while," I said, hoping to trigger some more talk.

"You mean the Carpetbagger State Police? Yes, in 1870 Governor Davis sent for me and asked me to organize and command a statewide police force. He was a Radical Republican, so that took me by surprise. 'I know you're a Democrat,' the governor said, 'but I also know there's no one else as well qualified as you for the job. I commanded Union troops in Louisiana when you were there, so I know.' I mulled it over and asked General Shelby what he thought.

"General Shelby urged me to accept. 'Lawlessness is out of control in Texas,' he pointed out. 'Something drastic has got to be done or soon neither life nor property will be safe anywhere in the state.' So I accepted. But when Governor Davis began using the police to help him establish political control and put the Democrats out of business I quit."

It seemed like he was through talking. "Corporal Rudd told us you were in the Strip in '72 working for some committee," Josh said.

"That was when the cattle war was first getting out of hand. Mexican ranchers in the Strip were in a cross fire, hard put to survive from day to day. If they fought the river bandits from Mexico, on the next raid the bandits came back and killed them. If the raiders overlooked 'em, Anglos swore they were in cahoots with the river thieves and drove 'em off or killed 'em. Some of the ones I persuaded to testify before the congressional committee sent to investigate the war were killed for it. I hate to think I was responsible for their deaths, but in a way I was."

Captain was silent after that, so we all turned in. The next night was our last one before we got to Burton. This was the only time we'd ever had Captain to ourselves and we wanted to know everything about him. Corporal Rudd had told us a lot, but that wasn't the same as hearing it from Captain himself. I recalled what Rudd had said about Captain trying to get the Taylor-Sutton leaders together to end the feuding.

"We heard you were in DeWitt County a couple of years ago," I said.

Captain shook his head slowly. "Big waste of time and money. There'd been so much violence there already the governor wanted to see it stopped without adding to it, so we didn't even have authority to make arrests. A more treacherous bunch of cutthroats I've never seen before or since. At least now we've got seven of the worst ones out of action if the courts don't turn 'em loose. But it's only a start, and barely that. There're about a hundred and fifty thieves and killers still loose in and around DeWitt County. The feud won't end until lawmen and the courts are able to see justice done without interference. You boys have your work cut out for you.

"When I first came to Texas it had the makings of a great state, and it was a good place to live—rich land and decent people. The land is still good, but since the war nothing else is the same. When I was with the State Police I made up a list of three thousand wanted men known to be in the state. Only a few hundred of 'em were Texans. The rest were fugitive criminals from other states. Later the list grew to five thousand names. The scum of the rest of the country had landed on us.

"Texans deserve better than the life they'll have as long as these outlaws are free to rob and kill. The Rangers are the only ones who can make it safe, but it'll take a few more years." He paused and looked from one to the other of us.

"I know you boys and what you can do. I'm not askin' you, but I'm hoping you'll both stay on at least a few more years, until the worst of it is over and sheriffs are able to keep the peace in their own counties. I may be back or I may not, but that doesn't make any difference. It's a job we took on together and it's up to us to see it through."

"Captain," Josh exclaimed, "when you come back you can count on us bein' there." I nodded in agreement.

"I'd like to count on you bein' there whether or not I come back," Captain said.

"We'll be there," I said, knowing I had no right to speak for Josh.

When we got to Burton, Captain stopped the buggy. "I'm goin' to try to get in a cotton crop, so I've got a few things to look after in town. I know you're needed in Clinton, so I won't hold you up any longer. Any time you're comin' this way, stop off at the farm for a visit. Carrie still talks about you gettin' George Hall out of Matamoros, Concho. I didn't tell her the whole story about Pete. You're both damn fine Rangers, and I'm proud of you. Now get movin' before I get sentimental."

"We know you'll be back when we need you real bad," Josh said. "You've never failed us yet." Captain smiled wanly and shook hands with us, but said nothing. We rode on.

Sarge Armstrong was at the Ranger camp outside Clinton when we got there. "I hear Lieutenant Hall has to take the prisoners to Austin," he informed us. "For a few days the folks here believed that story about us shootin' the prisoners, and naturally the papers picked it up. They said Captain was up to his old tricks. Anyway, it gave us a chance to round up twenty-one outlaws before the rest got wise and skipped out."

"We rode back to Burton with Captain," Josh told him. "He was feelin' some better by the time we got there, but he still needs to rest some before he comes back."

Sarge was silent. He started to say something a couple of times, but the words wouldn't come out. He shrugged and left us.

There were a lot of criminal cases on the docket, so when Lieutenant Hall returned he kept us busy rounding up wanted men and witnesses. The law-abiding folks took heart and made it clear that they supported us. A lot of bad characters had skipped out in a hurry when they saw that the judge and grand jury meant business, and there were too many for us to catch them all.

Right after Judge Pleasants had sent the Brazell killers to Galveston, he got another threatening letter. He had sent the wrong men, the letter said. "It was them Jermans that done it and the reason why they kill them was because the old man and his sons riten a hole lot of black-guard and put it all over the Shiloh church. Now there are two things that has to be done, and that is send after those men and bring them back and allow them bale, or you have got to die. There is twenty-five men that have you pick out, and they will give you two weeks to bring them back and allow them bale." Judge Pleasants ignored this letter and others like it, but Lieutenant Hall kept Rangers near him at all times.

In the meantime, raiding across the Rio Grande had flared up again. "There's only one way to end this," Hall said, "and that's to get the Army to help make a big sweep along both sides of the border."

"That's what Captain wanted to do," Josh told him, "but the Army wouldn't lend him troops or allow them to cross the river."

"If we clean up just the Strip the outlaws will head for Mexico and then come back as soon as we're gone. But it's got to be done sooner or later. I've written Captain King that I'm coming for a talk with all the ranchers he can round up. Get your stuff together and come with me, Josh. You know that country and I hear you have friends there."

Josh looked a bit flushed but jumped at the chance. He knew that Caroline and the other girls were probably away at school, but he aimed to make the King Ranch home when he quit the Rangers, and he didn't want Captain King to forget him.

Hall and Josh were gone about a week. "The ranchers are having trouble again," Hall told us when they returned. "But they say it's not nearly as bad as it was two years ago when Captain McNelly went there. Seems like they date things before McNelly and after McNelly."

When Josh and I had a chance to talk he seemed mighty happy. "I talked to Captain King every time I could," he said. 'You're the lad from Georgia,' Captain King said with a twinkle in his eye. 'Seems like there's someone 'round here who keeps askin' if I've heard anything about that big ole boy from Georgia.'

"Of course I turned kinda red when he said that, but at least he remembers me. One of these days I'll ask him for a job."

Governor Richard Hubbard took over in Austin that same January of 1877. He'd won the election partly because Governor Coke had organized the Special Force and had given Captain permission to follow raiders into Mexico. The East Texas men in the legislature had always opposed the Special Force, and some of the people in the Strip howled about it because—though that wasn't the reason they gave—it interfered with cattle stealing.

People in DeWitt County and Goliad wrote the governor and urged him to keep the Rangers on duty; otherwise lawlessness would get worse. There was still a lot of horse stealing, cattle rustling, and stage robbing, and Governor Hubbard knew the Rangers were badly needed, even though the idea of getting rid of us had helped him get elected. He ordered the Special Force reorganized and re-enlisted for six months, and raised our pay to forty dollars a month.

When the Special Force was reorganized, Dr. Cupples of San Antonio reported to Adjutant General Steele that Captain's health was no better than it had been in October. At that time he'd certified complete disability. So Captain's name was simply left off the company roll and Hall was named first lieutenant and commander. Protests against dropping Captain soon came in from all over the lower country. Steele defended himself by pointing out that Captain's medical bills used up one third of the funds spent on the whole company. Most of us didn't care about that, for Captain alone was worth ten Rangers. Steele went on to say that Lieutenant Hall was "in the full vigor of early manhood and health," and that the best of McNelly's men were still in the company. The Special Force was as effective as before, he declared, and it cost only half as much. I guess he was right, but Josh and I considered all of this a dig at Captain. After all he'd done for Texas, dropping him like that to save a few dollars was shameless ingratitude. It was the hard life he'd lived while trying to rid the Strip of *bandidos* that had worn him down. Josh and I were still convinced that Captain would make it back when we needed him, and that in the meantime he should be kept on the roll.

We all had a lot of respect for Hall, for he was a first-class lawman and afraid of no one, but when Captain couldn't be there we figured our commander should be a McNelly man. Sarge Armstrong was our choice, for he was naturally like Captain or had grown to be that way. There wasn't a man in the company who wouldn't have been happy to see Sarge named commander.

Old Orrill inherited his uncle's farm in Mississippi and turned in his badge. We shook hands with him before he left. "I sure hate to see you go," Josh told him. "Who'll I go to for advice now? Concho here is about as bad as I am."

Orrill grinned. "Shucks, you boys are doin' fine," he said, with his Adam's apple going up and down his long skinny neck. "Just keep on doin' same as Captain taught you. So long."

George Hall left the company about the same time, and Dave Watson, who'd been in the Army with Captain, was named sergeant in his place. Like Parrott, who replaced Orrill, he was a good Ranger.

Josh and I were pretty glum when we knew that Captain had been dropped like he wasn't ever coming back, for it left us feeling like orphans. I know Josh was thinking about quitting, and I was feeling pretty resentful. I guess Sarge Armstrong sensed how we felt, for he took us aside. His blond beard was neatly trimmed, and his light blue eyes looked us over for a few moments before he spoke. It was like the way Captain had looked me over the day I signed up with the Rangers. We shuffled our feet, figuring he was reading our minds.

"Boys," he said, "I know how you feel about Captain, and about the state letting him down after all he's done for it. I know, too, that you're thinkin' of quittin' the outfit." He paused. He had us dead to rights. We had nothing to hide behind.

"You also know how Captain is about finishin' what he sets out to do. Well, he's not in shape to do it now, and the job's not half done. There're still a heap of outlaws we need to run down before this part of the country's fit for honest folks, the way Captain promised it would be. You're both McNelly Rangers, and you know what that means. We need you. So I'm askin' you in Captain's name to stay on, at least for the six months of our enlistments. Will you?" He held out a big hand.

I grabbed his hand and shook it, feeling like the time I'd just signed on. Then Josh did the same, though he seemed a little reluctant.

"Good," Armstrong said and left us.

"If I hadn't promised Captain I'd stay on a bit longer," Josh said, "I'd head for Santa Gertrudis and show Miss Caroline my new duds."

XVIII

Sarge was right when he said the job wasn't half finished. The hide war was boiling in a lot of places from Refugio and San Patricio clear to Dog Town on the Frio. Cattle were bringing such high prices the hide men couldn't buy any but stolen stock. Thieves drove cattle to the hide and tallow factories on the coast, or killed and skinned animals on the range. The cowmen, especially on the big ranches, were losing hundreds of steers that could bring them thirty or forty dollars a head in Kansas.

The troubles were so widespread that Lieutenant Hall had to send men out two or three at a time, so the company was widely scattered. Only two Rangers stayed in DeWitt County, where a crowd of murderers still had to stand trial in Judge Pleasants' court. But those folks had learned to respect the Rangers, and two were enough. Lieutenant Hall and a few men escorted the Brazell killers from Galveston to Austin. Other Rangers were helping round up witnesses and protecting grand juries in half a dozen counties.

Stages were held up and horses were stolen almost daily. Fortunately, the Indian troubles had ended, except for a few small raids, after Colonel Mackenzie's cavalry routed the Comanches, Kiowas, and Cheyennes in Palo Duro Canyon. After that the Ranger Frontier Battalion had turned to hunting outlaws in North and Central Texas, and some of them were on the trail of train-robber Sam Bass. Because of the prices cattle were bringing, the Big Steal was on and cowmen everywhere were losing cattle, so rustling was the main problem.

In February the Special Force arrested more men than in any single month before, but as usual the courts let too many of them go. If they weren't released on bail, the juries were packed with their friends. We were on the go all the time, but it didn't seem that we were making much headway. A few outlaws resisted arrest and got themselves killed. A few others were given long sentences, but too many were released for what was called "insufficient evidence." That meant they'd been caught in the act only twice. It was hard to understand why the courts didn't support lawmen.

Lieutenant Hall sent Sarge Parrott and three men to Refugio, while Josh and Talley and I rode to San Patricio; both were hide war centers.

The ranchers were desperate, and Tom Coleman had wired Austin to send Rangers at once or they'd take matters into their own hands and stretch some necks.

San Patricio was a small town that had started as an Irish colony, but it had been abandoned during the Texas Revolution and wasn't reoccupied for several years. We stabled our horses and then got a room in the hotel before reporting to the sheriff. It was our old friend Sheriff Green of Brownsville, but he didn't appear glad to see us. In fact he looked shocked.

"Who sent for you? We don't need no damn Rangers here."

"The ranchers think you do," I replied. "They say they're losin' cattle every day. We're here to look into it."

"I'm sheriff of this here county, and I don't need any help. You young squirts git on your horses and clear out."

"We get our orders from Austin, and we were sent here to see what's goin' on. We aim to do just that." We left his office.

"What do you make of that?" Talley asked. "I smell somethin', and it ain't roses. Let's check with Tom Coleman."

We rode out to Coleman's Chiltepec ranch next morning. Tom wasn't there when we arrived, but his wife told us to wait, so we tied our ponies in the shade and squatted near them. He and one of his vaqueros rode up an hour later and unsaddled their horses. We told him who we were and shook hands. He was a big man with steely blue eyes and a gray mustache that curled up on the ends.

"They sent you pretty quick," he said, "but only three? Damn. I was hopin' they'd send ten or twelve."

"Any idea who's doin' it?" Josh asked.

"Hell, must be everybody in the county but us cowmen. Every time we turn our backs our cattle disappear. There's about fifty acres of brush over yonder"—he nodded his head toward the southeast—"and cattle grazin' near there one day can't be found the next. Me and José just come from drivin' a bunch of steers away from it. The thorns in there are so bad men can't go ten feet."

He paused for a moment. "Who's *not* stealin' would be easier to tell than who is. I wouldn't be surprised if all our county officials are in it, includin' that fat-ass new sheriff."

"We met him before in Brownsville but he didn't put out a welcome mat for us here," I said. "Told us to saddle up and git."

"We had a damned good sheriff, but he was murdered. Then this buzzard Green come here from Brownsville, but he's as useless as tits on a snake, and things are worse than ever." He frowned. "Since they only sent three of you, I'm meetin' with the cowmen tonight. We'll round up all our hands and ride into San Patricio and stretch a few necks."

"Don't do anything tomorrow," Talley said. "Give us a day or two to see what we can come up with. We'll check back with you in the afternoon." Coleman agreed, and gave us directions to the brushy place, eight miles away on the edge of his range.

With Talley leading the way we stayed on low ground, out of sight of anyone who might be watching. We hid our horses in some oaks, and climbed the nearest mound. Toward the top we hunkered down and crawled.

"Look," Talley said, pointing to the left. A couple of cowboys were hazing a dozen steers toward the brush. The men kept looking back to see if anyone was following. "Let's catch 'em and see what they have to say."

We slipped back down the rise and mounted our ponies. I shook out a loop in my rawhide lariat while Josh and Talley drew their pistols. Walking our ponies, we got in position. Only one of the riders came into sight. When Josh yelled "Reach!" the rider turned his horse and dug in his spurs. My mustang shot after him and brought me close enough to drop a loop over his head. He stopped his horse fast. The other rider then saw us and left like his wife was in labor and he was goin' for a doctor.

The man wouldn't talk. "Let's turn him over to the sheriff," Talley said. The man half smiled. Behind his back Talley winked at us. When we got to the sheriff's office there was a sweating cowpony at the hitching rack; he looked like someone who'd been in a hurry to see the sheriff.

"We caught this man stealin' Coleman's cattle," I told the sheriff. "Hold him for trial on a charge of rustlin'."

"Those men, I mean this man wasn't stealin' nothin'. Cowboys got a right to cross a range without bein' attacked by Rangers. If somebody's steers get in the way it ain't their fault. You leave folks around here alone or I'll throw you in jail. I told you to git once. I better not have to tell you again."

It was late in the day, so we stabled our ponies and headed for the hotel. Before sunup we were on our way back to that brush country. We rode around it for an hour or two before Talley stopped and rode in close. "Looky here," he called, pointing to a narrow cattle trail coming from the brush. "You hide here and watch for anyone comin'," he said. "I'll go in on foot and backtrack."

Half an hour later my mustang pricked up his ears. "Someone's comin'," I whispered to Josh, "and it ain't Talley." We drew our guns and waited. A seedy-looking cowboy rode up holding a half-filled gunny sack. We stepped out with guns levelled.

"We're Texas Rangers," I said. "Hold it right there and get your hands up." He dropped the sack. I pulled his pistol from the holster and threw it down. "Get off your horse." He dismounted.

"Who do you work for?" Josh asked. He didn't answer.

We waited until Talley came out. "What'd you find?" Josh asked.

"There's a clearing and a corral. They pile rock salt in the center of it, and that draws the cattle. No way they could drive 'em in."

"We used to bait 'em out of the brush that way," I said. "Beats gettin' torn up." I looked in the gunny sack that the man had dropped. It was half full of rock salt.

"He doesn't want to talk," Josh remarked. "Let's show Talley the way Haysoose unlimbers tongues. Works like magic."

He tied the hombre's hands behind his back while I slipped my lariat around his neck and pulled it tight. I tossed the other end over a mesquite limb and handed it to Josh.

"Who do you work for?" I asked. No answer. Josh pulled him a couple of feet off the ground and dropped him. "The sheriff'll get you for this," he mumbled. Josh hoisted and dropped him a few more times, after which he looked ready to talk.

"Who do you work for?" I asked again.

"The sheriff and the county attorney."

"Where do you take the cattle?" He told us they had several hidden corrals. They put a bell on a tame cow, and the steers followed her when they moved the cattle at night. In three nights they got them to a hide and tallow factory at Rockport. With a little more persuading he told us the names of everyone he knew was involved. I pulled an envelope and pencil stub from my shirt pocket and wrote the names. They included the sheriff and county attorney and ten others I didn't recognize.

"The ranchers are goin' to have a big roundup of cow thieves tomorrow," Josh told him. "Those they catch are goin' to do some dancin' at the end of a rope. If you're willin' to testify, we won't charge you with rustlin'." He was real eager to cooperate.

We took the prisoner to Coleman's ranch. "What'd you find?" he asked. I showed him the list and he copied the names. "Can you hold this man for us?"

"I'll lock him in the shed and have one of the boys keep an eye on him. The ranchers are all ready. They'll meet here with their hands at eight in the mornin'. We'll be in town at ten o'clock for a showdown if you haven't rounded 'em up by then."

On the way to town we caucused on what to do next. "If we let 'em

hang those men it'll mean we ain't done our job," Josh remarked, "even
if they deserve it. Captain would fire us for that."

"Let's wire the names to Austin and let the sheriff find out about it,"
Talley suggested. "That should smoke 'em out fast."

The sheriff was standing outside his office when we rode past. We all
smiled and howdied him like he was good news. He squirted a stream of
tobacco juice our way. "We'll be leavin' tomorrow," I called, "but we'll
see you before we go."

"Don't bother."

Next morning we took our time eating ham and eggs and biscuits at
the cafe. A couple of the sheriff's deputies sat at a table near us. "I
wonder when the telegraph office opens," I said. The deputies stopped
eating. "We got to wire Austin before we leave, and let 'em know." I
lowered my voice and mumbled something. The deputies finished eating
and left in a hurry.

We waited till nine-thirty, then went to the telegraph office. "There's
a deputy watching us," Talley said.

In the telegraph office there was a message pad on the counter. I
wrote Ranger Headquarters, Austin, on it, then the list of names. The
telegraph operator was tapping out a message. When it was finished he
came to the counter.

"Send this list to Ranger Headquarters," I told him. He tapped out
the names. When he came to the county attorney and sheriff, he
stopped.

"What's this here list for?"

"Finish it and you'll know." While he tapped out the last names, I
wrote on the pad: "List of men involved in San Patricio rustling." The
operator hesitated.

"We're Texas Rangers," I said. "Send it." He did.

"Sheriff ain't gonna like bein' called a cow thief. You'd better light
outa here fast, even if you are Rangers. He's killed men for less."

"I believe it."

As soon as we left, a deputy headed for the telegraph office. We sat on
a bench in front of the general store, with our backs against the wall.
Josh and I had our Winchesters across our laps, and Talley held his
Sharps. The deputy ran past us carrying a sheet of paper. He didn't
even glance at us.

Pretty quick the sheriff and two deputies came charging out of his
office and stomped toward us. The third deputy followed with the
county attorney.

The sheriff was carrying the list, and his jaws were working like he'd bitten off a piece of suet and found it hard going. We swung our rifles in his general direction. "What's this about a telegraph?" he sputtered.

"You mean telegram?" I politely asked.

"You know damn well what I mean. The one you sent callin' honest citizens and public officers cow thieves. You won't get away with that in my county."

"Are there any names we left out?" I asked.

The sheriff sounded like he was garglin' with salt water.

"Where's your proof of this charge?" the county attorney demanded. "Who's your witness?"

"One of your men is missin', Sheriff," Josh told him. The sheriff looked at his deputies.

"Jake disappeared," one of them said. "We ain't seen him since yesterday mornin' when he was takin' salt." He stopped as the sheriff glowered at him.

"He gave us the names and agreed to testify if we don't prosecute him," Josh said.

"You won't need no witness. Ain't none of you leavin' here alive. Folks here don't like bein' called rustlers. Round up the others," he told the deputy, and the man left on the run.

I saw a cloud of dust west of town. "Looks like we won't need a witness after all," I said to no one in particular. "I thought Coleman said the hangin' bee wouldn't start till noon."

"What hangin' bee?" The sheriff spun, saw the dust, and turned the color of a snake's belly, which seemed proper for him.

"They were comin' in yesterday to clean up the town," Talley explained. "They said they'd give us till noon to talk some sense into you. Rangers don't go for private hangin's."

The sheriff looked wild-eyed. The other men, I guessed the ones on the list, ran up with the deputy.

"They can't hang Ranger prisoners," I said. "If you're smart you'll drop your guns and surrender pronto."

They got rid of their guns like boys shucking their pants to see who'd be first in the swimming hole. Josh and Talley kept them covered while I walked down the street to meet Coleman and his war party. There were around thirty of them, all carrying rifles.

"We've arrested the lot of 'em," I told Coleman. "We'll turn 'em over to the sheriff at Corpus to hold for trial. You might want to let 'em know they're lucky to be in Ranger custody."

"We never thought you had a chance of roundin' up the whole bunch," Coleman admitted, "but we knew Captain McNelly didn't worry about big odds. He must've trained you boys pretty good."

They rode up to the prisoners and sat on their horses, staring at the pale-faced crowd. "You're lucky we didn't get here sooner," Coleman told them. "Now you'll just serve time. You deserve worse than that." They all winced when he slapped the coiled lariat tied to his saddle. He turned his horse, then he and the other ranchers all rode off.

In Corpus we wired Lieutenant Hall, and he ordered us to meet him in Austin. The day we arrived a character named Ham White had robbed stages going both ways between San Antonio and Austin. He didn't get much loot from the one bound for San Antonio so he'd waited for the one coming to Austin.

He'd gotten the drop on the guard and made him throw down his shotgun. Then he ordered the passengers to line up and empty their pockets. One man handed him three hundred dollars and a gold watch. "My brother gave me that watch," he said. "He's dead now, and I hate to lose it."

"In that case I wouldn't think of takin' it," White had replied. "That'd be like stealin'." He chuckled and handed it to the man along with a ten-dollar bill. Then he made the passengers cut open the mail bags and hand him the registered letters. He tore them open and took whatever money was in them.

He was still chuckling. "Don't you folks know it's against the law to tamper with guvamint mail? If I had time I'd stay and testify against you." He swapped his nag for a big bay horse from the stage team and left. All the while a young man on horseback had been watching, and he rode off with White.

"That bay horse has a broken shoe," the stage driver told Lieutenant Hall. "Should be easy to track."

The stage company offered a reward of $1250 for the capture of White, and Hall agreed we'd split it if we caught him. The four of us left Austin at two in the morning and at daylight saw the mail bags and letters scattered over the ground. We gathered the letters, put them in the bags, and left them by the road. We picked up the tracks of the two horses and followed them to Lockhart. At the livery stable we learned that two men had left their horses to be fed, and later got them and went down the road to Luling. One of the horses was a big bay.

Many horses had been over the road to Luling and covered the tracks, but riders we met had seen a big bay that fitted the description. In late afternoon we reached Luling and put our horses into stalls. At the end of the lane between the rows of stalls a man quietly started saddling a big horse. The stable was too dark for us to tell the horse's color. The four of us walked toward them.

"Don't you come near me," the man said. We kept walking.

"You seem scared of somethin'. What is it?" Lieutenant Hall asked.

"It's enough to scare a preacher to have four men surround him. What you want? I ain't got anythin'."

Talley grabbed his wrists and Josh snatched his gun. "You're under arrest for stage robbin'," Lieutenant Hall informed him. His saddle bags were full of money, watches, and jewelry.

We told the liveryman we'd hold the prisoner there overnight. "Ain't you goin' to question his brother?" he asked. "He went out to see when the next stage leaves."

The young man was easy to find and he meekly surrendered. His name was John Vaughn. "You don't look like you were cut out to be a highwayman," I told him. "You must have good folks somewhere."

"True enough," he replied. "I was lookin' for excitement, not money. It was exciting while it lasted. I was goin' to take the next stage and head for home. I'd rather be dead than have my folks know I'm a jailbird."

Next day we took them to Austin. On the way Ham White leaned over and spoke quietly to Lieutenant Hall. "This here kid ain't no accomplice of mine," he said. "I'm a lone wolf. I just let him come along to watch. I'd appreciate it if you'd let him go."

Hall glanced at Vaughn's pale face. "I'll think on it."

In Austin we entered the jailer's office. "Got a prisoner for you," Lieutenant Hall said. "This is Ham White, stage robber."

The jailer took White by the arm. "What about the other one?"

"He just came along to keep us company," Hall said. As the jailer led White to a cell, the robber turned his head.

"Thanks, Lieutenant," he said.

Vaughn shook our hands like we'd saved him from drowning. "I can't thank you enough," he said. "I'm goin' back to St. Louis and settle down in the tamest job I can find. I've had enough excitement to last a lifetime."

"I figured as much," Hall said with a smile.

XIX

King Fisher was a real challenge to us, for he seemed untouchable. We didn't doubt that he was mixed up in the rustling and horse stealing, but whether or not he was boss of the whole outfit like people figured he was we couldn't be sure. He had so many friends—even good men like Doc White, Charles Vivian, and Santiago Trinidad—that he was a puzzle. They were honest ranchers, not the kind to associate with outlaws. Trinidad had bought an expensive horse in Mexico and it soon disappeared. He described it to King, and it was back in his pen within a few days. And whenever his men came to town on a rampage King always paid for the damage they caused. "He has a good heart," Trinidad told us.

Hall spent some time in Eagle Pass in March, getting ready for the court term in May. He tracked down everyone who might serve on the grand jury, promising them that the Rangers would protect them if they would hand down indictments when the evidence was conclusive. When he returned he was optimistic. "Some men are goin' to be in for a surprise. Judge Paschal and the district attorney both have backbones, and they know what needs to be done."

Late in April, Hall divided us into three squads to hit Eagle Pass from different directions. Josh and I went with Armstrong and four others. Talley was in Parrott's squad. Hall took eight men and stopped by Fort Clark, about fifty miles north of Eagle Pass, to caucus with Colonel Shafter about a big roundup of outlaws on both sides of the river

When we rode into Eagle Pass and started making arrests there was a stampede for the border. We rounded up nineteen men we had warrants for, but many made it to Mexico. Armstrong and Parrott crossed over to Piedras Negras, arrested three of the outlaws, and persuaded the alcalde to hold them in jail until they got extradition papers. When Hall arrived the three of them went after the prisoners and brought them back. In Piedras Negras they saw another outlaw and brought him back, too.

After they jailed the prisoners in Eagle Pass, Hall learned that King Fisher was in town. Just like before, King surrendered without a fuss, but he was shocked to learn that the grand jury had nerve enough to indict him for the murder of William Donovan as well as for horse stealing. Donovan was a rancher who'd let it be known that he was heading for the Pendencia to settle a dispute with King. Friends had warned him not to go, but he was hardheaded and went anyway, and was never seen again. If King didn't kill him he had to know who did.

Some folks we talked to in Eagle Pass said they considered the charges against King to be without basis, which made us wonder some more about him. He was a likable man who just naturally inspired respect, but he was too close to a bunch of thieves and killers to have clean hands. Because the area was full of outlaws and he was regarded as their leader, like Cortina he was blamed for every crime in the whole region. Charles Vivian, a relative of King's wife, was foreman of the grand jury that handed down the indictments against King. He was also one of those who guaranteed bond for him. All of this made King more of a puzzle than ever.

No one could be found who would testify against King. Hall ordered Josh and me to take him to San Antonio for trial while other Rangers escorted prisoners to six counties. There were still lots of wanted men on the loose, but we'd made a good start.

On the way to San Antonio, King told us his life story. His family had moved from East Texas to Goliad when he was eleven. Even as a boy, he admitted, he'd always attracted characters like Charles and Wes Bruton who were inclined to get into trouble, and he'd always stuck by them. We had a number of warrants for that pair, mostly for rustling, so we knew who they were. When King was sixteen an older man talked him into helping him steal other people's property when no one was home, and they'd gotten caught. King was sentenced to two years at Huntsville, but after four months the governor had pardoned him because of his age. "That should have straightened me out for all time," he said. "It did for a while."

He'd made friends with good folks like Doc White and the Vivians. Doc White had led a bunch of families to the Carrizo Springs region, which was great ranch country but visited by Comanches and by raiders from Mexico. When he was seventeen, King joined them there. Because of the troubles they were having they appointed Doc White justice of the peace and told him to get some protection for their stock. When King arrived Doc hired him to guard the stock against raiders and Comanches.

King was already a good shot and practiced until he was accurate with either hand, and it wasn't long before raiders left the Carrizo Springs country alone. King located a ranch for himself on the Pendencia and registered his 7D brand. Men on the run from the law found that they were safe on his ranch, and it soon became a refuge for outlaws. Some of them worked for him, and others showed their gratitude by branding other folks' stock with his 7D.

"By the time I was twenty everyone from Goliad to the upper Nueces knew who I was," he told us. "Men looked up to me, and what I said was law. I tried to keep it from goin' to my head, but everyone figured I was the boss, and it turned out that I was. One thing led to another, and before long I was nearly as bad as those around me, but I never admitted it to myself or anyone else. My family had been poor, and now I got to liking fancy clothes. But since everyone thought I was boss of all the bad men around Carrizo Springs, pretty soon every theft or killing was blamed on King Fisher or his men. Luckily, some good people didn't believe anything bad they heard about me. That's why the Vivians were willing for Sarah to marry me, just a couple of months before Captain McNelly took me to Eagle Pass."

The more we listened to him the more we liked him. He was good-looking, tall and well built, with black hair and mustache. Through the respect he'd inspired in some, and the fear others had of him and the men around him, he'd carved out a little kingdom for himself by the time he was twenty. Eagle Pass was known as King Fisher's town, and as near as we could tell that was true. Some honest men there, both Mexicans and Americans, swore he hadn't committed the crimes laid at his door, and after you'd talked to him you wanted to believe them. But he certainly knew what those outlaws were doing and he shared the loot, so even he knew he was no better than them.

On the way he asked about Captain. "What's it like working for Captain McNelly? Everybody says he doesn't ever let the law get in his way, but he didn't look like that sort when I saw him. They also say he doesn't take prisoners and shoots men trying to surrender." We straightened him out in a hurry.

"He took you and that bunch of wanted men with you to Eagle Pass," I said. Josh broke in, saying, "And what happened?" Then he answered his own question: "Some of the worst thieves and murderers in the state were turned loose. Captain knows that when outlaws put up a fight we have a chance to make this country a better place for decent folks." Josh and I both got a bit hot any time anyone said anything bad about Captain. King was silent for a while.

"I'm sorry," he said at last. "I didn't know how you both feel about McNelly. All I know is what I've heard, and that's all you know about me. I guess the answer is that none of us should believe everything we hear." We had to admit he had a point.

We rode on in silence for a while. "McNelly said something to me that I've thought a heap about," King continued. "When I told him I'm no outlaw he said, 'Anything that walks like a duck, looks like a duck, and runs with ducks is most likely a duck.' I've tried to put it out of my mind because I didn't want to believe it was true, but it keeps coming back. Change ducks to outlaws and see how it sounds. My wife is from a good family and she deserves better." We rode on some more without talking.

"There're still indictments out against me in Laredo and I don't know where else. It's not goin' to be easy to get clear away from those ducks, but for my family's sake I aim to do it. I'm selling my ranch on the Pendencia and movin' to Eagle Pass. That'll be a start. And you have my word on it—there'll never be a reason to hand down any more indictments against King Fisher."

Josh smiled at that, for he really cottoned to King. He reached over and shook King's hand. "I believe you," he said, "and I know you can do it." I didn't feel as sure as Josh did but I was willing to wait and see. King was a likable cuss, no question about that. I just wasn't at all sure he could shed his old feathers and grow new ones.

"Where's the man called Blackie?" I asked.

"He cleared out right after McNelly arrested us. Said he was goin' back to the lower country."

Our enlistments were for six months, which meant our time was up in July. From all of the counties where we'd served, men petitioned the governor to maintain and increase the Rangers. Three hundred people signed the one from DeWitt County. If the company was disbanded before all of the indicted criminals were tried, they said, the outlaw bands would never be suppressed.

Governor Hubbard was under the gun—East Texas legislators still wanted the company dismissed. The funds for it had been spent, and it looked for sure like we'd be turned out in July without our last two months' pay. Ranchers in the Strip now came to our rescue. Until the legislature met, they wrote Hubbard, they would contribute money to keep us in the field. The Southwestern Cattle Raisers Association met in Goliad on June 11. Cowmen from twenty-five counties were there, including Captain King and Tom Coleman. They told the governor he couldn't allow the Rangers to be disbanded.

Josh was the only Ranger who accompanied Lieutenant Hall to Goliad. When he returned he looked like he owned a ranch and had no poor kinfolk. "I talked to Captain King again," he told me. "This time he even remembered my name. I told him I was goin' to ask him for a job when my time was up with the Rangers." He paused a minute, blushing a little. "Captain King said he hoped I'd stay with the Rangers awhile longer but I can go to work for him when I quit the company. 'If I didn't hire you Miss Caroline would never forgive me,' he said. 'She wonders if that big ole Ranger has a girl waiting for him in Georgia.' I'm ready to quit right now, but I'll hang on awhile like I promised Captain."

Sarge Armstrong wasn't with us for he'd been accidentally shot in the leg and couldn't ride. Sarge Watson had also been wounded, and he'd be laid up for a month. Both were badly needed, but they'd be out of action for a while. Shorthanded as the company was, Josh naturally couldn't think of quitting just when it looked like the Army and the Rangers were about to make a big sweep of the whole Rio Grande valley. On June 1 General Ord had been authorized to let his troops cross the border in pursuit of raiders. That's something Captain had asked the Army to do.

Border troubles had increased because of revolutionary activity in Mexico. Porfirio Díaz was president, but he still wasn't strong enough to control the whole country. General Escobedo had crossed into the Strip, where he started recruiting an army to overthrow Díaz. Major Price had arrested Escobedo but released him on his promise to stop recruiting. Escobedo's army had disbanded, which meant that three hundred more troublemakers were on the loose in the Strip.

When Porfirio Díaz learned that U.S. troops would follow raiders—bandits or Indians—into Mexico, he was in a bad spot. He'd promised Texans who'd helped him in Brownsville that he'd put a stop to the raids. He wasn't strong enough to do that right away, for Lerdo supporters were thick along the border. But if he allowed U.S. troops to enter Mexico after raiders without fighting back, every Mexican would turn against him and he'd soon be back in Texas if he was lucky enough to escape.

Díaz sent his most trusted general, Ramón Trevino, to the Rio Grande with fifteen hundred troops. This was to prevent Yankees from invading the fatherland, he announced. That made most Mexicans support him. Privately, he sent word to his friends in Brownsville that he'd ordered Trevino to put an end to the raiding and to avoid any U.S. troops that might cross the river after Indians. Soon after Trevino landed in Matamoros there was a rush of outlaws, both Anglo and Mexican, into the Nueces Strip. Trevino got in touch with General Ord, and they agreed to cooperate and put an end to the raids.

At the end of July Lieutenant Hall took all available men to Eagle Pass again for another roundup, for thieves had flocked there after leaving Escobedo. On the way Sergeant George Arrington of the Frontier Battalion joined us with eighteen men. Arrington was as tough as they come, and we were glad to have him with us.

In Eagle Pass we quickly filled the jail with outlaws, but a lot more left town in a hurry. A hundred or more were said to be in big camps down the river, but someone warned them we were coming, and they didn't wait. They scattered so fast we caught only eleven.

Early in August Lieutenant Hall called Josh and Talley and me to his tent. "Boys," he said, "I want you to take six desperadoes to Austin, all of them killers. Their friends are on the run, but if they find out what you're doin' they'll likely pay you a call. After you deliver 'em go down to Corpus and check with Sheriff McClure. There's big rustlin' over around Ban Katy, and it sounds like Americans, not border raiders. When you get through there, wire me for orders."

It took six days to reach San Antonio, and we had to take turns guarding the prisoners every night. At San Antonio we put them in the old Bat Cave jail on Market Street overnight and got a good sleep. The Bat Cave jail wasn't really a cave, but the bat part was correct. It was the courthouse, the city hall, and the jail, built in 1850. The jail was in back of the building and had a high stone wall around it, with pieces of broken bottles lodged along the top. Anyone who tried to climb over that wall would get cut up some and maybe lose his valuables in the process.

The district court met on the second floor, which was also where the bats lived. They hung upside down and slept through the proceedings. That would have been all right except that jurymen sometimes got hit by bat droppings, which made them impatient to get trials over in a hurry. I wondered how many men had gotten speedy acquittals on days after the bats had eaten lots of insects the night before.

We pushed on next day, and late on the third afternoon delivered the outlaws to the Travis County sheriff in Austin. Without taking time to rest, we headed for the coast.

As we rode to Corpus I thought of the first time we'd gone there over two years earlier. That time we traveled only at night, and Captain was with us. Josh and I had been green kids then; now we felt like old-time Rangers, able to take on any assignment. Following Captain changed boys into men fast. Josh must have been thinking of that first trip, too.

"I wonder how Captain's doin'," he said. "He must be rested up by now, and he ought to be comin' back any day. We promised to visit him, but there ain't been one time we could."

In Corpus we called on Sheriff McClure. "You're McNelly Rangers," he said, shaking hands with the three of us.

"They are," Talley said. "I wish I could say I was one."

"How's Captain McNelly doing?" McClure asked. "I'd sure like to see him back in this country. We need him 'bout as much as we did when he came in '75."

"We haven't heard any news from him lately," Josh replied. "But Captain always bounces back after he's had a good rest. We used to think we'd never see him again, but he always surprised us, and he will again. What can you tell us about the rustlin' over around Ban Katy?"

"It's not river bandits, I'm sure of that. At first it was only Mexican ranchers who were losin' stock. That's not true any more. The only lead I can give you is to check on a man named Rabb. He's a hard customer and a killer, so don't take any chances around him."

"Where's he located?"

"Over west of Ban Katy, on a ranch that used to belong to the Vásquez boys. Still belongs to their family, but they don't dare claim it. Rabb's got two–three drifters workin' for him, and they're all handy with guns."

We headed for Banquete. On the way I remembered where I'd heard of the Vásquez brothers. They were the two Mexicans we saw hanging from the bridge over the Little Oso.

Old W6 Wright was still at Banquete and talkative as ever. "You're McNelly Rangers, ain't you? I never forget a face.

"I could have won some money if Captain McNelly had been a bettin' man," old W6 told us. "I picked out eight of that crew he had and offered to bet that nary a one of them would go through with him. I know seven of them didn't because they came out through Ban Katy." The eighth one was Blackie. He'd stayed in the Strip.

"From what we heard around here, I'd say that following McNelly was a hell of a way to make a living. That sort of work ain't got any future. How many men have you lost so far?"

"One," Josh told him. "Only one."

"I'll be damned. That's one bet I'da lost. I figured you got shot up bad when you went to Las Cuevas, and that's what I heard."

"You don't know Captain."

"You remember them Dick Heye saddles?" W6 asked. We nodded. "Tom Noakes over at Nuecestown is the only one who appears to have made any money on 'em. The bandits took eighteen of his, and Tom has already got back twenty-six, last count I had. But he sure can't sell 'em right now. Can't even give 'em away. No one wants to be caught straddlin' one of 'em. What brings you boys here? Rustling?"

"That's it," I told him. "What can you tell us about a man named Rabb?"

That set off a string of cussing that was impressive both for its length and its number of colorful expressions. Anywhere else he'd be mistaken for a member of the legislature. If he wanted to convince us that he didn't think much of Rabb, he made his point. "The Meskin ranchers hate him, 'cause he's grabbin' their land and cattle. Now he's stealin' from American cowmen, and he swears no lawman will ever take him. He's got three men who are as bad as he is. One of 'em was with King Fisher a while back."

"I guess we got to try," Josh remarked. "That's what we was sent here for."

"Betcha a hundred you don't take any of 'em alive."

"We don't have warrants for 'em, so maybe dead is better. How do we get there?" I asked.

"It's over toward Agua Dulce. Stay here till mornin' and I'll show you."

In the morning he saddled a horse and stuck his Winchester in the rifle scabbard on his saddle. He led the way, keeping off the trails. After an hour of riding he stopped near a rise. "We'd better hide our ponies and go on foot," he told us.

We tied our ponies in a clump of oaks and followed him, crouching low. At the top of the rise we hid in the brush. Beyond was a log cabin, a big corral full of cattle, and a smaller one that held half a dozen horses.

"I know that roan steer with the crooked horn," W6 whispered. "He's mine. Wonder how many more of mine are there. They're waitin' for dark; then they'll put 'em in some trail herd to Kansas. We got to stop 'em."

Three men were squatting near a saddle shed. "Should be four of 'em," W6 said. "Wonder where the other sumbich is. What you aimin' to do?"

"I reckon we'd better circle around where we can take cover and tell 'em they're under arrest," I said. "If you want we can deputize you and you can cover us from here." He agreed.

"Let's swap rifles, son," W6 said to Talley, handing him his Winchester. "You'll need to shoot fast. I'm an old hand with a Sharps. Give me a handful of shells."

Talley said he'd get behind the horse corral so they couldn't mount up and make a run for it. I'd get into a bunch of oaks on the far side of the shed. Josh would slip down the rise to a big tree at the bottom. When Talley and I were set he'd yell at them to surrender.

It took me fifteen minutes to get in position. Talley was already behind a big post on the far side of the corral. Josh levelled his rifle.

"We're Texas Rangers," he shouted. "Throw down your guns. You're under arrest."

"The hell we are," Rabb yelled, firing his pistol at Josh. Talley and I opened up, dropping the two men with Rabb. Rabb ran for the horse corral and reached the gate when Talley fired twice and knocked him down. Remembering Sonny Smith, I waited a few minutes before Talley and I approached Rabb. He was sure enough dead.

We walked toward the two sprawled by the saddle shed, and were halfway there when Josh yelled "Concho! Watch out! Blackie!"

Talley and I hit the ground as a rifle bullet whistled over my head. I spun around on my elbows and fired my Winchester at Blackie, whose body was almost hidden by a big corral post. I nicked him, but he kept on shooting. Talley and I both got off a couple more shots that knocked splinters off the post. Blackie staggered back a step. Then the Sharps roared, and Blackie went down for keeps.

Josh and W6 ran down to join us. "Blackie just popped into sight and I saw he had a bead on you," Josh told me. "Way he was standin' I couldn't get a clear shot at him."

"Same for me," W6 added. "Couldn't get a bead on the sumbich till you two backed him up a couple of feet."

I was sure glad to see the last of him. "He swore one day he'd get the drop on me and kill me for sure," I said. "Today he almost did it. But that's one thing I don't have to worry about any more."

We went after our ponies, then W6 rode to the big corral and opened the gate. The steers trotted out, and W6 headed them toward his range before he rode back and rejoined us.

"Do you know where the Vásquez folks live?" I asked him.

"Sure do. One of the boys works for me. I'll tell him to round up his folks and get out here. I don't think anyone else is goin' to jump their claim."

"Wait for me at Ban Katy," I told Josh and Talley. "I'll get the sheriff out here as quick as I can." My mustang loped the fifteen miles to Corpus. McClure and a deputy rode back with me while another followed in a spring wagon.

"There may be rewards for some of these men," the sheriff said. "If there are, I'll have them sent to you boys."

We spent the night with old W6 in Banquete, then rode to Corpus to wire headquarters. Our orders were to report to Austin. We stopped to say goodbye to McClure.

"A man just rode in from Austin," he told us. "In Burton he heard that Captain McNelly's barely hangin' on. Knowin' how you boys feel about him, I thought you ought to know."

Josh and I could hardly believe that. Captain had always picked up when he had a chance to rest and eat regular. "It don't seem possible," Josh said. "Remember after we hid out in that Norther we figured we'd never see him again? Then he showed up lookin' great and took us into Las Cuevas, and when we needed him in Clinton, there he was. All this time I was sure he was on the mend and we'd see him back in charge any day. Barely hangin' on? My God."

We took the road to Burton and traveled as fast as we could without wearing out our ponies. Thinking of Captain, we didn't do much talking. Talley sensed our feelings and also remained silent.

We made it to Burton just after noon on the fifth day and stopped at the post office for directions. The postmaster shook his head. "I hear he's pretty weak. Maybe you're too late. He may not be conscious."

We rode in silence to the farm, dreading what we might find. The suspense was worse than crossing the resaca at Palo Alto in the face of all those rifles.

Josh was ashen-faced when we dismounted and dropped our reins. We walked to the door, and Josh gently knocked on it. Carrie looked pale and worn when she opened the door. "I wasn't sure I heard a knock," she said. "Josh, Concho, it's good to see you. Lee has asked about you often, hoping you'd come. He knew you were busy and wouldn't let me write. I guess you heard John Robinson went to Virginia and fought a duel. They killed each other. What a waste! I didn't dare tell Lee, but he wonders why John hasn't returned."

We hadn't heard that news. Finally I remembered to introduce her to Talley.

"Can we say hello to Captain?" Josh asked. "I mean is it . . . ?"

Carrie's face had a pained look. "I'll see if he's awake, but he may not recognize you. Sometimes he doesn't know me when he first wakes up. You won't recognize him, either, and you may wish you hadn't come."

She entered the house and soon returned. "He's awake. I told him two of his favorite boys were here to see him. Come in."

We followed her on tiptoes to the bedroom and entered. Talley stood by the door. The curtains were open and sunlight was streaming in. Captain lay propped up on pillows, looking at us. His beard had turned nearly white and his hair was gray. His cheeks were sunken, his eyes hollow. I was terrified that he wouldn't know us.

"Why, its Josh and Concho," he said, and weakly held out his hand. We shook it as gently as possible. "I haven't seen you since, since— where was it?"

"Clinton," Josh said.

"Oh yes. Clinton. I'm glad to see you boys. You both made good Rangers."

"We owe it to you," Josh told him. "You made us. We'll always be McNelly Rangers and proud of it." Captain smiled weakly.

"I haven't forgotten what you did, Concho. I still have the pin. I wish . . ." He closed his eyes and lay back on the pillows, and we heard his labored breathing. We quietly left the room.

"Thanks for coming, boys," Carrie said softly as we left. "I know it meant a lot to him to see you two, more than anything in the world."

"If there's ever *any*thing," I started to say. She shook her head.

"There's nothing anyone can do." Her voice broke and her eyes filled with tears. We said goodbye and mounted our ponies. Talley led the way and never looked back at us, for which I was grateful. We hardly spoke all the way to Austin. I don't know about Josh, but if I'd opened my mouth I'd have blubbered.

Lieutenant Hall was expected at headquarters in a few days, so we waited for him, checking in every morning. Lieutenant Armstrong arrived in Austin with John Wesley Hardin in tow. He'd gotten assigned to tracking down that killer earlier. The governor wanted to bring all of the DeWitt County outlaws to justice and had offered a four-thousand-dollar reward for Hardin. Rangers were allowed to accept rewards, and Armstrong hoped to buy a ranch. He'd sent Jack Duncan, a Ranger detective, to live on a farm next to Hardin's kinfolk, and the man had learned that Hardin was in Alabama. When Armstrong and the detective went there they found that Hardin had gone to Pensacola, so they followed him there. Though he walked with a cane because of his wound, Armstrong entered a railroad car and subdued Hardin and three companions. Hardin's friends had tried to rescue him, but Armstrong eluded them and made it to Texas, where he and Duncan collected the reward.

On the morning of September 5 Sarge Parrott met us at headquarters. "Bad news, boys," he said. "Captain died yesterday. We'll never see his like again."

Josh and I went outside, breathing like we couldn't get enough air in our lungs. "Why him?" Josh asked. "Why not someone who deserved to go?" I had no answer to that and couldn't have talked even if I'd had anything to say.

"I've been wantin' to turn in my badge and head for the Santa Gertrudis," Josh told me. "But knowin' how Captain felt about finishin' what we start, reckon I'll stay on awhile longer. I can't let him down now."

X X

We were back in Austin, early in December 1877, when Lieutenant Hall got word that train robber Sam Bass had left Denton to buy cattle in San Antonio. Hall had known Bass earlier, when he was a lawman in North Texas and Bass was a young cowboy. "He's about five feet six or seven inches," he explained. "Got black hair, brown mustache, and brown eyes. His voice is kind of high-pitched. You won't mistake him if you hear him talk."

Sarge Parrott and Josh and I rode with Hall to San Antonio. Bass had been there, we learned, still spending the fresh-minted twenty-dollar gold pieces he'd gotten from the Union Pacific express car he robbed up in Nebraska. Wells Fargo offered a ten-thousand-dollar reward for his capture, so we were hoping for a chance to collect it. But he'd already left for Castroville when we got to San Antonio, and in Castroville we learned that he'd headed for Frio City. Hall left us, for the trial of the Brazell killers was about to start in Cuero and he had to be there. We hunted for Bass some more, but his trail turned north, so we rode back to Austin.

The next thing we heard was that Bass and his boys had robbed a stage at Mary's Creek just west of Fort Worth. Sheriff Everheart of Grayson County had caught Underwood, one of the Bass men, but Bass and Frank Jackson knew all the hiding places and soon held up another stage between Fort Worth and Weatherford.

They hadn't gotten much money robbing stages, so in February they held up the Houston and Texas Central train north of Dallas. Governor Hubbard had offered a five-hundred-dollar reward for the capture of each of the robbers, and the Texas Express Company and the Houston and Texas Central both matched it. All this did was to triple the number of men who were after the Bass gang.

Hall was back in Austin the day of the robbery, and he got the railroad to give us free passage to McKinney. The place was crawling with Pinkertons, railroad detectives, sheriffs, and citizens, all after the reward. While these people were milling around McKinney, the Bass gang robbed another train, this time at Hutchins, south of Dallas. Some of the passengers were armed and fought back, so Bass didn't get much loot. Early in April he and his boys held up a Texas Pacific train at Eagle Ford, between Dallas and Fort Worth, and a few days later hit another train at Mesquite. The papers had a great time covering the robberies. Bass was becoming a local hero—a lot of people, especially farmers who were hurt by the railroads' high freight rates, enjoyed the railroads' troubles. The papers also said that Texas lawmen were bumbling idiots or worse.

About this time Hall had to leave again. By now he'd received his commission as captain, and Armstrong was first lieutenant. Judge Pleasants had moved the trial of the Brazell killers to San Antonio after the jury at Cuero had acquitted Dave Augustine of the murder of Dr. Brazell. He still had to face trial in the murder of George.

Sheriff Everheart meanwhile had arrested Jim and Bob Murphy for harboring Bass and other outlaws, and had taken them to Tyler. Major Jones had a talk with Jim Murphy and promised to drop the charges against him if he'd help capture Sam Bass. Murphy agreed and was let out on bond so it would look like he'd jumped bail and was on the run. We learned all of this from Captain Hall later.

We didn't hear much more about Bass until early June, when his men fought off Sheriff Egan and a posse in Grayson county. It must have been right after this that Murphy joined Bass, Seaborn Barnes, and Frank Jackson. By this time things were getting too hot for them in North Texas so they headed south. Josh and I had stopped in Austin after arresting a rustler in Oakville, and we were at headquarters when Major Jones got a telegram from the town of Belton. We didn't know it at the time, but the wire was from Murphy.

Major Jones moved pretty fast, so we figured something was about to break. We stayed out of his way but kept our ears open, and heard him tell Corporal Vernon Wilson to get to Lampasas as fast as he could and tell Lieutenant Reynolds to bring his company to Round Rock on the double. The only Frontier Battalion men in Austin at the time were Dick Ware, Chris Connor, and George Harrell. The major ordered them to ride to Round Rock, stable their horses, and keep out of sight.

The major asked Deputy Morris Moore if he'd accompany him to Round Rock for a few days' work, and Moore said he'd go if there was money in it. The major thought there would be, but didn't say what the work was. They took the train to Round Rock.

"You two stick around and be ready to ride," Lieutenant Armstrong told Josh and me. "We may have to head for Round Rock on short notice." By then we were hoping we'd be ordered there, for it looked like there'd be action.

Sure enough, when the major got to Round Rock he learned that

Reynolds' company was on the San Saba River a hundred miles away. He added Deputy Grimes of Grayson County to his force, pairing him with Moore. Then he wired Hall to bring some men from the Special Force.

"Let's go," Hall said, and in minutes he and Lieutenant Armstrong and Josh and I were loping north. On the way Hall told us that Murphy had wired the major from Belton that they aimed to rob the bank in Round Rock. We set up camp outside of town, and soon Lieutenant Reynolds and six of his men arrived. They and their horses were worn down after covering a hundred miles in twenty-four hours.

We stayed in camp while Captain Hall went to the hotel to check in with the major. Bass, Barnes, and Jackson would recognize Hall immediately, so he stayed in the hotel and kept out of sight. The major had sent Grimes and Moore down the main street to look for suspicious characters. They still didn't know who they were looking for, but they knew it was someone wanted by the law. They may have figured it was Sam Bass, but I doubt it.

From what Murphy said later, we know that Bass had sent him and Jackson into town to see if there were any men who looked like Rangers. It was a sweltering hot afternoon and no one was stirring. Knowing that Bass wanted to look over the bank and buy some grub, Murphy told Jackson to go back to camp while he checked on Old Town. When the International and Great Northern Railroad had come through Round Rock in '76 it built the station on higher ground nearly a mile from the town. A new settlement was growing up around the station, but some folks and stores hadn't moved. Murphy admitted he'd been plenty nervous, for Barnes was suspicious and would have killed him if Jackson hadn't interfered.

Rangers Harrell and Connor were hiding in the livery stable and watching the street, while Ware was getting a shave in the barbershop across from Henry Koppel's store. They saw three men ride into town and tie their horses to a hitching rack in the alley, then go into the store.

Moore and Grimes were also watching. Their orders were to look for suspicious characters, but the three men didn't fit that description. "Those men are wearing guns," Moore said. "Over in Travis County I usually take their guns till they leave town."

"I do the same thing," Grimes said. "Sure cuts down on gunplay." The two deputies walked to the store. Grimes stood in the doorway, hands in his pockets.

"Are you men wearing guns?" he asked.

"Yes," one answered as all three drew their pistols and shot Grimes down. Moore fired five times at them but missed and fell with a bullet in his chest. Ware, the nearest Ranger, ran from the barbershop and opened fire, while Harrell and Connor rushed from the livery stable, also firing their Winchesters. Moore arose and followed the three men to the door.

That sleepy little town was awake in a hurry, but the smoke was so thick around the store it was hard to see a target. Hall heard the gunshots and ran from the hotel to join in the shooting. Major Jones was at the telegraph office a few blocks away, but he came on the run. We also heard the shooting and galloped into town, but all we saw was a cloud of smoke and citizens milling around in the street.

The three strangers had run down the alley toward their horses in a hail of gunfire. One of them fell and another was hit. The third man held the Rangers off and helped the wounded one onto his horse. They galloped out of town side by side, one holding the other to keep him from falling. By then it seemed that every man and boy in town who had a gun was in the street peppering away at the fleeing men.

Hall mounted Grimes' horse and followed, along with Connor and Harrell. The major mounted the first nag he saw and joined the chase. We followed them through Old Town. Murphy had been standing in a doorway when Bass and Jackson dashed past, but he stepped back and they didn't see him. Hall and the others came along a few minutes later. By the time we caught up with them they'd lost the trail in a cedar brake, for it was getting dark. We rode back through Old Town, where Murphy joined us.

"That was Bass and Jackson," he told the Major. "Bass is hard hit. He can't go far." He identified the dead man in the alley as Seab Barnes.

At sunup we assembled in front of Koppel's store. Murphy led some of Reynolds' men to where they'd camped, while the rest of us went with Sergeant Nevill and Deputy Milt Tucker of Georgetown to pick up the trail where they'd lost it the night before. Near the railroad track we saw a man stretched out under a tree and figured he was one of the section hands earning his pay. Another railroad worker was coming along the track with a pick over his shoulder.

"Have you seen a wounded man?" Tucker asked. The worker squirted a stream of tobacco juice that barely missed his boot, wiped his chin, and said. "That's him yonder." He pointed to the man lying under a tree.

We approached him cautiously, rifles ready. "Who are you?" Tucker called.

"Don't shoot," the man answered in a weak, high voice. "I'm wounded and helpless. I'm the one you want. I'm Sam Bass."

Tucker looked at his wound to see what could be done for him, but shook his head. He'd been drilled good, and a couple of fingers had been shot off his left hand.

"Where are you taking me?" Bass wanted to know.

"To town to a doctor, I reckon," Tucker replied.

"I've seen you before," Bass said, handing Tucker his gun. "In Georgetown, right?" Tucker nodded.

"I'm not scared of Rangers," Bass said, "but I don't want to be grabbed by a crowd."

About that time Murphy and the other Rangers rode toward us. Tucker walked in their direction, motioning Murphy to keep out of sight. Murphy got a good look at Bass without being seen. "It's him, all right," he said.

"Where's Frank Jackson?" Sergeant Nevill asked Bass.

"He wanted to stay with me, but I told him I'm a goner and made him leave. He tied my horse over there in the brush." One of the Rangers went after his horse and gear. "I tried to find water," Bass continued. "Anyone got a canteen?" No one did.

Nevill sent one of his men to borrow a farm wagon. "What brought you here?" he asked Bass.

"Money. We thought the bank would be easy, but it didn't turn out that way."

"How many men with you?"

"There were four of us. Three who meant business and one turkey."

Neville sent a man to tell Major Jones that Bass had been captured and was badly wounded. The major wired Adjutant General Steele about the capture; then he and Dr. Cochran got a buckboard and came to bring Bass to town. We stood around while the doctor examined the wounds and Tucker told the major about finding Bass. Then we all headed for Old Town. Everyone was lined up along the street to get a look at the famous train robber as we rode through on our way to the new town.

The major sent someone to borrow a cot from the Hart House and we put Bass on it and carried him into a small building. "He doesn't have much time," Dr. Cochran told the major. "He's in bad shape. I give him a few days, a week at the most. If you hope to learn anything from him, don't delay." The major had us take turns standing at the door, not to keep Bass from escaping but to keep curious people from bothering him. Dr. Cochran dressed his wounds and stayed with him most of the time.

The telegraph operator trotted up and handed the major a wire from Steele. "It is claimed that your dispatch is an election trick," Steele's wire said. "Bring Bass if possible. Reply." When the major finished reading it, the operator handed him another message; this one said, "It is a positive fact about Bass being captured."

"I knew you were out of town," the operator explained, sort of apologetically, "so I took the liberty of replying for you. I hope I did right."

"You did fine," the major assured him. "The State Democratic Convention is in Austin, and Governor Hubbard's facing an uphill battle for re-election. They know he supports the Rangers, and some smart politician suspects us of pulling a hoax to help him."

Word of Bass' capture spread quickly, and people arrived by train and on horseback from all over just to gawk at the famous train robber. I watched them, trying to figure out what had brought them and what sort of satisfaction they got out of seeing him, but I couldn't figure it out. A reporter from the Galveston *News* came on the two o'clock train, and it looked like he was given special treatment, for the major allowed him to question Bass. No one else was given that privilege. The *News* was the leading paper in the state, and I guess the major figured that if it said good things about the Rangers it would help us stay in business. Reynolds and his men returned to the San Saba and the others headed for Austin. Only the major remained, but he kept Josh, Ware, Harrell, and me with him.

When the Galveston *News* reporter questioned Bass I was on guard and heard what was said. "Yes, I'm Sam Bass," Sam said in his weak voice, adding that he'd kept track of what he and his men were doing by reading the *News;* this made the reporter smile a bit proudly. Bass corrected a couple of mistakes the paper had made, like saying he planned to break a couple of train robbers out of jail. "All I intended to do was make a raise on the bank here and then head for Mexico," he said. "We were flat broke."

"Do you know who wounded you?"

"The Ranger with the lather on his face shot me." That was Dick Ware.

After Bass had rested, the major tried to get some information and had pencil and notebook ready. "Who were the men with you each time you held up a stagecoach or a train?" he asked. "We need to know and will appreciate your cooperation."

I peeked at Bass, feeling a bit embarrassed for him. His wound was hurting, and he turned his ashen face toward the wall, breathing heavily for a few minutes. "Let them be forgotten," he said with a sigh. "Telling you would hurt too many good men. Whatever you think of me, I'm not one who will tell on his friends. You know I'm dyin', so let me go in peace."

The major felt it was his duty to learn what he could, I guess, so he kept asking questions. I moved away from the doorway, not wanting to hear more. I knew the major was only trying to get information from a dying outlaw, but his questioning of Sam made me uncomfortable.

"I won't blab on my friends," Bass said. "If a man knows something like that he should carry it to his grave. Can't you understand?"

When asked about the shooting in Koppel's store, Bass said, "Grimes asked me if I had a pistol on me. I said I did, then all three of us drew our guns and shot him. If I killed Grimes, he was the first man I ever killed."

Thinking Bass might want to talk to a preacher, Dr. Cochran asked if he was a church member.

"Why ask me that? I'm goin' to hell, you know."

"You're goin' to die soon, Sam," the doctor told him. "There's no way we can save you. Why don't you make a clean breast of it and die with a clear conscience?"

"Don't be too sure of that," Sam said, smiling weakly. "I may be tougher than you think."

About noon on Sunday Sam felt intense pain and asked the doctor to do something to ease his suffering. Cochran did everything he could, but it was clear that Bass was sinking. The major stood by his cot.

"Sam," he said, "you've done much wrong in this world. You've got an opportunity to do some good before you go. You can give us the information we need to clear up some robberies. I'm askin' you once more for the names."

"No!" The major shrugged and left.

About three that afternoon I heard Cochran tell Bass he was dying.

"What day is it?" Sam asked.

"Sunday."

"I mean day of the month."

"July 21."

Sam smiled wanly. "I'll be damned. It's my twenty-seventh birthday. In on the twenty-first, out on the twenty-first."

"Is there anything you want to tell us?"

"Let me go." He closed his eyes.

About half an hour later he called for the doctor, who'd stepped outside to smoke a cigar. He hurried to Sam's side.

"The world is bobbin' around," Sam said, and breathed his last.

The major sent me to the telegraph office with a message for Steele asking if he should bring the body to Austin. I waited for the reply.

"Hold an inquest then bury Bass," was the answer. The major sent for the coroner and told him to take charge.

The coroner's jury tried to decide whose bullet had killed Bass. They finally concluded that Harrell had fired the fatal shot. Moore, who'd been watching, was sure it had been Ware. That agreed with what Sam had told the reporter, that the Ranger with the lather on his face had shot him.

There was some talk that Grimes and Moore had known that Bass was in the store and were trying to beat everyone to the reward, but that didn't make sense. If they'd known who the strangers were they'd have had their guns out when they entered the store. Grimes wasn't expecting trouble or he wouldn't have had his hands in his pockets when he asked if the men were armed.

A farmer told the major he'd seen a stranger hanging around outside the town and thought it might be Frank Jackson. If it was, he was probably waiting to see if he could help Bass, for he was one loyal man. The major sent Ware and Connor to look for him, but they didn't find him. Then the major and his Rangers took the train to Austin. Josh and I were to follow after the funeral.

That night, while a carpenter was building a coffin of good pine lumber, some of the local men held a wake for Bass. I think everyone except maybe the major admired Bass for not telling on his friends.

The next morning a small group of men, both blacks and whites, followed the coffin to the little cemetery, where a grave had been dug next to that of Barnes. As the procession passed the home of the Reverend Ledbetter, he saw us and came out. "I see no minister of the gospel," he said. "If you wish I'll officiate so at least the poor man can be buried with Christian rites." He joined us.

Mary Matteson, a young black girl who'd cooked meals for Bass when he'd been lying wounded, watched the burial from a nearby cornfield. She came to town half an hour later and told the minister she was surprised there were no women in the party. "After you all left," she told us, "a tall young man on a bay horse rode over to the cemetery from the Georgetown road. He got off his horse by the grave, took off his hat, then threw a few clods on the grave. Then he got back on his horse and rode away to the west like he was in a hurry."

"That must have been Frank Jackson," the minister said. "They say he was the most loyal to Bass. It was his way of saying farewell."

Josh and I were ready to head for Austin. "I reckon we ought to run that feller down and see if he's Jackson," Josh said. "I say we leave him be, and I think Captain would have agreed. If it is Jackson he'll probably start a new life like King Fisher and go straight from here on. Better that than us havin' to kill him." We mounted our ponies and jogged south down the road to Austin.

XXI

We were scattered all over the Strip, but there weren't half enough of us to check the Big Steal. Captain Hall and a dozen men were after rustlers down around Oakville, while Cavin and Holden, a couple of nervy cowboys, had hired on with rustlers to get the goods on them. Corporal Rudd and three Rangers recovered hundreds of stolen cattle and gathered enough evidence to indict a dozen thieves. But no matter how many we arrested, the reports of thefts kept coming in. Unless the number of Rangers was at least doubled, we were fighting a losing battle.

Running down Sam Bass got the Rangers a lot of attention in the papers, but that didn't generate much support for the Special Force. We heard rumors that the funds the legislature had appropriated for the company were nearly gone and would surely run out before the legislature met again, but we didn't have time to worry about that. When the money gave out in '77 the cowmen of the Strip had gotten together and raised enough to keep us going. They needed us now more than ever.

"What do you reckon will happen if we do run out of money again?" Josh asked Lieutenant Armstrong.

"Hard to tell. The state can't do anything unless the governor calls a special session, and he won't do that unless he has to. Some of the cowmen are down on us for protecting sheepmen and for helping Mexican ranchers recover their stock. Railroad officials think we should spend most of our time lookin' after their interests. East Texas legislators would like to see us disbanded. All honest folks in the Strip want us bad, and our only hope is for them to rear up and demand that the state support us. But it ain't likely that's goin' to happen."

In October Rudd, Josh, Maben, who was back with the Rangers, and I were closing in on some rustlers below Goliad when Parrott and his men rode into our camp. "We've orders for everyone to report to Austin immediately," he told Rudd. "That means you and your men, too."

"Damnation! We were fixin' to round up some skunks. Can't we do that first?"

Parrott showed him the order, and it said all Rangers and immediately. We packed our war bags and all of us headed for Austin. Along the way other Rangers who'd gotten the same order joined us. I guess we all figured it meant the end of the McNelly Rangers, and we rode along in silence like we'd ridden that time Pete Marsele had tricked us into hiding out while raiders cleaned out the country.

By the time we got to Austin the rest of the company was there, and next morning we lined up outside headquarters. We looked like a bunch of culprits standing before the judge's bench waiting to hear their sentences and hoping he wouldn't order them hanged. Captain Hall came out and faced us, unsmiling. He cleared his throat a couple of times.

"Bad news, men, as I'm sure you've guessed. The money's about gone and we've been ordered to reduce the company to one lieutenant, two sergeants, and fifteen privates." He stopped, like he was having trouble talking, while we stood there shuffling our feet. "There's no fair way to do what's unfair," Captain Hall continued, "but we'll go by seniority. Those who've been with the company longest have first choice. I hate to lose any of you—you're all good Rangers and the state needs every one of you." He paused again, while we mulled this over. Thirty-two men hadn't been near enough to do the job and now there'd be only seventeen of us. I wondered bitterly why they didn't just sack the lot of us.

"Those of you who're let go keep in touch with me. As soon as word of this gets out all hell will break loose and lawlessness will spread like the yellow death. Within six months the state will have to recall every last one of you. I'm dead sure of that."

Parrott, Rudd, and others of us had been with the company from the start so we stayed on, but Talley and a lot of other good men were dropped. Cavin and Holden were still working as cowboys for rustlers' bands, gathering evidence to send them to the pen. Both were supposed to serve as witnesses when the next court term opened in Uvalde. Now it looked like they'd been risking their lives for nothing.

We all felt like we'd been sold out. We shook hands with the ones who'd been let go, but there wasn't the usual joking. Luckily Captain Hall didn't give us much time to mope around—he sent us off in pairs to escort prisoners and protect witnesses. Few were left to make arrests.

Cow thieves welcomed the news and unlimbered their lariats. A few raiding parties even crossed over from Mexico again, but the Army now had permission to follow them across the Rio Grande. Lieutenant Bullis and his cavalry company chastised a few and the *Rurales* of Porfirio Díaz made it hot for others. Anglo rustlers in the Strip were the real problem, but the Army couldn't help us there. They were the state's responsibility.

Captain Hall hadn't forgotten King Fisher, and once sent Josh and me to arrest him on a charge of horse stealing. We knew the charge

wouldn't stick, but we headed for Eagle Pass. Soon after we got there a
young dude from the East saw our Ranger badges. He patted a pistol on
his hip that was about as big as he was. "I want to help you Rangers
arrest outlaws," he told us in his squeaky voice, "even King Fisher. I
been practicing and can shoot pretty straight, and I ain't afraid." He
patted his cannon again, waiting eagerly for us to seize this grand opportunity to avail ourselves of his valuable services.

Josh glanced at me and then gazed down at the little feller. "You
ought to be plenty scared," he said. "Shootin' a man is different from
shootin' a tree stump. If you point that gun at an outlaw he'll blow your
head clean off at the neck. Don't you have a mother?" The little out-
law-hunter looked at his shiny boots and admitted he did. "How do you
think she'll feel when your corpse is delivered to her in a cheap wooden
box?"

He thought about that some and looked like maybe he was fixing to
cry. "You take the first stage out of here in the morning," Josh ordered.
"If we find you here by noon we'll throw you in jail with King Fisher.
Now git!" He got.

"You've done your good deed for today, Josh. You just saved an
idiot's life." We headed for Bruton's saloon.

King Fisher was there and came to shake our hands. "I reckon you
want me, don't you?" He handed us his gun belt. "Are you gettin' as
tired of this as I am?" We nodded.

"I hope you don't think it's our idea," Josh told him. "We just follow
orders."

"By the way," King said, "there's a big fandango startin' soon. What
say we take it in? There'll be lots of pretty girls, and I won't run out on
you. I give you my word on that." We agreed.

It was some fandango. Those señoritas were all decked out in their
best finery, and the way they whirled around showed us some of the
sights we'd dreamed about in camp. I'd seen fandangos before but Josh
hadn't, and he was big-eyed. The dance we'd gone to uninvited in
Brownsville had stopped the moment we entered the room, so this was
the first real Mexican dancing he'd gotten to see. We stayed until it
broke up about daylight, then had breakfast and delivered King to the
sheriff. He made bond and was out the same morning.

When the legislature met in the spring it voted funds to restore the
company, but new Governor Roberts vetoed the bill. That caused a real
uproar all over the Strip, and the governor got more letters than if he'd
been popular. Warren Goodin, whose cattle-stealing band we'd broken
up, escaped from jail in Lee County and was soon back in business. The

protests from cowmen got so strong the governor couldn't ignore them any longer.

In June he backed down and called a special session of the legislature, which quickly ordered the Special Force for the Suppression of Crime and Lawlessness reorganized and increased to twenty-seven privates. Major Jones, who'd commanded the Frontier Battalion, was named Adjutant General. He was about five feet seven inches tall and didn't weight over 125 pounds, but he'd been a great cavalry officer during the war and was a first-rate Ranger. With two or three men he'd ended the Horrell-Higgins feud in Lampasas County without firing a shot. He'd rounded up the leaders of both parties and made them sit down and work out a truce. We knew he'd be a good choice for Adjutant General.

Lieutenant Armstrong went on leave to get his ranch started, about fifty miles south of the Santa Gertrudis, but he promised to return. T. L. Oglesby took his place as first lieutenant. He was from the Carrizo Springs area and knew everyone there. Hall sent word for us to meet at Carrizo Springs to reorganize the company and swear in the new men. Most of those who'd been dropped came back, but Talley wasn't among them, for he'd taken a job as a guard for a mining company in Mexico.

"I ought to quit right now," Josh said, "but I'll stay on for a while and maybe collect a few more rewards."

After he'd talked to Oglesby about what to tackle first, Captain Hall called for me. "Most of those men we rounded up at Eagle Pass in '77 are out and causin' trouble. I've got new warrants for some of them. Let's slip in there and see who we can catch." We got there about dark, left our ponies at the Sunset Livery Stable, and checked into the hotel.

Next morning we walked down the street to see who we could find. We were moseying along when ahead of us an hombre dismounted at the general store. He didn't look in our direction, but we both stared hard at him, for he looked familiar. "I think that's Frank Porter," I told Hall. "At least that's the name he was usin' when Captain McNelly brought in King Fisher. Always boasted he'd never be taken alive, but he couldn't face Parrott. You probably got a warrant for him under some other name."

"I have, under the name of Burd something or other. He's poison. Let's get him." When we entered the store I had my pistol out, for Porter was a cold-blooded killer when he had the drop on anyone. He was reaching for a box of cartridges on a shelf.

"Hand over your gun belt," Hall ordered. The startled outlaw dropped his hand to his pistol butt and looked around into the barrel of my gun. He shrugged, unbuckled his gun belt, and handed it to Hall. We turned him over to the sheriff, then returned to the street.

A rider galloped past toward the river, but we were too far away to recognize him. A bunch of men were already swimming their horses across, not waiting for the ferry. Hall swore. "Didn't take long for word to spread that the Rangers were in town."

Someone had seen us with Porter, and that set off a stampede for Mexico. Hall handed me the rest of the warrants. "We probably got the worst one of the lot, but you stay here during the court session. If any of these men show up, arrest 'em. Get the sheriff to lend you a deputy if you need help. I'm going to make a swing down around Corpus and see where we're needed the most, then I'll come back."

The court session was like most of the others. The grand jury ordered a few men held for trial, but all of the charges against King Fisher were dismissed. The men on the jury were probably his friends, but most of the indictments were a year or two old. In each case the foreman of the jury said there was insufficient evidence. Maybe there wasn't much evidence to support the charges, or maybe no one would testify against King or the others even if he knew something. It was hard to tell.

I saw King afterward. "There're still a few indictments out against me in other counties." he remarked. "No more here. I'll be glad when they're all settled one way or another. Like I told Josh, there'll never be any more issued for me. I've gotten particular who my friends are."

When Hall returned we headed for Oglesby's camp at Carrizo. "Things are really out of hand, about like they were when Captain McNelly first went down there," he observed. "Only now it's not only river bandits. With beef bringin' high prices in Kansas our own brethren are the worst ones. Some cowmen have lost every animal."

He still hadn't given up on putting King Fisher behind bars, and there were indictments for him in Laredo on several counts of horse stealing. Hall sent a Ranger named Allen to arrest King and take him to Laredo, mainly because no one else was handy at the moment. Allen hadn't been with the company long, and he'd made it clear he wanted to do something he could brag about for the rest of his life. He was busting to be able to say he'd arrested the famous desperado King Fisher. He took with him a man to handle a couple of pack mules.

As usual King surrendered quietly, but he must have been fed up with being arrested. Allen tied him onto a mule and the three of them started for Laredo. There was no need to treat him like that and Allen knew it. Naturally King didn't like it.

They were riding along the river when King managed to spook the pack mules, which galloped off with Allen and the other man after them. King swam his mule across the river into Mexico, then went back to Eagle Pass and surrendered to the sheriff. His mule had run away with him, he explained. It was a Mexican mule, and homesick. He couldn't keep it from crossing the river.

Everyone, especially the Rangers, had a good laugh over that, for we were all tired of Allen's bragging. "I'm damn glad that happened," Josh said, slapping his thigh. "King's the better man."

Allen asked Hall to let him try again. "This time I'll get him there one way or another. He won't get away from me again and live to tell it." But Hall sent Parrott, figuring Allen would claim that King tried to escape and he had to shoot him, and Hall wouldn't be party to anything like that no matter what he thought of King. In Laredo the charges were all dismissed, for the evidence was mostly hearsay. These were the last indictments against King. Allen quit the Rangers soon after that, and no one was sorry to see him go.

King's first daughter had been born on his Pendencia ranch before he sold it, moved to Eagle Pass, and bought an interest in a saloon. When his second daughter was born he sold his share of the saloon and became the partner of a man named Bates in the Sunset Livery Stable. "It's no credit to my daughters to have a father in the saloon business," he admitted.

Later we heard he'd bought James Vivian's ranch along the Nueces and moved his family there. "Looks like he's settled down to live like a family man should," Josh remarked. "I hope so. He may have done some of the things they say he did, but so far no one has made a single charge against him stick. He stood trial for the killing of Daugherty, but the two were sworn enemies. They met on the prairie and shot it out and King won. If he'd lost you can bet they wouldn't have arrested Daugherty and charged him with murder." As an afterthought he added, "I hope he don't let any of that old crowd of outlaws hang around his place."

Some time after this the Austin *Statesman* reported the rumor that King had accidentally shot himself in the leg. We knew King was too handy with guns to do that, but the editor pretended to swallow the story. "King Fisher, the desperado of former years, is now a quiet, peaceable man," the paper said. "He began to feel the devil getting the better of him a few days ago and rather than shoot anybody else, he shot himself through the thigh and is now lying up to cool off. He may be a priest yet. There is nothing like self-punishment and 'mortification of the spirit,' if you don't have to submit to amputation." When I showed the paper to Josh he snorted.

"King's goin' straight now. Why don't they leave him be?"

Our main camp was at Cuero for a while, but outlaws steered clear of the county when they heard we were there. Parrott hauled in Bill Taylor and several other wanted men around Goliad. Taylor had killed his share of Suttons and robbed banks in his spare time, but once in the Rangers' custody he was as meek as a newborn heifer. He offered to turn state's evidence, named his accomplices, and described their hideouts. He even promised to lead them into a trap by setting up a bank robbery in Victoria. In the hope of catching a bunch of outlaws, Hall took a chance and let Taylor go.

There was organized cattle-rustling all around us, and we recovered hundreds of stolen steers. Warren Goodin's outfit covered DeWitt and several other counties. Jim Moon's gang was operating on a big scale above Fort Ewell. One of the worst was the Dunn bunch in Nueces County, for they'd killed sixty men in two years, mostly Mexican ranchers who didn't like having their cattle stolen. The sheriff there was a good one, but no more than three men in the whole county had the guts to join his posses. Hall hired a man to work for the Dunns and collect evidence, but when he asked the Mexican ranchers to go with us to identify their stock they refused. They knew the Dunns would kill them if they did. By November they realized we were there to protect them and they agreed to testify. Hall took ten of us and set up camp in Nueces County.

Hall's scout came in and reported that the whole Dunn outfit was camped at La Rosita, getting ready to gather a big herd of stolen cattle to trail north. We loaded up with bullets and set out about dark, with Hall's man guiding us. When we got near the Dunns' camp we left our ponies and moved into position around it on foot.

Just as the sun was appearing over the horizon, Hall stepped into the open with his Winchester at his shoulder. The rest of us also walked forward, rifles ready. One of the Dunn men arose, yawning and stretching.

"Texas Rangers! Up with your hands!" Hall shouted. There was a wild scramble as they all hopped up and grabbed for their guns. They looked around and saw the rest of us with rifles trained on them. Then they dropped their guns fast and raised their hands, cursing savagely. We gathered up their artillery, loaded all fifteen of them onto their wagon, and hauled them to Corpus. That was one bad band of thieves we managed to put out of business, for there was too much evidence against them for any slick lawyer to get them off.

Sheriff McClure had a message for Hall from headquarters. One of his scouts who was working with rustlers in Atascosa County had written that some of the men aimed to rob Campbell's store on November 21. Hall sent for Josh, me, Graham, and Martin and told us the story. "Campbell's store is at Wolfe City, about twenty miles north of Pleasanton," he said. "It's no city, just a little settlement, but Campbell serves all the cowmen around it. He sells their herds and holds the money for them. That's what these men are after. If you hustle you should get there in time to surprise them."

We were camped a few miles from Wolfe City on the night of November 20. Next morning we split into pairs and headed for the store from different directions. Josh and I hid our ponies in the brush and got behind a mesquite fence where we had a clear view of the storefront. Later Graham and Martin walked into the store and hid.

We waited for hours, wondering if the men had changed their plans. Late in the afternoon four rough-looking customers rode up and dismounted, throwing their reins over the hitching rack. They looked around in every direction but we kept out of sight. A few minutes later one of them came out, pushing Campbell's clerk in front of him. Martin and Graham came out of hiding and ordered the three in the store to raise their hands. Instead they started shooting, and it sounded like twenty men all firing at once.

One man fell in the doorway. The other two jumped over him and ran, but Josh and I dropped them. The one holding the clerk used him as a shield until he was out of range and got away. Even with all the shooting none of us had been nicked, but two of the robbers were dead and one wounded. We turned him over to the sheriff in Pleasanton to hold for trial.

No Ranger said anything about why we happened to be at the store that day, but a reporter for the Pleasanton paper wondered if the Rangers had a spy system. When our scouts read that they pulled out while they could. Hall swore and said he felt like shooting the reporter. He could have gotten our men killed, and it meant more trouble for us in getting evidence to convict thieves.

Early the next year we noticed that Hall seemed to be quieter than usual, like his mind was on other things besides Ranger business. He made a number of trips to Oglesby's camp near San Antonio, where he was after the Warren Goodin gang. We figured that Hall was sore that Goodin had escaped and was determined to put him back behind bars, but he didn't say.

Corporal Rudd stopped at our camp near Cuero one night on his way to Victoria after a fugitive. "Did you know Captain Hall has a galfriend in San Antonio?" he asked. We didn't. "She's Bessie Weidman, a real beauty, and folks say he's smitten. Sounds serious."

None of us mentioned this to Captain Hall, but we weren't as surprised as we should have been when he told us he was getting married soon. "She made one condition," he said a bit sheepishly, "and that was for me to quit the Rangers. I agreed so I'm headin' for Austin to make my last report and turn in my badge. Got a job managing the Dull ranch over in La Salle County. I hope you men will stay on and finish what we started. Lieutenant Armstrong's comin' back to take command."

We shook his hand and wished him well. He was one good Ranger, no doubt about that, and we'd never hesitated about following him into a scrap. But Captain McNelly was still special to those of us who'd served under him, and no one could ever take his place. Lieutenant Armstrong came the closest, and having him in command would be sort of like having Captain come back to lead us.

Josh had visited the Santa Gertrudis every time he was in that part of the Strip, and he knew Captain King would hire him whenever he left the Rangers. He'd been lucky enough to find Caroline there a few times. "I told her I was comin' back to stay one day," Josh said, "and I hoped she'd be there. She promised she would." Now he figured the time had come. "I'm goin' to Austin with Captain Hall and call it quits. If I wait too long someone might come along and make her forget me. I'll let you know what happens, though I ain't much on writin' letters and that kinda stuff." That was a long speech for ole Josh, and he had to catch his breath.

"If you or any of the Rangers are down that way and need a hand, just let me know. I'll always be a McNelly first, and I ain't likely to forget what Captain taught me." He stopped to catch his breath again. That was a lot of talking for a Georgia boy. "I'll appreciate it if you'll let me know whatever King Fisher does. I still got hopes for him turnin' out right."

When we shook hands I felt like a part of me was cutting loose and heading down the road. We'd been through a lot together since that day five years earlier when we signed on with Captain. We'd never had much time to think about it, for those years had flown by. It still seemed only a few months ago that we'd set out from Burton. A flood of memories tried to pour through my mind all at once: Captain riding Segal across the *resaca* at Palo Alto and holding his fire, Josh's horse falling and him slogging ahead on foot, the fight at Las Cuevas, and our last visit with Captain.

"Good luck, Josh," I said. My voice sounded like I was talking into an empty barrel. Afraid to say more I shook his hand again, then turned away so I wouldn't have to watch him ride off.

XXII

It was strange not being paired up with Josh, but I didn't have much time to think about it. After about six months a letter from him caught up with me. Captain King had hired him at seventy-five dollars a month, which was almost double Ranger pay. "He asked me what I was good at," Josh wrote. "I told him chopping cotton and rounding up cow thieves. He said to forget the cotton. One of his best vaqueros is teaching me to handle cattle and use a lariat." The last thing he said was what news did I have of King Fisher.

It was in the fall of '82 that I finally had some news of King. It took four pages of foolscap to tell the whole story, and I had to rest my arm afterward. I'd been talking to Baptist preacher Bruce Roberts, a circuit rider who made the rounds from Eagle Pass to Carrizo Springs, Uvalde, and Laredo. I'd run into him occasionally before; everybody knew him, and he knew everybody, so he always brought us the latest news.

He camped with us between Eagle Pass and Uvalde one day in November, and that night we got to talking about King. "I'd heard about him—everybody has—but the first time I met him was at the convention of the Rio Grande Baptist Association at Carrizo Springs last July," the Reverend Roberts remarked. "King Fisher is a fascinating person. If I were a betting man I'd wager that almost everyone who walked out of his presence did so with the feeling he'd like to say something nice about him." I had to admit he'd win that bet.

"At our meeting the Reverend O. C. Pope delivered a sermon on the perils of drifting into lawlessness and sin by choosing the wrong companions," Reverend Roberts continued. "Pope is superintendent of our missions in the state and a most effective preacher. After this sermon Mr. Fisher drew him aside, and what he told Pope made so profound an impression on him he told me the whole story, word for word."

"Dr. Pope," Fisher said, as told to me by Reverend Roberts, "I want to bear testimony to the truth of what you said today, for I know too well how easy it is to drift into sin. I was just a boy, away from home and with poor advantages, but I still had a pretty good idea of what I wanted to be. I foolishly drifted into bad company, and there didn't seem to be anything much to hold me back from doing wrong. Some of the older people seemed to like me, but it appears they didn't know how to tell me to go straight. Of course they probably thought I wouldn't pay any attention to anything they'd say, but I wish they'd tried me out a little more.

"Captain McNelly and his Rangers came and took me and some other fellows in, but afterward he gave me some mighty good talk. I've heard he always carried a little Bible with him. Anyway, it seemed like the Captain was on the right road. It made me think of a preacher I heard once talking about being on the Lord's highway. I remembered that I said to myself, 'King, it would be a lot better for you if you could be on the Lord's highway.' I never saw Captain McNelly again. He had a bad cough at that time, and in little more than a year I heard he was gone. I've often wished I'd talked with him about his road, but being a prisoner . . . you know, well, I didn't.

"Dr. Pope, I still remember the Captain's talk, and I'm going to remember your talk today. I've been trying to shape things up and to travel a different road."

The Reverend Roberts and I talked some more about King Fisher. I could see that Josh had judged him right, and now I was convinced. I only wished Captain could have known that his advice to King in Eagle Pass had triggered some thinking that finally got him on the right track. Josh wrote back right away, real excited. When I could, he said, I should get word to King that Josh was still sure he could straighten out his life.

The next thing I heard was that King had moved his family to Uvalde, where another daughter was born. That county had more than its share of hard characters and outlaws, and they were more than Sheriff Boatright could handle. But when he asked King to be his deputy, King said no thanks. When we heard about it some of us Rangers sent him word that he ought to accept, and that changed his mind. He told Boatright he'd serve as deputy until the '84 election, and then he'd run for sheriff. King wasn't used to being second to anyone, but the sheriff didn't object—he needed help bad.

Not long after King became deputy, the San Antonio–El Paso mail stage was held up. From the description of the robbers, King figured Tom and Jim Hannehan were the culprits, and the sheriff told him to follow their trail. It led to their mother's ranch on the Lerma. King called on them to surrender, but they were wild as well as stupid, and put up a fight. After King killed Tom he captured Jim and recovered the loot from the stage.

King was soon the acting sheriff, for Boatright had some legal trouble and left Uvalde. King set out to clean up the county and made so many arrests a flock of rustlers left the area. Two men he'd known on the Pendencia were indicted in Llano County. Thinking King still harbored wanted men, they fled to Uvalde, but they were in for a shock. He told them he wouldn't arrest them on one condition—that they return to Llano County and surrender. Glumly they agreed.

Sheriffs of other counties who had difficult arrests to make often called on King for help. People in Uvalde said that in two years he'd done more to reduce rustling and killing than any other lawman in West Texas

Early in '84 the Southern Pacific reached Uvalde on its way to El Paso, and at about the same time the legislature outlawed fence cutting. Barbed wire had come to Texas in '76 and after cowmen saw that it could actually hold wild longhorns many began buying land and fencing it. But some of the big ranchers got greedy, and fenced state land without leasing it and ran fences across public roads without putting up gates. They were asking for trouble and they got it.

The summer of '83 was dryer than usual, and when the grass gave out and the creeks and water holes dried, many small cowmen had to move their stock. When they discovered their way blocked by barbed wire there was a rush for wire cutters, and the Fence War broke out. Bands of small cowmen and their cowhands rode out at night and cut hundreds of miles of fences. There was no law to stop them, and most folks sided with the little men, especially against syndicate ranches owned by Britishers and Easterners.

It got so bad that Governor Ireland called the legislature into special session in December, and in January it outlawed fence cutting. The law also required gates every three miles and wherever fences crossed public roads, and it prohibited fencing land not owned or leased. Now there was work for sheriffs and Rangers.

Uvalde County was one of the worst places for fence cutting. In March, King Fisher took the train to Austin to get some instructions about enforcing the fence law. Before he left the capital he had the bad luck to run into Ben Thompson, who'd been Austin town marshal a few years earlier. But he'd been gambling at the Vaudeville in San Antonio, and had accused gambler Joe Foster of cheating. Joe was a co-owner with Jack Harris of the Vaudeville, and one thing had led to another. Harris had tried to gun Thompson down with a shotgun, but he wasn't quick enough on the trigger. Ben was tried for murder but acquitted. He resigned as marshal and got to drinking and doing crazy things. He and King had been friends for some years, but they fell out over the shooting of Harris, who'd also been a friend of King.

When King took the train to San Antonio on his way home, Ben

decided to go along. He told King that Joe Foster had invited him back
to the Vaudeville, "but they don't catch me in that trap. I know if I was
to go into that place it would be my graveyard."

At one of the stations where the train stopped someone wired Foster
and his partner Billy Simms that Ben Thompson was on the way to San
Antonio. They apparently got pretty active, for in San Antonio a friend
warned King he'd be in trouble if he stayed with Ben. But King wanted
to smooth over the trouble between Ben and the two partners, so he
didn't follow his friend's advice.

According to what the San Antonio paper said, King and Ben had
gone to the Vaudeville, which had a bar on the first floor and a variety
show on the second. The two went upstairs and sat at a table to watch
the girls dance. Then Billy Simms, Joe Foster, and Jacob Cox came
along. Cox was a special policeman who worked at the Vaudeville. Ben
offered to buy Foster a drink and to shake hands, but Foster bluntly
refused. There was some unpleasant talk, but King explained that they
were all his friends and that he wanted them to shake hands.

Simms and Foster swore afterward that Ben had drawn his gun but
Cox had grabbed the barrel. A lot of shooting followed, and Cox, Ben,
and King went down. Cox had a slight wound; the other two were
riddled with bullets. Foster received a leg wound.

The first I knew of the shootout was when I saw the Austin *Statesman*
the next day. The headline said: "Ben Thompson, Hero of Many A
Bloody Fight, Has Fought His Last And Died Last Night. King Fisher,
Faithful To The End, Yielded Up His Life To Save A Friend." The
coroner's jury had declared the killings justifiable because they were in
self-defense.

I showed the paper to Rudd, who'd been promoted to Sergeant.
"This sounds fishy to me," I told him. "A couple of tinhorn gamblers
gunning down the best gunfighters around. It doesn't make sense." He
read the account and agreed.

"Let's hop the train over there and talk to witnesses before they all
scatter," he said.

We found two men, Alex Raymond and John Sublett, who'd seen the
whole affair but hadn't been questioned by anyone. Rudd took out his
notebook and we retraced King's and Ben's movements from the time
they'd entered the Vaudeville. Simms had welcomed them, and they all
shook hands. "Ben, I'm awful glad to see you," Simms said. "Let's
forget the past and be friends."

Ben was in a good mood and told him he wanted to be friends, and
had come to talk it over and reach an understanding.

"Yes, Ben, that's right. I know we can be friends." Simms then invited them to go upstairs to see Foster. Raymond and Sublett followed them out of curiosity. Simms took them to a table he seemed to have reserved for them. Jacob Cox joined them there, and Ben ordered drinks for all.

"I thought you brought me here to see Foster," he said. "Billy, don't play any games with me. I didn't come for any fuss and don't want one, but you must treat me fair." Simms rose and said he'd find Foster.

"Yes," King said, "get him. I want to see you fellows friends before I leave. I invited Ben here. He didn't want to come, but I told him to come and talk it over and bury the past. Ben's willin' and I want Joe to meet us halfway."

Simms soon returned with Foster. "I want you and Ben to shake hands like gentlemen," King told him. "You're both friends of mine."

"I can't shake hands with Ben Thompson nor can we be friends," Foster answered. "I just want him to keep out of my way."

Simms and Cox both stepped quickly to one side, several feet away from King and Ben, and Foster moved back on the other side. Sensing a trap, King and Ben leaped to their feet, but before they could stand they were riddled by a volley that sounded like a dozen carbines. It came from a curtained box a little above the two men. Neither had drawn his gun.

After they fell, the witnesses told us, Simms or Cox had drawn Ben's pistol, held it close to his head, and fired twice. Then he put two more shots into Ben's body. The other man, using his own gun, shot King the same way. "It was monstrous," Raymond exclaimed. Foster had tried to draw his gun but it caught. He gave it a jerk and shot himself in the leg.

There was no doubt that the two were killed by three hired assassins hiding in the curtained theater box above them. They were, we learned, a bartender named McLoughlin, a gambler called Canada Bill, and Harry Tremaine, a performer. Each was paid $200, and all three sneaked out of town in a hurry.

We returned to Austin and reported to headquarters, and our account of the killings was published in the *Statesman*. The witnesses were still available for the grand jury to question, but they were never called. San Antonio's officials accepted the coroner's verdict and the story that Simms and Foster had told. Not a single indictment was handed down.

San Antonio's officials may have been satisfied, but the people of Austin were outraged and the *Statesman* echoed their feelings. Among other things, it said: "Fisher was personally popular in the West, and his death will be regretted by many. It is the irony of fate that men with the reputation for personal prowess possessed by the departed should be shot down like dogs and butchered like sheep in the shambles, without one life in exchange for their own. There never was, and we trust never will be, such a cowardly act committed in our own city. San Antonio is alone in this great country as a place where hired assassination is endured and approved by the people and the press, and it is welcome to the glory."

All witnesses agreed that Ben Thompson had been in a friendly mood, and that Foster wouldn't have dared talk to him the way he did if he hadn't known that three guns were trained on Ben. In Austin it was discovered that some of the bullets in Ben's body were from a Winchester .44 rifle and some were buckshot.

Foster and Simms had laid a trap for Ben Thompson, not for Fisher. Because he'd tried to patch up the differences between Ben and the two partners, King had to die. The only act of justice in the case was accidental—Foster died a week later from his self-inflicted wound.

I'd gotten about one letter a year from Josh. By '82 he knew cow work well enough to be made foreman of the El Sauz division, and Captain King had a house built there for him and Caroline when they married. The next year they had a son, and ole Josh just had to brag on him a bit. I'd sent him news of King Fisher from time to time. I knew he would read about the killings and wonder how a couple of gamblers could shoot down two expert gunmen like King and Ben. I got out a pad of foolscap, sharpened my pencil, and sat down to tell Josh the final chapter in the life of King Fisher.

ABOUT THE AUTHOR

Don Worcester is a professor emeritus of history at Texas Christian University, and winner of the 1988 Western Writers of America Saddleman Award. He lives in Aledo, Texas, where he raises Arabian horses. This is his first Double D Western.